Distracted

Distracted [1]

STATION HILL

[1] by Jalal Toufic

Published by Station Hill Literary Editions, a project of the Institute For Publishing Arts, Inc., a not-for-profit tax-exempt organization in Barry-town, N.Y. 12507. Station Hill Literary Editions are supported in part by grants from the National Endowment for the Arts, a Federal Agency in Washington, D.C., and the New York State Council on the Arts.

Distributed to the trade by The Talman Company, 150 Fifth Avenue, New York, New York 10011.

Cover: Frank Auerbach's *J.Y.M. Seated* (1987-88).

Library of Congress Cataloging-in-Publication Data

Toufic, Jalal.
    Distracted / by Jalal Toufic.
      p. cm.
    ISBN 0-88268-059-5
    1. Aphorisms and apothegms. I. Title.
PS3570.076D57 1991   91-33365
818'.5402--dc20   CIP

Manufactured in the United States of America.

Author's Note & Acknowledgements

Regarding this book as a second edition (1991): a shorter version — basically, the first sixty pages of the present edition — was sent to a dozen publishers and to the Register of Copyrights, Library of Congress (registration number TXU 310-041) on March 15, 1988. It was rejected by the former.

The two books, *Distracted* and *(Vampires)*, should have been published together:

Chapter I: Distracted & (Vampires).   pp. 1-199.
Chapter II: Distracted & (Vampires).   pp. 200-450.

The publisher advised against it due to the length of *Distracted*.

Thanks to Omran Toufic Omran, Jim Calabrese, George and Susan Quasha, Peter Rose, Daniel Shulman, Charles Stein, and Jason Watts.

Acknowledgements to Ralph Gibson for permission to use the photograph that appears on page 79, which originally appeared in *Tropism* (Aperture 1987); to Rizzoli for permission to use two photographs with their captions, which appear in Edward Lucie-Smith's *Lives of the Great Twentieth Century Artists* (1986) and to use two reproductions of paintings form Jean Leymarie's *Balthus*; to Le Muse for permission to use four photographs with their captions, which appear in *Yves Tanguy; Retrospective, 1925-1955* (1982); and to Frank Auerbach and Marlborough Gallery for permission to use *J.Y.M. Seated 1987-88*.

To the forgetful grateful

— Are you saying this to me?
— Also to myself. One should speak only when also speaking to oneself. Only then is there a dialogue.

J. T.

That shiver of cold down one's spine, and not due to the cold, is the only lightning.

Seven in the morning, sitting in a cafe, having read for four hours. The sky a pure violet, and yellow street lights. The traffic lights: green, orange, and red. How much time passed while they succeeded each other, cars passing like changing newspaper headlines? Yet as this went on, the sky became brighter and brighter, and one felt younger and younger.

It's those that want to fish that have knots all over them.

Nomad: to flee the flight of the world.

boat
cloud
lake

a sound
fish? Gull? — the moon! the moon!

Wrote a page. Felt dissatisfied with it. Began crossing out. Crossed out an infinity of pages.

By listening to one's emptiness, it becomes space needing, yet unable, to throw up itself. It becomes time vomiting itself. It becomes stillness.

I like most, I'm best at, play. I hate games.

Not too much, yet overflowing.

a way: away

Paris. When I miss New York, I go to a cafe at 5 a.m. People, half-exhausted, half-asleep, half-drunk, half-"clairvoyant" (I know that's already four halves, but at 5 a.m....).

Light coming from outside and inside the room to illuminate what I scratch out.

From the same mouth, saliva as eyebrow make-up, and the "no."

It's at the point when the semen cannot but be ejaculated, it is at that point of no return, or rather it is between that point of no return and the ejaculation itself that I disappear. And all the kissing, holding to, and pressing against means that I cannot find you. But it also means that I am trying to hold to myself in you, for you still believe in me, unaware as you are that at that moment I have vanished, and all that remains are sperm going through you like rain falling on the mist.

She has long hair and short memory.

Since where one begins is the beginning, one should begin at the end.

Glacial cold. I put fire to a forest.

Experimenting on the instincts with the instincts.

Loneliness, for one cannot meet people any more. Utter loneliness, as one has lost the ability to meet streets, words, images. Then loneliness disappears, for one no longer meets oneself (except sometimes a drop of rain passes slowly all the way from hair to lips).

For a long time now I've been working in silence. That is, during all that period, I talked only in quotations.

long journey
looking at lake's surface —
drops of sweat

— Are these ruins?
— Yes. Why do you ask?
— They keep on disintegrating, into ruins.

The real question is: Will one ever be able not to answer?

Music moves us. It also moves with us, but only as it's passing us forward to proceed or backward to lag. Living the moment means we don't give music or life the time to proceed or lag: We make the moment of passing infinite.

Whitman knew how to stay just long enough to leave too early (that is, not too late).

High above, a man on a tightrope. People admire his sense of balance, when in fact he is fear-frozen.

A thing, however light, has a sound. Only absolute heaviness has no sound.

Never buy a city map. For without it there is no city, just streets that intersect, and others, obstinate, that don't — becoming dead ends.

To X — is this a dedication or the beginning of a letter? Both? Most probably, for dedication presupposes distance.

Arriving at a crossroads, they decided each should go his own way in solitude. How pretentious. As if each were not walking on a road that multitudes before him had passed over, and multitudes after him would pass over. One goes one's way only if one is away from roads.

A walk takes place not in one's shoes but in the world.

a frog
a leap —
the fifth leg!

Putting on her shoe, she lifted her foot a little off the ground. The lace, suspended, slightly moving, was a bell.

A bookstore. The board has the inscription, "Old and New Books." Yet how old is the board itself.

— Who do you think will win?
— I don't know.
— Who do you think will lose?

To become a rumor on nobody's lips, in nobody's mind.

A story is always too long. Which means its summary as well is always too long.

Words?! Yes, I will leave some behind only if they take as little space as the ashes of that half of my body that will be burnt, and as little time to read as the time it will take to bury the other half.

Five minutes before the train moves. To the left, to the right: more trains. The whole station a huge train whose compartments lie not front to back, but side to side. No horizon. Inside the compartment, no faces, just newspapers, and from time to time a nail sticks out, like a magnifying glass for eyes too old, weary, dull. The train moves. The world!

On adjoining tracks long as a vampire's fingernails, dead animals. Their necks a faint thin line of black blood reddened by the setting sun. A car cemetery and, much further, human cemeteries. It is right the two should be separated. None of those too lengthy phrases that join a crushed car and a killed human being. One thing following the other not causally, but because the road happened to pass here and not there.

The white paper limitless as a sterile field. A sterile field can absorb all the rain of the sky without being soaked. Only seed and plant, and hence the field in which they grow, can be soaked. The flood occurred when the whole ancient world became fertile.

Knowing nobody in France, I went to Versailles alone. I was lucky out of necessity, for Versailles crushes groups.

I'm amazed to hear of people committing suicide by drowning in the Seine. But for the Seine, I may have committed suicide.

"I know you" is merely a fade in or out.

I don't like it when a subject is reduced to a subject reduced to an object.

Shedding two skins: snakes shedding their old skin always fascinated him, and he tried as hard as he could to do the same. In the end he succeeded! He shed the one part of the human body that can be shed: the blood. What remained was an absolutely pale body: a skin. Had he been no more than two skins?

Out of reach. We've left "No Trespassing" to others.

alone at night
the mind blank like a white paper
and the white paper
the world is far away it is my eyebrows: no more dust
inertia vanished even as transparence

The resting place of travelers is the edge.

All changes happen in the three points of the etc. To know how to detect in every phrase, in everything, its three points — that place where it becomes so slow it can proceed only by leaping. One must remain in these three points as long as they persist, and precisely because one is a nomad; for all continuation toward the one point that ends is nothing but a drifting along a circle whose center is this one point.

All courage resides in walking to the very edge. Beyond is a dizziness. Has anybody gone over the edge except by slipping? But there, beyond the edge, the world itself slips. Thus one remains steady.

Lightness: Wings themselves have become heavy, cumbersome, something to be discarded.

Sterility: A heavy emptiness, for there exists a container, and the lightest container is still too heavy.

Twenty-four years old, and still not one book written, not one feature film made, not one suicide committed!

— Do you know what I mean?
— No.
— I know what you mean.

5:30 in the morning. The sound of a passing car. Yet, outside, in the utter darkness, no car to be seen. One hears sounds best at night, for then they are not mixed — with their sources.

6 a.m. My head feels as things look when rain has just stopped. Yet, outside, it's still raining.

The in-between is never a go-between.

He repeated the question over and over. Was it his chewing gum?

Where you see a planter, I see merely a man planted, stuck. Those unable to grow, grow plants and projects. The road is that place where nothing is planted (not even car plants).

There is no choice where all the alternatives are given, for choice is the creation of the alternative.

I asked her twice. Twice a "no," one for each ear.

Clothed by their infinitely fast movements.

The beginning and end of a line are not points, merely extremes. Hence their sterility. Still, every point on the line can create its own extreme. If this happens with even one point, the line is undone. Hence a real beginning.

A sudden sadness, as if one has become a well.

A laugh larger than the mouth.

Is it too early or too late? For it must be too something.

Patience is the biggest obstacle to the attainment of serenity.

Suddenly he felt he could endure loneliness no more. He spoke to the first woman he met in the street. No response. "But what do I lack?" "Nothing. You lack nothing." And then, with a certain tenderness, "Not even a woman."

A corpse floats. And yet its nauseous, thick smell drowns all the space around. Its fixed constant gaze that does not travel makes of everything a grave. The blind man does not use a stick to find his way, but because his eyes and consequently he himself have become too heavy: his stick is first and foremost something to lean on.

Never summarize. Be brief.

Sunrise: A red sun. A yellow sun. A white sun.

Practice makes practical, not perfect.

Always arriving too early, that is, too late to act.

They regard themselves as different because of their failure to imitate. Unfortunately, they all fail to imitate in the same way.

Trying to join two cliffs with a phrase. But the phrase itself has a precipice, stops in the middle.

A resort. Old people dancing. Only part of their bodies is moving at all. The major part is still sitting on comfortable chairs looking at the dance. They are always in the company of their "children."

How cruel of you to describe him, for he's no more than a description of himself.

It was a silly question, but not a silly remark.

Sunday, March 2, 1986. I touched a branch.

— Thank you for your present.
— Thank you for your birthday.

The wind is moving round and round like a dizzy drunkard, and it is we who fall.

At times, one can preserve one's right movement only by making a wrong move.

12:30 at night. Waiting for the ferry. People, some sitting, others buzzing like the lights one sees through the windows of a moving train. Yes, it seems I am waiting for the ferry in a moving train.

It is that which is irreplaceable that is so early and so easily replaced in the replaceable.

Huge rooms. Nobody present. One is dust falling on chairs, tables, and carpets. A waiting not so much for a human presence as for the expectation of a human presence: for the janitor coming to clean the rooms in preparation for the coming of others.

I was in a hurry to meet her. She was not in a hurry to meet me. How could we not miss each other?

Dancing: The flying bird opened its wings more than usual.

Generous: Parting, she gave him a melancholy smile. In the melancholy itself, he saw her eyes.

My apology turned out to be unnecessary, for he had already forgiven my age.

Your smile makes your eyes close a little in a gesture of yielding — to your smile.

All are sleeping and I don't understand their dreams. Dreams are the clichés of the sleep world. My mind has become blank. Yet, I can't sleep, for it is the blankness of someone trying to remember — the margin. Everything I am writing is far away, as if one has run after distant objects, and now one's breath is distant. I accept writing wholeheartedly when I am refused sleep. She had disheveled hair, disheveled books, disheveled crotch. She looked in my direction as I spoke, her eyes becoming bigger and bigger. They didn't suddenly grow bigger out of anger, joy, or surprise. It was a slow expansion at a constant rate no matter what I said or did. Was she masturbating in front of me? No use fleeing, for her eyes would go on expanding until the whole universe is swallowed in them. No use speaking about love either, for I have become merely another item among the infinity of items that have disappeared in her. I was suffocating, for her expanding eyes were making the world smaller and smaller, until my veins burst and I felt them sweat on my skin, and my heart became the alternation of her warm breath and the cold air. As I froze into silence, everything went back to normal, that is, to her ears, to her craning neck. Also present was a painter who had a huge mouth. For a long time, she did not speak, and yet one had the feeling she was always repeating the same words, "I have a very big mouth." She spoke of the waiter having, "Can you believe it?" a very good collection of paintings. Well, believe it or not, I can believe it. But let me see those legs on which you walk, on which you stand. The melancholy of those legs, there, like closed curtains. My head feels a strange emptiness as if it has become the coldness of white marble. The lamp too old for the light issuing from it. The comb a beach. I look at Allen sitting by her. He's very tall, as if he has not yet wakened. He says to me, "Stop enjoying your own intelligence." I look at his eyelashes. They are jutting out. I feel like plucking the ones on his left eye one by one and muttering, "He's not my friend. He's my friend," then do the same with his right eye. He having no moustache, I would then lay them above his upper lip and write about autumn as they fell to the ground. I look at the painter and say, "Shut your mouth," "It's shut." I draw a smaller mouth on her big lips with three of his fallen eyelashes, "Now it's shut." The most nonsensical thing is those people who are still speaking sense on the radio at 6:18 a.m. Whoever wants to speak or perform (late) at night, should not sleep during the day. We walk to her house. She gives me a thick notebook of poems she wrote. She waits for my opinion. Mediocre poems. How can I talk at all when my lip is suspended at the edge of her lip? She's putting fire in the hearth. I throw the notebook there, give her a pen and tell her to write a poem not as she looks at the notebook burning, but with eyes closed. I forgot her pseudo poems very quickly, her clothes instantly. She wants me to go inside her vagina and come out a baby on the stream of her menstrual blood. Then she'll clean me with her kisses' saliva. Balthus' Katia is reading: she has her book open, her legs open. The book has no words on its covers; neither does it have any words inside. How dark must be a book on which nothing is written. Noises in the night's darkness, but no objects. Darkness itself an object making its own sound. Certain parts of me are present, fully awake, while others are hidden in their dreams. Men masturbating before Katia's virgin vagina. Her pupil swims in their semen. A blind man has no shadows. Rivers flow toward waves. Red lips, red wine, and pale red cheeks.

The director was such a perfectionist that, having a close-up of a person's palm, he redistributed its lines with make-up, so that a palm-reader watching the film would be able to predict what would happen to that character.

A powerful person would never do this, only a mere powerful situation.

"I like the way you sound." That was your reply to my letter. Now, it's the envelope as it's torn that makes a sound. Could it be, then, that you mistook the envelope for the letter? Or is it — which is even worse — that being too heavy yourself, you searched for a letter inside the letter, that is, mistook the letter itself for an envelope. "I like the way you sound." What about the five other senses?

Walking always at the edge of waves. The only footprints the feet themselves.

I looked at her for a long time — until I became a photograph. Beautiful women are nostalgic.

I balanced myself on one of her hairs. She felt tickled, laughed hysterically.

Puzzles demand, to be (dis)solved, that pieces be removed rather than added. Remove so many pieces that empty roadlike spaces form. Go from house to universe by extraction.

Transparent, hence no mud, dust to let fall from one; and, yet, this weariness! The sky itself must clear, the landscape become a desert, then reflections too will "fall" from one. Transparent.

His fat hand moving up and down her fat jeans/legs as if scrubbing the floor.

I can hear his words and it feels to me that if I were hearing them a few months from now in Winter, when it's really cold, they and the breath carrying them would be visible not as white air but as saliva.

I am not just modest, I am completely humble when I am tired-resting (tiredness is already rest).

To forgive is to forget. A pessimist would add, to forget is to forgive.

Darkness. The sky become a huge eyebrow swallowing the eye.

As if having the ability to run meant automatically that one had also the ability to walk!

After forty hours without sleep, you begin to sleepwalk.

the blood still, the veins circulating

None of the sound lost, for nothing absorbed or deflected it: Nobody was there to hear it. Santûr music listening to itself.

Barren branches like disheveled hair; one feels the rain would comb them. Nothing of the sort happens. You ask me to write you a letter, when I don't have a place to cover me. A letter needs an envelope. I stood in the park inhaling darkness. Later, I walked into the day as into deafness.

Resting alone in the bark. Faint ripples, formed by the play of light and shadow rather than by the breeze. Too faint. The additional breeze of eyes closing; one felt them. Then he began rowing.

It is difficult to resist easiness, but what is even more difficult is to resist the easiness of the difficult.

Night. Don't sleep, don't close the lids on the whiteness in the eye that like the snow falling in the darkness, has its day in itself.
Slowly, the eyelids closing on the body as on a claw.

The sound of water against my chin, against the towel. A caw. Through me flew a bird. My apprehension that it would perch inside me, that I might become rooted in its tired wings.

The sweat all over my body. I've become a cloud.

Short people are amazed when a person is both tall and serene. They always imagine tall people gasping from the effort of climbing up there.

An aristocrat-artist goes on inventing his repetitions.

Sunset. Water's sound going through my veins.

Dancing is forgetting the eye, is the eye's rest.

Quicker than the possible.

We listen only when listing sounds.

When one says of a ball that it came to rest, one means it stopped. In contrast, saying of a nomad that he stopped means he was resting.

Space falling on them like light.

5:30 a.m. The bums are still sleeping under the park's lights, which have remained on all night. I have often left the light on while I slept. It dawns on me I should not be hard on myself for doing this. 5:35 a.m. The cold: I feel like one of those jackets one can wear on either side; I must be wearing my clothes on the inside and my body on the outside. The cold: that most Christian of all afflictions. Because of it, saints slept even with lepers. Christ rubbed stones against each other, but no fire was produced, not even with a miracle. Fire belongs to hell (and cold to the Christians). The Devil was tempted by God to tempt Christ with becoming hell's master. He did not succumb. So Christ turned the other cheek. Only a slap could give him some red warmth.

Winter. Windows veiled by breath, and for once breath not held back. Fingers leaving in their wake a transparency. There, at the other mist's shore, rain, driven mad by the drunken wind, falls in harsh verticals against all that is liquid. But it never touches plants, nor anything rooted. In that heavy universe of theirs, water always ascends. There, rain falls twice to reach the roots. Only then does it touch ground. But we, have we been touched by the rain?

Just one's two walking legs echoing each other against oblivion.

You must not write yet, for though you have something to write, this something still does not have you.

the branches a net to catch the air
and they do:
the wings have closed

Either you have this inability or you don't.

He's no good at it, for someone else could have done it.

The wind mocked the lake for being muddied. That's you, Sarah, and me.

Sarah, you have a lover. You ask me to withdraw. But in *withdraw* there is *with* and *draw*.

Laconism has little to do with writing short phrases; it has everything to do with being short of inessentials.

That solitary person, Nietzsche, knew that one either uses the dash to introduce merely an interlocutor's words, or uses it instead in the phrase itself to introduce a subtlety in the monologue.

Not hard, but detached, for hardness is still sensitivity.

The taste of your body. My lips at last have become nude.

The clapping of two hands is mere noise. Applause is the clapping of the hand against one's forehead or one's cheek.

Sky. Trees. Road. This sand attached to the tattered shoes resting in the moving car. This yellow colorless sand is the limit to what I would accept as a house, as a home.

Night. Closed eyes. Black. The eyes open. A pure gray room. Light turned on. Colors.

Water. To swim between one's shadow and one's reflection and be lost to oneself.

So cold. My hands become gloves.

Most people have no instincts, merely habits.

Unlearn how to count, for one counts only one's debts.

Fighting for a cause?! A cause has an infinity of effects, and one usually wants only one or two of these. All the others one calls by-products. One fights for an effect. Someone who accepts a cause and consequently its myriad effects is no fighter.

One has become indistinguishable, utterly defenseless, like snow buried, floating in snow. Also, one has turned into a cold, white bubble that goes on becoming wider and vaster as it falls until it turns into a universe — a universe settling down to become indistinguishable, snow exposing snow.

It is late at night... perhaps.

Il promenait les mains dans les poches.

This vacant cross one finds on graves. What? Is one supposed to nail oneself to it?

A bell sound and one no longer knows who one is: a child running in a Christian missionary school; a Tartar sacking a Russian monastery. The cold wind, the hand-turned-rigid become more persistent in moving the bell, as if it were knocking on a doctor's door.

At the request of his friends comma he repeated a certain phrase as quickly and for as long as he could period The silly phrase disintegrated into sounds that re hyphen formed as funny words period They all laughed period Yet he knew one should go further and dissolve the prearranged result period Sounds period It is then that one laughs wholeheartedly comma for one's laugh will not be repeated period
To do this too quick repetition not only with banal phrases but mainly with those that are necessary period Absolutely against the actor comma precisely because he takes too seriously comma that is comma not seriously the lines of the author period One knows better than to hold them too high dash that is comma to be a tightrope walker on them period For comma slowly comma one has acquired the necessity of walking on a tightrope made of the line traced by one's steps period One will repeat these lines more and more quickly until they dissolve comma and all that remains is the clown laughing behind his make hyphen up period One has become that non hyphen existent

point at which the two parallel lines of writer and clown meet period

Perspiring veins.

There. No, there. This white calm lake in the sea. Why do the waves still travel toward the shore of sand, pebbles, and rock, and not toward it?

The eye taking all the light, the eyelashes taking all the shadows.

One kills the shepherd in oneself only if one is not one's own son. Then and only then, there won't be a shepherd's rejoicing over finding his lost sheep. The lost sheep was a wolf and therefore can never be found — to be a sheep. This lost one will find the sheep again and again; and not one but many of them will be lost. All that will remain are clear and distinct trails leading to where they cannot be found, trails made of bones and blood, trails made of bones drunk with blood.

One is a constellation of contemporary incarnations. Nomad: to encounter the meeting of world and shoe shedding their skin, to experience that which is between the incarnations, and that answers not to a world, but to a world shedding its skin, to the shedding itself. Totally nude, now that the world also is nude. A real breeze.

You parody it to bring it to its end. Fine, but remember that a thing is not completely dead so long as its parodies are alive.

Always liked that vapor of darkness one glimpses through the windows of moving subway trains. The fog of dirt on the window, on which falls the rain of light. The train moving away from time into noise, and I dissolving into that eternity between two heartbeats.

The subway, the darkness outside, and these yellow and blue lights that do not illuminate, that are the twinkle in a blind man's eye. Darkness all around, and one no longer knows whether one is in a tunnel or on a plain and about to perceive the moon behind two clouds.

The fertilizing sterility of water.

He always loses you and others win, for they have no difficulty seeing the white ball one strikes the other balls with. Is love a game of billiards? If so, he is never part of it, since he does not see the white ball, only the one to be struck.

The loved one is made merely rare, not by the multitude of balls to be struck, but by the presence of this dialectical ball that makes every shot carry two balls. And, the uniqueness is not dispensed with for every shot in a unique "once and for all," but twice, in that at no point is the possibility present the white ball may acquire a color; hence, one cannot confuse which ball is which in the moment they strike each other.

I'm following my pen as one follows a woman's legs through known and unknown streets. Do you follow me?

There is a movement, a walking in tallness.

Is there nobody, nothing to bombard this sun?

Sarah, you said, "Let us not meet." I walk streets where I know you'll never get lost and pass along. I swim in deeper seas, for I'm the taller of the two of us. But if, nonetheless, we meet, can you ask me not to follow you like the wind blowing through your hair?

They separated us to put each out of context. To go on with the process of extraction, not ending it at a paragraph, a phrase, a word, or even a sound. Going further than the merely enigmatic word or sound selected as the password between friends who have forgotten each other's name and face. We'll meet again without a password, though we'll have different faces now, names, and thoughts. If sometimes one chatters with the guard it is so that a prisoner who has planned to escape may find it easier to do so.

To hear the silence of the sea, one must become a wave.

In the street. Brutally cold. A feverish man is pissing. His hot urine. I feel warmer.

At times a modicum of help is necessary! Without it, that which, in us, we were trying to let wither away would be all too happy, in order to save itself, to offer us its help; and we, grateful as we are, would then offer it in return ourselves.

In most books, one must look for the digressions; for in the digression from the digression, one may still find something necessary.

The surface of a table, a shoe, hair on my arm: Is it because I'm becoming colder and more detached that I'm able to get in touch with, to touch, their coldness and detachment? The mist. This feeling from my feet the earth is near. This sterile mist I love. Has one to move up, turn into a cloud, in order to become fertilizing? Now that I'm closest to this sand, to buildings, to their stones, I feel most sterile. Now, like the mist I have become, creativity lies in dispersion, so that a traveler lost to the world may exclaim, "the world!"

I keep staring at the misty red of your lips. Whereas, I always think of you as wearing some red clothing: I can't undress you completely. This is your shyness. Your shadow extends your dress. I try to undress you even of your shadow. My eyes look down or aside. This is my shyness.

Malcolm Cowley writes about «Whitman's old-age habit of never saying in three words what might be said in six.» One who accepts the two sides of the coin on one face needs more words than one who chooses either the head or the tail, or, which is the same — in *better* there is *bet* — that is, worse, chooses both, one in a first bet, the other in a second, and only knows how to bet on two out of three, that is, on three out of four, on three out of five, on four out of six, on four out of seven, on five out of eight, on five out of nine, on six out of ten, on six out of eleven, on seven out of twelve, on eight out of fourteen — He thinks laconism lies in using the etc.! No, laconism lies in using the etc. — on eight out of fifteen, on nine out of sixteen, on nine out of seventeen, on ten out of eighteen, on ten out of nineteen, on eleven out of twenty. He fell asleep. Sound asleep. No sound could wake him. Indeed, some count to sleep. As if counting were not already a variety of sleeping! Rather, to be open to sounds, voices, thoughts, snow, nothing; to anything that can cause you to make a mistake or forget the number you arrived at in your counting; to all that would interrupt your etc. To become an insomniac even during one's sleep.

The writing that strikes us is writing that underwent a becoming leaner and leaner until it became leanest: an exclamation point. This lightning separating sunset from night.

Kings are less aristocratic than nobles, for they must wait for their subjects to cross the large room where they themselves sit, must wait for them to kneel and bow. Waiting is servility.

One comes to New York to be crushed. One does not want to die as a grain of wheat dies, with that thrifty death that does not squander itself: It wants to give life and so must have a prudent after-death. Rather to be utterly crushed, so that one may experience both the dizzy speed of that which strikes and the amazed speed of that part of oneself that suddenly flies away. One has become this play of speed and randomness.

Not yet time to write. At last, time to write no more! Not yet time to write. At last, time to write no more! Not yet time... There is no such thing as the right time to write: a period that would take place between the "not yet time to write" and the "time to write no more," between writing as promise and writing as compromise. That period in between is just the point that marks the end of a sentence.

A shy painter is looking just above you, glancing from time to time directly at you. Slowly, he becomes aware that what he's simulating he's looking at is an amazing painting. You are attractive, but are you seductive? For that you should have sat in another place. Seduction is not generous; it is a company that does not accompany. In contrast you...

> the moon
> the melancholy of looking away
> white leaflets tickling the river!

I can't lose you, I, a nomad, going in the four directions: They frame, no, not a painting of you (your brows, shallow? Your feet, small?), but the white smoke drifting from someone's pipe and making me think of your blond hair. I try to touch it. It disperses, not in the four directions, but the four directions. I can't lose you, but will I ever find you? Still trying to stand at that non-existent point at which your eyes are focused. On the chair next to you lies a pale, white towel, and you look so fragile, always as if coming out of a bath into the air. My look's drizzle moves up your leg. I stare at your two small breasts, like young birds waiting to be fed, and I know you won't bear children. Love: moving through you toward you.

Words absent in your absence, silent in your presence.

In a cafe. Late at night. To my left, someone laughing, adjusting his watch, eating with a fork: making sounds. Next to him a drunk person; he spoke only to slow down the rate at which he was drinking. Heat a coarse layer of dead skin covering a wound. Closed my eyelids. Darkness powerless to efface the hot atmosphere. From time to time cars' lights, like gold teeth. Three men are sitting at the table by the window. One of them says: "If we're not ready yet to be enlightened, then at least dazzle us. You see, little did I know then..." How little does a person who says "little did I know" know; and how talkative he is. The one addressed begins speaking. Suddenly, I feel pity for the words he's uttering so vehemently. As suddenly, the pity disappears: I become those words, detached from his masturbatory voice drowning in saliva, from a self-satisfaction that paralyzed him, making him able to sleepwalk only in his dreams. He had to be awakened twice. I wait, to no avail, for him to say: «If anyone slaps you on the right cheek, let him slap your left cheek too». The two dazzled listeners keep on saying "unbelievable" to everything he says. I walk up to them and say, "Unbelievably true or unbelievably false?" Two film students are speaking by the door. You hear the word *industry* more from film students and teachers than from Chrysler workers. Would anybody please tell them we've already been living, and for a long time now, in the post-industrial age?

I go outside. As long as one has not seen the sun rise in a city, one has not visited it, let alone lived in it. I hear simultaneously the sounds and the silence. Silence now a transparency against which, unaware, one collides with shattering sound time and time again. One has entered the delirium of silence. Suddenly, silence becomes a transparent sound. And then, not what.

Reverence for oneself, never self-satisfaction.

All they do is comment on their quotes from one author by paraphrasing what another author wrote.

Joan of Arc in the presence of the king dissimulating his identity: a test for both of them, and the king knew this. There is never an acknowledgement, a meeting except between those without proofs.

Autumn leaf joins its shadow, buries its shadow.

So dry one threw dust in one's eyes. At last, tears! One saw light falling with a tear and breaking as the tear splashed.

Speaking to myself in front of the mirror. Suddenly, that which I saw in it became a living person. One puts a mask in front of the mirror precisely to have a mask in the mirror.

"It is midnight, time to…" That's how both vampires and most people reason, the former waking up, the latter going to sleep. As for me, it's never "time to…"

Sadness: tears fall without reflecting anything.

You trip. They laugh; without tripping themselves, despite the multitude of crevices their laughter has dug around their mouths and eyes. One goes on a trip only by tripping.

The wind can move a whole. It can break it into pieces. But it can never move a piece.

Pathos is not, as Eisenstein thought, just a leap; it is being swept up by a flood as one is leaping.

One used to come to school late every morning, not because one was too sleepy, but because the class made one so. The classroom: listening to one's not listening.

The strangest: the familiarity with which language met me halfway in my attempt to meet a new thought dawning on me.

My corpse burnt. There remain the ashes. The air's stillness. I've become the wind that will disperse them.

A Renoir painting of a vase full of flowers. How pale are the flowers compared to the vase. A sculpture of a girl putting on one of her stockings. Is she sculpting herself?

Unadapted: A piece on which, in miniature, is the (dis)solved puzzle, discarded because it does not fit in the puzzle!

Touched the lukewarm water with its cold transparence.

I walk. Left tragedy to my tattered shoes. Left dance to the sweat on my body, where the cold breeze is reflected. I laugh at those who look directly at the sun, see utter darkness, then, on seeing light again, exclaim, "Another dawn!" For these "men of many dawns" have never seen one dawn in the night. Sunset. This cold. Why am I feeling warmth penetrating, the sun already rising? The sun simultaneously sets here rises there. The traveller in his distraction, "sets here rises here." Someone yells, "Have you heard? The sun sets."

Sleepy. Someone seeing me closing my eyes said I was struggling to preserve the last remnants of my patience.

White cheese green lettuce red tomato brown bread. Late at night. I am eating a garden.

The nomad, as against the sedentary, refuses to learn how to fix things, how to intervene to halt, at least for a while, the natural process of disintegration. He accepts nothing more than dissolution. Yet, it seems, always comes the moment of the dissolution of dissolution, the moment when dis-solution begins to ask for a solution. Then he goes away.

Yes, the food is better in Beirut than in New York. Yet once you abstain from eating for a more or less long period, once you go on some kind of diet, once, that is, you begin eating yourself; then you discover that you taste better here than in Beirut.

They keep repeating the same infinity of things.

— This film is not about X, it is about his relationship with Y.
— X is an eclipse. An eclipse eclipses all that is not totally blind. Since you don't know what an eclipse is, stand in any street late at night, no people buzzing around the street lights; and look. The falling snow, the lamp. An eclipse.
— You said it, not I: It takes two for an eclipse to occur.
— It is said in a Tarkovsky film: A drop of water falling on another drop adds up to one drop, not two. But this is because the first drop is not falling on the other, only on its shadow-reflection on it. How can a splash occur?
— The blind person has no shadow.
— Blindness would do, but only if it is total. Then, it is an eclipse. The hand-stick, and not only the eyes, must become blind. If not, the hand-stick would turn the world into a shadow: something one cannot collide against. But now, it itself is that which the body is always colliding against; so that the world now has to become a stick to shield us against colliding against the hand-stick. The hand-stick of the blind person is eyelashes guarding a blind eye. The eyes and hand-stick must become blind simultaneously.
— The mirror doesn't break, it is only the glass that does.
— The mirror breaks if in front of it one is totally blind, a shadow-reflection, but of nothing: an eclipse. Collision abolished: a splash. For collision is not what causes a splash, but what ends it. In the splash everything is in flight. Simultaneity undoes unity. The simultaneity of an explosion? A race beginning at the crossroads? No, not even that! For everything that has to come to a halt in order to begin has at least one end: the stasis that precedes the beginning signal. Every other end is the nostalgia of this stasis marking the superimposition of the beginning and end signals. Why, then, are they panting? To hide that normal breathing is a panting, the real one. Not to prevent the explosion, to interrupt it? An endless race beginning at different

places and different times? No, not even that! Rather, to become simultaneity, through becoming quicker than speed; and hence to be outside even of roads: collision abolished. "Where the fuck am I?" flashes through one's mind. The mind having emptied and become one with all space, this flash is not one's own question, not at all, but the wake of the collision that ended the race. A winner is chosen, for the kind of race was chosen. The applause he hears is the sound of the running feet of the other contestants arriving at the end mark.

I took my hand in her hand.

Wrote several lines. A blank page replaced by a blank mind.

As soon as I become silent, which happens so often and for such long periods, you go into a reverie that does not exclude me but, infinitely worse, goes back to when I talked.

How talkative are those designated as excellent listeners: Their silence is an interruption of silence, since they always reduce the latter to *someone's* silence.

Do things drown to flee the air?

One is just only when one *has had enough*.

— Tu es fou.
— Non (I am a no-mad), je m'en fous.

If I wrote to you about lamps illuminating blind men, streets walking in the footstep sounds one hears at night, music's dance among exhausted people, wouldn't it be the same as remaining silent with them about you?

The heat making her take off some of her clothing; the heat my ally, I, a desert man.

What does it mean to have a fade-out in Wenders' *The Goalie's Anxiety at the Penalty Kick*, where everything and more is shown, where nothing is overlooked and discarded except overlooking and discarding, except to add, rather than subtract, one more thing, the fade-out itself.

Eyes looking, looking, like plants soaked by the never stopping rain.

Mircea Eliade says one burns in yoga one's states of consciousness, the world.

But these, according to Heraclitus, are fire. To burn fire!

The surface is the most difficult place, for one must, in the same movement, balance oneself on it and keep it in balance by maintaining its constituent imbalance.

Hero: one who does not adapt to his victory.

Finally footsteps submerging talk no more, for, at last, no more talk.

This almost audible sound: detachment striking against inertia.

Her lips and my distraction often interrupted by her tongue.

My blood hitting against my blood. What will be spilled?

Revulsion: distance lacking distance.

Withdrawn are you, like your body falling behind, falling back under my very fingers, lips, in a diet that suits you more than your clothes, more than your jewelry, more than that third language I hear you sometimes speaking, of which I understand not one word except your meaningless name.

It's not only the banana skin that makes one slip; every skin does.

The sheep were gone. The shepherd's voice searched for them until it, in turn, was lost. The shepherd was alone.

Suffocating, and not because there is no air, there is plenty of it, but because the air one is exhaling falls steeply as soon as it leaves the body. One needs a savage wind to scatter it obliquely; yet a savage wind suffocates.

Slap yourself in the face to discover the hand that is ever in it.

If your yawn is not an earthquake, keep your mouth shut.

Swimming: becoming the still water's breeze.

I want to see you, and not just to watch you; that is, I want you to see me, too.

Helpful: the assurance help has been sent and will arrive too late.

Lebanon. Nothing left, not even leaving.

Three quarters of an hour into 1986. The subway train has been frozen in the station for the last fifteen minutes. Someone shouts, "What are you waiting for, 1987?"

Waiting for Godot: An Unadaptation
Since all New Yorkers who would go to see a performance of Beckett's *Waiting for Godot* have already read the text... Bad argument. Begin again.

Since... Bad: since an argument. Never explain. All explanations are excuses. Unless — after a sober, awkward preparation of oneself (nothing comes quickly, certainly not quickness. Everything happens suddenly), and by an unexplainable metamorphosis — "to explain" becomes to make something ex plain. Continue the interruption.

No text. No actors. No audience. "Just a cashier, then, counting money?" No. Something is occurring without taking place. No stage. No stages. No act one intermission act two. One no is enough to take leave of all stages. Their redundancy.

Color spotlights sweep the stage, auditorium, hallway, lobby, toilets, and as far as possible outside the theater. After forty-five minutes, they are replaced, except in the toilets, by flat white lighting. Five minutes later, color spotlights resume everywhere for forty-five minutes except in the toilets where flat white lighting is to be found. Then, the color spotlights are replaced by white flat lighting everywhere except in the toilets and outside the theater.

Ticket collectors, in official attire, enter the auditorium and declare in the most neutral, matter-of-fact manner, "Time for the intermission. Please follow us." People are conducted outside the theater. Later, other ticket holders (if most of the tickets didn't remain unsold) begin to show up and either enter the theater or remain outside, whichever they prefer. Those who don't have tickets, whether because they didn't buy one or because they already used it, can still, either in the area covered by the color spotlights outside the theater, or if they so wish, in the area further away lit by street lights, sit and/or stand and/or sleep and/or yawn and/or shout and/or fuck and/or sneer and/or snore and/or perforate and/or applaud and/or leave and/or and/or — do the same things those inside could do, except perhaps be unable to admire the interior design of the theater; on the other hand, they can get a fever if it's cold and raining outside — a thing those inside cannot do.

People feel at ease in the presence of ushers, for the latter ask them to take a place. This assures them both that something will take place — that there will be a stage — and that this something is different from themselves, for they have a place already.

People earn money by working from one specific hour to another specified hour. They spend that money only on that which begins and ends at prescribed times (almost everything has the inscription "Sell by…"). Hence, each ticket will specify the beginning and ending time — only, people will quickly discover that this is not a performance, but a perforation. It has always already perforated the wall of the beginning-end (no more horoscopes. Horoscope: anything that states the same will happen to whoever is born between two prescribed dates; to whoever attends a performance taking place, as all performances, between two prescribed hours), and is continuously perforating the wall of the etc.: of the endless. To let the house crumble. Not to restore it. Someone began digging the earth to lay the foundation of a new house! Once the first house (that one built and/or occupied, if one is a sedentary; that one met, if one is a nomad) has crumbled down, one will, by digging the earth, find and found only graves. To let the house go on crumbling until all there remains is a wall. A wall cannot be demolished. The one who tries to demolish it turns into a normal person, becomes himself a wall, «I actually stand where I've always stood, behind myself» (Wim Wenders). To perforate the wall. The dangerous necessity of becoming a rat. They heard, "art." They detected a defect, pitied him his having only one eye: the hole. Didn't each with his two eyes see (blind as they had become in that endless dark tunnel, the eyesocket. How to get to the light? Dying is encountering a strange light that has nothing to do with the sun, its brightness and its shadows, or with the grave, its darkness and the whiteness of bones and tombstones) the large number of walls he had perforated, of holes he had created (holes in which not oneself, but the walls fall), and hence, the myriad eyes that had occurred to him. Perforation should go on until one reaches the most terrible, best hidden of all walls: one's teeth. The teeth themselves must get perforated, become vampiric teeth, through which the whole universe circulates. Only then does respiration occur away from the masturbatory diastole-systole of the heart, away from the endless beginning-end of the most mechanical of pumps. To become a vampiric rat. (The thing I like most about New York is the subway. It perforates both city and difference of day and night. One sees, sometimes, amid its tracks, a rat). Now, talking with his bad pronunciation to a French woman — her beautiful black and white eyes. A white that overexposes all films, a black that underexposes all photographs — he hears himself say to her, "C'est dans le même mouvement que je suis devenu et écrivain et cinéaste." "Il faut avoir d'énormes dons, n'est-ce pas?" The suspicion he feels now she may be like most other whites, 18% gray. "La réalité est fluide, et non pas solide; alors les dents, on n'en a pas vraiment besoin."

Still almost everybody will go on telling one, "You want to get her? Make her laugh. And don't forget to laugh yourself." Only a woman and a man showing each other they have teeth, and strong and healthy ones at that, will assure all concerned — above all the baby to be born — that they can bite into, chew and digest the world. But what if, when the priest asks whether anybody has an objection to their marriage, someone tells a joke that makes them laugh so much tears overfill their eyes? Why, this is the last test, isn't it (after which, no more tests. More tests: They've become the testers themselves): whether they are such excellent swimmers as to survive any flood? They've rehearsed this already! For like most people they believe in the past and its TAKE 1 flood. Maybe they'll be the ones to perform the miracle: a baby who upon falling from her vagina laughs instead of crying.

They mistake perforating with biting into-chewing-digesting. The wall is that which is still undigested after everything has been chewed and digested. The wall is that which remains, the undigestible. It is the truest shit. Hence it has to be perforated. But if we ourselves go on shitting, isn't it because so much of us digests yet is never digested? So much of us is shit, walls that have to be perforated.

Rocks withered by the waves. Waves withered, heated into air by the rocks. Perforated teeth and universe have withered each other. Particles, like when you slap yourself in the face — all kinds of particles, from photons, which cannot be felt, to snow flakes; even nothingness particles:

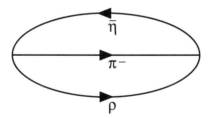

Everywhere particles, but also waves: One has experienced, outside all physics labs, many a thing as both particle and wave. Waves and hence distillation. For it is waves, not particles, that distill (weariness is the blockage of distillation). Everything digests and is digested now in the same movement. No more shit, not even the shit of *no shit!* Death? Not if one has intuited, and by this intuition constituted the, only then, already present absent-minded body that is always in the most relaxed position: a cyclone's eye in the midst of which, not around which, now, particles interact and waves distill.

Have you stared at people having a discussion? The movements of their hands, in their faces, and simultaneously, the immobility of their legs, knees, buttocks (or other parts). Look at people in subway trains. Don't merely deduce that parts of the body are distracted from the plot, plotting against it. Intuit that the body is always absent-minded: It is always in the most relaxed position however awkward one's pose, however strenuous the thing one is doing. It absents itself from nothing except rest, that is, from *absence*. Hence it has no parts made of shit, never shits, doesn't need rest rooms (*rest room* is the right word to designate the place where one shits, for rest is shit). And it is in the same movement one intuits this absent-minded body and one knows one is *always* tired, with a weariness that admits of no rest. Only the weariness of workers, that is, of almost everybody, can be alleviated by rest. I am tired of their weariness, for I am tired with a weariness that admits of no rest: I have become a reflection (of nothing), and hence cannot fall from the surface to *rest* on the ground. Nothing is ever created without weariness, and hence without partial insensitivity, without weariness at last rather than making one heavy, making itself heavy, and distilling. In most cases, it is this weariness admitting of no rest that interrupts inertia.

It is aphoristic writers that have intuited the most intensely this absent-minded body, since they are the ones who hate the most the inertia of deduction (deduction has nothing necessary about it: It may be made by anyone, even though not everyone can make it — it is made by itself. Deduction is imitation), and the restless rest of ex-*plan*-ation (Cain, the "restless wanderer" (unclean situation: Cain is driven away from God's presence while having God's mark to protect him. It was all too natural that this compromise(d) God should give the lowest breed of the wanderer: the restless), ended up building a city on the *plain*. And *since* explaining remains empty without deduction, «Cain lay with his wife, and she... gave birth to Enoch... To Enoch was born Irad, and Irad was the father of Mehujael, and Mehujael was the father of Methusael, and Methusael was the father of Lamech... When Lamech had lived 182 years, he had a son. He named him Noah...» By deduction we got to Noah. With him (*Noah* sounds like the Hebrew for comfort) deduction changes into itself, into subtraction, «So God said to Noah... I am going to bring floodwaters on the earth to destroy all life under the heavens».

One understands nothing about aphoristic writers if one finds distance, silence, whiteness, and suicide only between the aphorisms, and not also in the aphorisms themselves. With the distracted, even though the creation, by perforation, of an opening in the wall is simultaneously the creation of a less perfect eye — an eye that does not adjust automatically, that underexposes and overexposes, that unfocuses —, the two are superimposed, for one is active, the other receptive, an act of grace. Hence gratitude. Generosity (whose? The distracted person's? Distraction's?). A change from active to receptive, like any change, presupposes a time in which to occur; it is, here, an untimely time in the simultaneity itself. It is this strange time that makes it possible for things separated by one's preparing oneself to occur at the same time. Preparing oneself, taking one's time, is giving things the necessary time to reveal whether they drown or distill in one, that is, whether one drowns, or distills in them. That which drowns falls to rest on the one and only ground: the *imaginary line*. That which distills is continuously crossing the imaginary line (*the imaginary line* crossed (not just once, but continuously), one is struck by how one's dialogues with others disintegrate into monologues, people facing one with their backs; but also how one's monologues are simultaneously, now, dialogues), hence not falling, and if we believe it is doing that, moving in one direction, it must be because we still have an eye that adjusts perfectly.

The fragile total trust one has in oneself (fragile for one is disappearing), the refusal to get distracted from distraction, is what permits one to perforate the blindness of the wall. A blindness constantly colliding against one, against everything, but that most people don't feel, since they are leaning against it, since it is their stick. One perforates it with nothing to sustain one except the fragile total trust in oneself and the feeling one's teeth are being perforated. That this should end in the creation of an opening in the wall, but also that this latter should in a simultaneous movement that comprises a superimposition, and hence by an act of grace, become an eye that does not adjust automatically; this may lead one not just to have faith in oneself, but, unfortunately, to become one of the faithfuls of oneself. Editing is almost a necessity here, for it is in editing in the case of the distracted, much more than in writing (the opening in the wall become an imperfect eye: this receptively receptive or receptively unreceptive state) that one senses how little control one has on the material. Still, editing, unlike writing, is a kind of rest, though one rests in it much less than in most other things. Hence, it exposes one to the danger of trying to join: The rest less becoming the rest-less. Yet one must not cry wolf too quickly — one may be the wolf oneself. One knows that finding many an *and* and *therefore* in the aphorisms need not necessarily mean the writer became restless, needed to explain — and not only to the readers — but that... Her constant shy smile, a fall trying to prevent a trip.

"I'll have a cup of tea and a bowl of soup." Her being a waitress is so ironic, it becomes a parody of irony. For it is I who is waiting, even though the cup of tea and the bowl of soup have long been on the table. Nietzsche wrote, «To say in ten sentences what everyone else says in a book — what everyone else does not say in a book.» I've already used a sentence; I don't care. Thriftiness counts. Everything that counts does not count. Laconism is generous. Generosity is in not counting, in being awake.

How words withdraw from the one who tries to withdraw from his withdrawal. Can't she feel my feelings? All I feel, in her presence, is an obscurity in which words become bats that hear me, strike me, without my being able to hear them. An obscurity that blinds me, making me touch things to find them to touch them. In this obscure blindness I've touched her skin. Were she to ask, "Why do you want to speak [?] to me?" I could answer that it is because of the touch of her skin, except, my neck is words' noose. I try to write to her in this obscurity. The words bury the words. I rip the page from the notebook; it leaves behind torn pieces (her hair gives the feeling of something torn). She looks at the page. If only her pupil would swim in the page's whiteness, then there would be need neither to speak nor to look; both pupil and words have been overexposed by the page's whiteness become cornea.

Speaking is merely peeking through the hole of the mouth. Whereas it doesn't matter to me you're speaking to him. Your voice reaches me. It gets lost in me. Now, I meet you: only the lost can meet the lost.

You smile when I say *lost*, for I walk with no hesitation whatsoever through the myriad paths of this library and sit in front of you who are ever lost in it. (Never cared about most shelved books. I like the ones I find on toilets' floors, including those I don't deign to read).

How easy it is to reduce someone to muteness: your red earphones. You bow your elbow and lean your hair on it, and lean your face on your hair on it, in a gesture of sliding in water. I stare at you like a shy blind man. Your eyes, what color? Eyes that make me forget everything else; so what is it, then, that each time makes me forget to see their color? "Brown." Your stretching words makes them instantaneous. Your stretching words is a second tongue.

Your long still hair, like curtains blowing in the wind.

Will my shadow ever get jealous?
A woman enters the café where I am sitting, and smiles. Someone must be waiting for her. Yes. Did the solitary person I am ever smile on entering a café? Did I ever come running into any place; that is, when not racing against a heavy rain? Except for a few films, I now go to the cinema — rarely — only to rediscover that most social of feelings: *being late* (it presupposes, for one, adjusting one watch to another, even if this adjustment occurs too late) — late in going out of the cinema (a few fade-outs in the film. An infinity of them during projection, for the eyes keep closing from time to time).

My mind is as blank as this pond. I can disturb the pond by spitting in it. How to spit in one's mind?

Metaphor: not *as* but *like* (liking). The second term is a new sense organ (there aren't only five) that makes it possible to perceive-experience the first term. A vision occurs when the two terms are the same.

You can't catch someone by surprise. His surprise surprises you. Your surprise, however short, gives him the chance not to get caught.

He may in turn be surprised by your surprise. It is this second surprise that renders him fragile, opening the realm of surprise proper where anything can happen, and not merely his eluding being caught by surprise. It is this second surprise that abolishes the possibility of an infinite static progression — each being surprised by the other's surprise — in which both would get caught.

Table edges cutting the air. Fire burning things to continue to burn the transparency in it.

Ever the waves, for the hugeness of the sea is a storm.

— Prove that you hate explanations.
— I accept misunderstandings.
— I thought you abhorred films that are the story of a misunderstanding.
— A story is an explanation.

The tourist is not someone who doesn't find the places he is searching for; he is someone who, on asking "Where is the place—?" always gets the answer, "But you're in it!"

Falling snow. One moves in order not to be completely buried by it. Bleached sky. One moves so that dust won't cover one totally. Yet I often yield to the temptation to remain still until dust or snow buries me vertically. Whereas the axes get dizzy, move, the horizontal to become the vertical, the vertical to become the horizontal. During the axes' movement, everything is freed, me included.

A figurative painter should suggest the light in his painting will fade out some time in the future. This has nothing to do with the intensity of the light illuminating the things in the painting: whether it is midday, sunset, or whether everything in the painting, including the candle, is lit with a candle.

The past? Yes! But only in so far as one lives no more in terms of obligation, but of extravagant supposition (and its "am obliged to you" of gratitude): no more "he must—," but "he must have—!"

She began cleaning the table, throwing away the remains. It was a removing of her make-up, a taking off of her clothes in front of me, but without all the awkwardness. One was losing a prejudice with every item she disposed of. Her slender pants.

One antagonist?! Only an infinity of them would answer to a bomb exploding into myriad shells. A conflict with them?! One wages war not against the problem but to safeguard it by hiding one's antagonists with the clarifying dust raised by war.

The desert night. The moon reflected in a mirage.

"He's of normal height." They overlook that he's standing on quicksand, and hence, that his height should be measured from the quicksand's bottom up and not from its surface up. What height is one whose head is quicksand?

Nothing is missing even though everything is in excess.

A branch entered my room through the window. If, when it rains, rain does not also fall in my room, I'll burn the whole tree.

I've been in Paris now for three weeks. Both hotels and universities are full. All the better. On the thirteenth day I had the apprehension I might get acquainted with a human being. Nothing of the sort happened. When I feel the need to have a discussion (an old habit that has not yet vanished completely), I see a film twice and have a dialogue between my two views of it.

On diet until the *a* becomes leaner and turns into an *e*: until *meat* becomes *meet*. Until one becomes a layer of skin over skeleton, dust on a mirror. Combing one's short hair.

The Fourth of July. Children on branches, like rotten fruits (a musty smell); drivers on cars paralyzed by the simultaneous red, yellow and blue of the fireworks; people on the comic magazines' bubbles of their thoughts; women copulating with men just so they can lie on top of them (the men accepting so as to deploy their white transparent fireworks in the vagina's darkness). Everybody is trying to have a better view of the huge artificial flowers, yet nobody is dazed by their odorless smell.

To Derrick and Edward:
You can be used for both the singular and the plural.
My father is no more. I don't miss you, since you've changed me (I think I too changed you) and hence will remain with me like things' odors carried along by the wind, which has left the things themselves far behind; a wind so violent one can smell nothing, except sometimes that odorless smell of the nose's hair. One misses only that which was altered by one but did not alter one.

I will try to call you (one *talks* on the phone, one *writes* a letter). Wrote this letter very quickly, so that you should not be forgotten in too slow a process of writing it (in some cases, that sadness (sometimes crowded, sometimes deserted), in other cases, that joy one feels on beginning to forget those who will remain with one; on knowing one will be accompanied by people who can no longer exist as company).

Both of us under the shower. Who would have thought I would drink water from her breasts?

Forty hours without sleep. Every moment, now, feels as a wake-up-early ordeal.

So long as a man opens his mouth to eat and/or laugh and/or yawn and/or shout and/or suck nipples, he will continue to speak.

Corpses carried by the wounded to the most distant of places, the ground. The wounded ended up buried in their wounds.

Grand Central. The distant voices and sounds (a drowning man's bubbles) of an infinity of people (a drowning man's bubbles) merge at unlocalizable points — some extremely near, already taste-free acidic particles dissolving the cheeks, the arms, the feet, the fingers' bones, the tongue, the darkness under the tongue — beyond which the eye breathes or suffocates. Suddenly, all sounds withdraw, creating a movement of suction (like a soundless snoring) that makes the resultant emptiness slap one. Then, once again, dizzy currents of sounds creating waves moving toward the foam. (Foam: the bubbles of a drowning sea in which silence, not only sounds, dare not enter). Everybody has the same gestures and movements, merely at different stages in their enactment. Could one of them mistake the breeze on his arm for his breathing, this undoing the heart-clock, making him both forget the timetable and forget to remember the timetable? Not a one none nary one not any I'll be hanged if there is one far from it not by a long shot nohow not for the world no such thing of naught by no means by no manner of means on no account in no respect in no case under no circumstances on no condition at no hand never no way no nope nay nix unh-unh certainly not no sir no mam not a bit no such thing nothing of the kind nothing of the sort not so not to be met with nonexistent existless unexisting missing not a sign of not a like or smell no sirree shucks no! They move by running. As soon as they have the apprehension that they will get at the required place before the prescribed time, they begin to trip, to collide against each other. Anything is permissible (even becoming temporarily inefficient) so long as it allows them not to get too early somewhere, for then somewhere becomes nowhere, and time, long imprisoned behind the hands of watches, floods all clocks. Subsides that which these immortality-loving people fear most: Clock's hands become oars floating, no, not on eternity (eternity: working time's strike; a time that works 24 hours/day (it also has another job on the side), that rests only when the clock is being adjusted), but on the sterility of time.

A black woman sitting on the floor is speaking to herself and giggling: creating a fog of words and laughter so as not to get sucked into this vomited movement of sore feet, suffocating armpits and blinking asses. A fog that made many people collide against each other. A fog; yet nobody got lost. After a while she turns away in tired disgust, and begins drinking.

Someone awakens from a nightmare with a shout, only to feel the knife of a murderer plunge through his cry.

Time-lapse cinematography accelerates incredibly the decomposition of a corpse compared to how the human eye sees it; but, even then, the decomposition is rendered much slower than it is experienced in reality. For in a corpse all filtering devices that ensure most stimuli remain below the level of sensation have dissolved; everything is felt. The flood. And there is no way to flee the decomposition of a corpse, this horrifying *life after death*: suicide, heart attack, death of any kind, are not possible. I speak from experience. Why aren't corpses anesthetized?

When the situation is hopeless, he doesn't react to it with despair: a refusal to become an echo. Neither does he wait for things to become better. There is too much sterility, one's own and things', in waiting. He has the grace to become distracted.

But beyond the decency of neither regressing to an echo nor indulging in the sleepwalk of waiting, beyond the grace of distraction, is the most difficult thing: to withstand the sterility of time. To try to wait for waiting is to be already outside the sterility of time and into one's own and other things' sterility. One can wait in history, not in time. Trying to wait (for waiting) in time is as meaningless as waiting for something to happen after the end of eternity. The distracted is perhaps the only one who tries to withstand the sterility of time, for time is history's absentmindedness.

Time is neither dead nor alive, it is the dying process, that instant when the non-biological rates of composition and decomposition of a thing become equal, and beyond which — the decomposition rate by then become more prolific — death has already occurred without ever occurring, since the thing has already vanished into the life of other things (the sterility of time is this instant prolonged endlessly). Dying, at last, divorced from death, no longer the shadow of this shadowy climax. To withstand the sterility of time is to experience the absence of climaxes. When, on his death bed, the prophet was about to say who should follow him as head of the Moslems, Omar al Khattab told those present not to bother to listen to the hallucinations of a moribund. All last words are the hallucinations of people who have buried dying in death.

Blocked writer. Testament to be written. Repeating to himself: Any lawyer can do it. He should know better: a writer never writes a testament, only lawyers do. Blocked lawyer then.

Not to evade time as waste through wasting time.

If, like a cat, one has nine lives, one may be forgiven wasting one dying. Already with eight, no.

Standing on the platform looking at the train moving away. Five fingers swaying in the train-blown wind.

Non-anorexic women loathe shy people with their flushed faces. For them all blood is menstrual blood.

A scene in which I have no part is a scene in which I am not even a spectator.

Water distilling in its sound.

The hotel manager shows him around his room. Near the bed, a copy of a painting by Monet showing rain falling. Above it, an air conditioner that drips. Under it, a vase containing artificial flowers.

A few days later, he moves to another room. The manager shows him around his new room: a replica of the other one (yes, the air conditioner drips). The manager drops a piece of information about the presence of something that was also in the other room but that wasn't mentioned then. A hotel room cannot be known by scrutiny, but by a lateral movement from one room to another, from one account to another.

At home only in places that are in exile. The subway, most of the time under New York, is such a place (except in rush hours, when it regresses to become New York's subway).

Never an occupation. A preoccupation.

Walked for so long my shoes, in very good condition when I left, were in tatters. Bought new ones. Only then did the trip begin. Walking barefoot, that is, with no roads separating one from the ground. For company this colorless yellow sand falling from one's shoes through the air.

Teacher: one trying desperately to learn from a student.

I am your long hair you keep moving away from your eyes, mechanically.

Noise scratching the skin until skin no more. Noise scratching against noise until it bleeds noise. Heard only by an eye that no longer blinks and whose pupil no longer moves. A pupil that has drowned in its cornea. Noise withering noise until particles of silence detach, forming transparent pupils.

The teacher of English enters his elementary class, "This class is noisy. Safa, go to the board and write *noisy.*"

Don't promise, that is, don't compromise.

One cannot react to an action, since an action is always simultaneous with other actions; hence its newness. One reacts only to a reaction.

Equality is made up of two minuses (=).

They know a city best who have fallen in love with a woman who lives there. They go on desperate walks through an infinity of streets, not at all seeing the places where they are passing, nor reading the names of the streets, all the better to feel the differences in the pavements; to hear the clamor of a drunkard, the silence of a crowd; to stare at the frozen streams on branches. During such outstretched walks, the changes from street to street alter imperceptibly one's thoughts about what to say to her. And yet, one ends up with the same phrase one should have said, and did say, for one is by now standing at the same corner looking at her house, from which the walk began, "I love you: I know, I am sure of, nothing anymore, not even of whether I love you or not."

Gauguin's *Le Repas*. The shadow of three oranges forms a bird. Sometimes things don't have to disintegrate first before becoming something else.

Not to lag behind one's ever circulating blood; to walk in company with it.

Don't get lost in the myriad paths my sauntering created in my small room.

One has become undistinguishable: people cannot find one, are unable to meet one, lost as they are in one's crowd, "There were many people there, all strangers to me; also that porous impenetrable blue of a table seen on video, and a sound without an echo: without the other sounds. I couldn't find him."
The herd: too many, which does not mean many. To detach oneself from the herd, one must become many and do so by making summation impossible, by becoming heterogeneous elements that cannot be added to give one number (or one yawn, the yawn of the etc.); for whether this number turns out to be one million or merely one is immaterial: each is one number only and hence one.

How do you open up to someone knocking at the wall?

On the rocky ground, my feet, unmoving. Three ants move from the ground to these feet and then back to the rocks. The anticipation of moving the feet at will.
A bar. Someone sitting close by, his cigarette lighter deposited in front of me. I can't move it myself. Time until he moves it. Time.

The mirror on which he painted his portrait
was shattered.
In his eyes,
like snow floating on the surface of a lake,
were pieces of glass
dazzled by his blood strange as a new color.
In his skin and fingers lingered,
moved like a snake,
the dangerous freshness of the edge.
In his ears, shells,
was the sound of a waterfall,

rain falling from earth to earth.

One collides against something whenever one moves, whenever one remains still, be it nothing other than the air one is breathing.

Every liquid is transparent, even red wine, even saliva; except that most liquids carry their container, melted, in them.

First meeting. Almost always, she's a surface pregnant with a depth. Thus one is reflected on her: one automatically has introduced oneself to her, has told her a story. And shyness is the awkwardness of shedding, instead of a reflection, a shadow. She knows that once one sheds anything at all, one will sooner or later shed semen.

One cannot remain in touch with the surface except by not adding to it another surface, one's reflection or one's shadow, hence reducing it to a depth.

Only by becoming a reflection, but of nothing, hence a surface that can float on any depth, a surface that will not drown to become the depth's surface, can a woman not reflect one: for nothing is reflected on a reflection (of nothing).

Nothing follows except hunting dogs.

More often than not they ask you a question, not so much to hear your answer as to make you answerable for your answer.

Mute, to evade the cry's easiness (the cry: a deafening yawn).

The circumference is encircled by the center point, not the other way around.

She was naked. I knew that the snake at her side would quickly shed its skin for her as clothes, and become yet another umbilical chord.

The ancients bowed to each other before parting. The bow was a way of reminding themselves that being unable to see someone did not mean he was far away.

The train, in this sedentary film, serves only to stop the cars.

Don't take away from them what they reflect, for then they become a mere reflection.

People: mirror images that linger obstinately even though there is no one in front of the mirror, even though there is no mirror.

Ill. That too intense, impure yellow of my urine as it falls in the water: am I urinating or throwing up?

Rules are against fighters. Including rules on how to fight.

— I am in an upside down relation to society, like the foetus in a mother's womb. I must be on the point of birth to myself and to the world.
— Women believe in nothing more than in jealousy. To them, there are always at least two males, the father and the child. Jealousy; hence always an afterword. An afterword; hence always a foreword, an introducing oneself, the telling of a story. A story contains somewhere a climax. A climax; hence to a degree the assurance that you can give her a child.
I loathe bastards, glued as they are to anyone who agrees to be their father. Each has an infinity of fathers. One who believes in fathers will reduce even a prostitute to a mother. When in fact, every mother is a whore who has been penetrated by millions — of sperm. A sterile whore: Let the sperm and ovules copulate; let them give birth to as many healthy sperm and ovules as they wish. What have I to do with the sex life of another species? One is not born. Hence, one should stop talking about being reborn. Women, behind their masquerade of loathing it, love nothing more than talk of rebirth. A woman's dream: giving birth to a child and rebirth to a father.

Walking back and forth on one-way pavements, in empty subway cars at $2 < x < 5$ a.m., on electric stairs going up, in front of cars hypnotized by WALK signs, on sea waves moving back and forth on the sand toward the shoreless white of the foam. Is reality fluid? Is this back-and-forth movement a rowing (without oars, hands, boat, shore, or heart)? Is one, at last, breathing in a non-mechanical way?

The cool breeze no longer refreshes me. Only a gust of cold does.

Tightrope birds on telephone wires. Will they fall into the safety nets of their wings?

The traffic lights swinging on wires in the wind are the only children I like.

— Why don't ears get sleepy?
— Mine do as soon as the darkness of an open mouth appears.

Whenever one looks at the sea, it looks out of focus. One then has to take away one's bad eyeglasses, even though one is wearing none. Looking at the sea, the eyes themselves are unsuitable spectacles.

The noise of the moving subway. The noise of the train passing in the opposite direction. The wind always somewhere in the cumulative noise of the two trains, and one is a plant, probably a leaf… or her hair.

It's the flesh that laughs, never the lean teeth ever submerged in the nausea of an endless diet.

Tomber sur une solution. Heaviness.

They used to give one a feeling of *déjà vu*. That was still bearable. Unbearable solitude: this feeling, nowadays, even as one stares at them, of déjà-overlooked.

The highway, like dying of suffocation on finishing a bottle with one sip. I travel in the back seat of couples' cars: a free man. The car moving away to another lane, with me staring at the yellow line receding into the dwarf distance. I feel like saying goodbye (to it?). Above, in a sky the color of two veins, a bird, its wings making farewell signs to nobody and nothing.

Why don't they brush their teeth after uttering so many unnecessary words? Solitude: all voices have become *ambient sound*. The ear a garbage can for words.

Isn't it strange she gets jealous of any attractive woman I meet, but never of the cool breeze passing on my face.

Her fragility a mist-covered-desert where one can collide against nothing, except, not water, but the freshness of water; where one can never start, only be start-led.

Only people who often fast are fast.

He brushed his teeth, rinsed, spat. In the creamy saliva on the point of disappearing in the sink, he saw four words.

Night, trees under which darkness hides from darkness.

June 26, 1987: Something strange happened: I felt shy passing a tree and the grass.

The silliness of her smile went very well with the excess of oil in the meal I was eating.

I'm drunk. Something is separating me from this man I feel strongly like punching, probably my hand.

You attract me fully, for you attract both my writing and me.

All the liquid of the universe can't fill the infinity of holes in the saliva of one mouth. Thirst.

To see the white, the pupil should stop looking and float on its back in the cornea.

I spat out the words that were in my mouth. I vomited my throat. If only words, like migratory birds, had their seasons for leaving us, for going away. Migratory words.

The crowded dance platform: I am the air fleeing their respiratory systems.

Veiled by boredom, except for her flowing hair. Passing me on her way out of the library, she says: "I am sorry if my talk with my boyfriend distracted you." It was not their voices that distracted me, but her freckles that give the feeling it is raining, her lips of a pink so pure that when they touch one can see the red color at the beach of contact.

She sat on my knee like a notebook.

A dancer knows that to be quicker than music s/he must at no time leave it behind. S/he has to be quicker than it while still accompanying it, never letting it lag behind, for music exists in a realm devoid of directions, so that the moment music lags behind you, it is you who are lagging behind it.

A hunter living at one with nature died. Are the ones who found his corpse a heavy wind? No. They dig a hole; lay his corpse in it. They throw sand over it until the earth is level again. They keep throwing sand until a small hill is created out of no wind. His corpse has not become sand again, which would be the case were the grave level with the sand around it, but has displaced the sand, and now the sand itself protrudes, looks awkward, obstinate, as if it were in water and did not distill; now the sand has become a floating corpse.

Wind trampled by wind.

Nothing is left me but the hug of the subway's closing doors.

White balancing my eyes with her teeth.

Ruth, in your absence the world is *Ruth*less.
Your eyes small like the room I'm living in. That's how they appear to me from the cancerous distance between us. Them eyes. I am grateful to you for making me use the word *them* again.

Found *The Reasonable Price Motel*. The search for a motel continued, for though the price was reasonable, the room wasn't. A foot put down: sleeping; a foot raised: waking (or is it the other way around?)
Rain, as in Tarkovsky's films, did not fall but distilled through the air. The thirsty world's thirsty skin (the thirsty world's umbrella) drank. Storm; raindrops: the wind's teeth. Need to rest while moving, to become a vortex in a fast moving river.
Two-day walk on pool-covered stammering roads. Another motel; people! I look at them and see holes in the air, places where one cannot breathe. The foreigner's exile: spelling (foreigners don't type), "*J* as in *Jalal, a* as in *ash, l* as in *laconic, a* as in *abroad, l* as in *unlike.*"
Numbers put one in an absentminded state, hence the frequency of mistaking other motel rooms for one's own. Unfortunately, the other room always has the bad number of occupants: two instead of one or one instead of two or two instead of three or three instead of five or ten instead of three.
Hotel room: What one does when one does nothing. Not to describe the object, to let it describe you. All pushing has dropped: it is as if what is in the room were being listed from one side to the other: a bed, a wall, a crack in the wall, a young man, a window, books.
Late at night: objects are distinct but not their distance from us. The person next door is watching TV on the balcony. It takes me $1/24$ of a second of looking at the TV to feel a total aversion. Pan. Another commercial: the billboard gleaming in the darkness.

The new world record: hit myself on the face fifty-nine times per minute (the previous world record was also mine: fifty-six times per minute). Typist of another kind, typist on my cheek.

Your legs right beside me and that I cannot touch, like this long sublime highway I see from the moving train but cannot walk on. Your laugh that I can prolong only by doing something childish, and now it is a laugh at me.

People abhor solitude. Hence, they abhor experimentation, for experimentation is the solitude of the unexpected.
They abhor to share your solitude, since to do this they would first have to create their own solitude.

A one thousand page book might contain more necessary lines than a sixty page book of aphorisms (of what is interrupted by its own conciseness). It won't contain more silence (nor more blank space and time. Aphoristic writers don't accept blank checks, for they know they won't fill the space between their names and the giver's signature). The sublimest combination: snow falling, river flowing: distilling while moving away.

Her fragility can be answered only by awkwardness.

A secret cannot be revealed since its revelation introduces the *speaker* and the listener into another world (hence it is as dangerous to hear a secret as to tell one). The real secret is this furtive displacement.

Action: X slapped Y on the left cheek. Reaction: and in the same movement on the right cheek.
The first slap can be an action only if contaminated neither by the thought of a reaction to it, nor by that of the impossibility of a reaction to it; hence, if it is not, even as it is occurring, already a memory (memory is the only imitation. Between one aphorism and another is a stretch of forgetting. If one remains at this forgetting, one will often mistake others' (not many) thoughts for one's own. One must forget this forgetting. Only then does one enter simultaneity). Inertia: the real repetition: the extension of a phenomenon until it is no longer an interruption (laconism is the only valid precision. All other kinds of precision are those of cooks, of those who deal with corpses), its reduction to a re-action. Memory, the *I*, is the interruption of the interruption. Not really: a cycle (eating-shitting, drinking-urinating, «from dust to dust») can never interrupt an interruption.
«For every action, there is a reaction». Certainly Newton was not an angry person. A reaction, even a deferred one, is always on time, it always occurs after the action. Anger is untimely (walking while very angry, the refreshing breeze licking my face like a dog. I despise dogs. I don't want to be separated from my anger). It alone can detect and prevent all the stolen *yeses* (drinking

from a bottle, he noticed the gesture of *yes* that went, not with it, but in it, that is, lived on it as a virus: the movement of the head up and back then down and forward. He brought a glass and sipped from it); detect and make it possible for all the otherwise missed *nos* (he was brushing his teeth. He noticed the gesture of *no* he was missing. He held the brush steady and moved his head laterally. Anger makes one, no, not stupid, but funny (nothing is as sudden as laughter, except anger). One has become as funny as any inhabitant of a Homs not to be found in Syria) to occur. No choice can occur prior to this.

Going through an action at all the different speeds (without repeating any of them) has nothing to do with repetition. It is a way (maybe the only way) to undo repetition. At all the different speeds except the slowest one, this latter being the black hole that swallows all the others, that therefore is not a separate speed, but a blockage, the annihilation of all the others. One can still experience the slowest speed if one gets to the absolute one, that being the same as the slowest one, except that it is a separate speed.

In the case of those usually designated as "most people" (Alan spelling his name: "*a* like in *Alan*, *l* like in *Leonard*, *a* like in *Anthony*, *n* like in *Nancy*." There is such a distance between them and me that they have become mysterious points sometimes eliciting my curiosity. I dislike their taking this curiosity as an interest in their person), each speed, with the exception of the absolute one, is determined by the resultant of the quickest forces, i.e., the ones present then. A decision — however much time one may take to reach it — is the instantaneous determination of the resultant force. A decision restates the outcome, hence its redundancy. It is a wasting of time in the instantaneity itself; yet, since it takes no time to happen, it still occurs on time. Hence, it is never confronted with the absence of time, a thing that makes it redundant. Decision is the opposite of choice.

Choice presupposes the impossibility of a resultant force (this impossibility of a resultant vector-force is the absence of time). Each vector-force (→) turns out to have been/turns into three lines (metamorphosis is not so much becoming an infinity of others as being able to let go (the nomadism of *letting go*), not to prevent one's dissolution (anger is dissolution, not explosion. This is something no actor will ever understand, and it is due to their taking anger to be a mere explosion, that they find it the easiest thing to perform. Anger as dissolution is aristocratic) into myriad forgetful pieces). So many lines (who knows how to count beginning with infinity? Only then would infinity not merely be an *etc.*, a film/video dissolve): a labyrinth in which all palm readers, including oneself as (palm) reader (— To write is to become a coward, one who can quote specific phrases about oneself and other strange things. — Who quoted these phrases as reader, not as writer), get lost. One begins with words (*losing one's way, losing oneself*), for words, when lost, can be found again — in dictionaries (these have a much too long *half life*). But what actually happens turns out to be more humorous, dangerous and scary: June 23, 1987: Loss of my phone book. July 1: Loss of a video editing room's key (a forty dollar fine). July 4: Loss of my cash convenience card. July 10: Loss of my international driving licence. July 14: while moving to another small room, loss of a bag containing my fake passport and a notebook. Today I lost my room's key. If this process does not stop soon I am afraid I may *lose* my mind (his fear of losing things extended now even to the distracted parts of his body).

A long preparation is necessary before an interruption can occur. Preparation is the undoing of the race, hence of selection, the undoing of breeding: All the forces-vectors (time itself is a vector), and not only the quickest forces, must get to the beginning line (not to mistake the temporary immobility (but is it immobility? The reason I like monochrome backgrounds so much is that one never knows whether the camera is moving or not; whether one is seeing a static shot or a pan and / or a tilt and / or a zoom)(*post-industrial, post-modern*, but also *post*pone (to have a *supersaturated solution*)(nothing is achieved in the total absence of forcing. Forcing: postponing the quickest forces becoming the resultant force. Both Orson Welles and Omran Toufic Omran say no book is bad insofar as its author put the best of himself in it. False. It all depends on whether the person put the best of himself in it according to both others and himself-as-reader-of-his-book (the quickest force: talent) or whether, outside all value judgments, he put in it what answered to this: If what one has written is lost (not only the page(s) on which it was written, but also erased from one's mind), would one be lost? That is the criterion for whether it should have been written (necessity is not always accompanied by certainty))) with laziness. Not to mistake distraction with waiting) and, henceforth, be dissolved into lines (no longer any *to*)(not to force the forcing, not to reduce the line to so many points, each the center of a vicious circle). Preparation is, hence, the marshalling of the dispersion of forces: these can no longer form a resultant force (this first dispersion occurs in time). Soon afterward the vector time dissolves (extremists are quite often angry with themselves about their moderation. All they remember are the times in which they rested. Indeed they rested, but only in so far as memory itself was their rest, their moderation. No, they did not rest: memory is the cunning of their anger), there is no longer any *time to* (those who never feel it is *time to* find out that time is never on time. Time should logically occur during, before and after two simultaneous actions. If it always occurs between the two simultaneous actions, it is because time is always late. And then one can't even wait for time, since one can wait for time only in time) and hence, no longer any *on time* (synchrony is made possible by the race (the start signal). For a race is nothing but the insufficiency of time, but also of eternity, for all the contestants but one (the vector time?). An insufficiency never felt as such, since the reaction is on time (Brain washing: they steal from themselves not only time, but also its absence, leaving themselves merely with its insufficiency). The edit to be performed. Two video editing decks. The two tapes move backwards for five seconds in order to have the same speed (be in sync) when the edit takes place (with 5850 decks, the movement backwards can be set to last 2 or 5 or 10 seconds). Having moved backwards for five seconds, the tapes stop rolling. A producer stretches a hand as stiff and rectilinear as a tombstone in which he holds a check; actors dub his closed mouth, "show us the script." There is the script, this paralyzed image on each of the two monitors. Now, all (producer, actors, cinematographer, editor) are happy, for they can be in sync with you, since you would be then in sync with yourself. That's what they want above all for they intuit that all sync is dubbing. Actors all of them, wanting you too to be an actor (or a scientist, which is the same thing, «Science means controlled observation and/or experimental methods that may be replicated by others»). To be in sync (on time, and having the same speed) is to be late (Against talent. Talent is always in sync with society. Even the talent that is misunderstood and neglected by society, i.e., submerged by its ambient sound. Talent has to be returned to society); in video editing, 2, 5, or 10 seconds late). The back-and-forth movement begins, the simultaneity of phenomena separated by (the absence of) time.

The absence of time: with his phantom hand he is scratching a red blotch on his paralyzed leg. The absence of time: an action done by one person and that takes one hour in life, when filmed in a medium long shot with the frame fixed, with no music or cutting used, seems to take an inordinate amount of time. Most actions experienced henceforth in the latter form. The absence of time: the zoom-in ended on an image still in focus: the cold; Solitude replaced by the absence of time (in solitude there is still *sol* (too certain) and *tu*).

The fast-moving car, the world slipping by in the opposite direction (not a back-and-forth movement). This won't do. One has to perforate holes (film's sprocket holes, video's control track) in the world, so that it would flow through the projector of the mind. Anger is this creation of holes (after Griffith, Toufic reinvents the iris). Then, one can accept everything in the (video) insert mode.

Choice is accepting all the dissolved forces, all the speeds: sound-over (due to forced non-sleep, one is penetrated by everything, becoming one's own X-ray); vomit-over (due to prolonged insomnia and weariness, one has the intense feeling one is vomiting all the external things surrounding one). Choice is a back-and-forth movement: one chooses all the speeds (the full cup)(sound-over, vomit-over); one is chosen by a new speed (a new thought and/or a new line and/or a new affect)(the extremism of accepting the drop to fall where it cannot fit)(voice-over (The actor repeated the phrase over and over. The voice must get over this over, this again. The voice must become voice-over. The voice-over must turn nomad, must leave leaving from synchronous lips that take turns simultaneously)). Then only, one enters stillness. Stillness has nothing to do with quietness (quietness is the instantaneity of the becoming a resultant force of the quickest forces). Stillness: turning a page, another page is skipped distractedly (nothing is skipped except projections)(a leap without anybody leaping (for once, a real mountain)), one going from the middle of a paragraph into the beginning of another, or from the end of a paragraph into the middle of another. One has become quicker than oneself (in-*vent*-er)(quickness and slowness are not a matter of how much/many things one does in a given period, but respectively, of whether one is quicker-slower than or in sync with oneself), like the wind (I don't believe in floods (I've never seen nor heard of anybody drowning in his/her blood or sweat), I believe there is such a thing as the wind, for I've often hit myself against the walls of closed-window closed-door rooms (the bones striking against the gummy malleability of flesh)) by-passing one, leaving one behind in its company (it is the wind trying to pluck them out of the earth, that makes the trees so tall in this region)(Youth, often the devil's advocate, was nonetheless clairvoyant enough in that it was slowly quick, thus eluded creating a suction movement that would have made it suck back all it was leaving behind). The necessity, when one is not in sync with oneself, of trusting oneself.

A nomad never rents unfurnished apartments (he spends his first hour in the apartment removing much of what is in it to the basement).

√ is not the meeting of two lines. Neither is X. √ and X are each not even the meeting of the projection of two lines (explanation: the projection of both the person to whom a thought or situation is being explained and of the thought or situation. Projections can never meet. And, since there is no necessity to projection, there is no necessity to where the projection of the thought and the projection of the person en-*counter* (2 IDs needed for paying by check. I pay in cash. The waitress' smile is her period) each other, for projection is the absence of a meeting. A meeting is the undoing of measuring devices, while projection is the en-*counter* of two measuring devices alternating in the twin roles of measuring device and thing to be measured (nothing can be measured except a (potential) measuring device). The cry of the baby on being vomited from her vagina is the 0 db tone. The meeting is the pre-sneeze. Followed not by a sneeze (in the sneeze everything first goes back to one squinting point (the blinking red traffic light is a stop signal) from which then everything explodes. Nostalgia is *this* going back to this point (nostalgia, hence, is already present even before the forth movement even begins, let alone ends). This going back to a point to then explode is not a back-and-forth movement. A back-and-forth movement does not comprise two stages, one preceding the other, but is an undecomposable unit) but by the harsh rainfall (The shower's water: the body floats (am I confusing distilling with floating?); music: the mind empties. One has become rainfall).

√ is the reason almost all males want her crotch, for they are students, including the teachers among them. As for me, I don't care about the √ (always lost my umbrella). I like the back-and-forth movement of her two breasts going in opposite directions (people get dizzy and annoyed when I walk back and forth in their presence. Why is it then nobody gets dizzy and annoyed at the back-and-forth movement of her breasts? (her two small breasts, one smaller than the other, and the whiteness of her skin, make the stretch from her breasts to her crotch a desert)).

He had written, "It is necessary that one be a cinematographer at least once in one's life, so as to experience how difficult it is to accompany anything, whether in a pan, dolly, or even a static shot." He asked her, "If when you dance, you accompany the music [a poor dancer], what do you accompany when you dance to silence?" She said, "When I dance, music (or silence) accompanies me." He corrected what he had written, "It is necessary that every male should become a cinematographer at least once in his life…".

When a person is accompanying anything, the latter is, logically, a reference; thus, a lag, however infinitesimal, is introduced (it can be hidden, but not abolished, through perfect projection). Men accompany music in sync (hence sloppiness, however imperceptible it may be in certain cases. Sloppiness is not the same as awkwardness. Sloppiness is still in the domain of forces, it is an imbalance of forces: the body like an incompetent physics student forgets to include, overlooks, a number of forces while making a summation to get the resultant force. Awkwardness is already a matter of speeds (being quicker and slower than oneself. It has to do with simultaneity). Awkwardness is the genuine movement). Music accompanies women in simultaneity.

Women dance to themselves. Dancing, they are at the same time seducing you (you've become her mirror. A woman does not believe in such a thing as "the mirror's objective view." To her the mirror is something to be seduced. She begins to believe in the mirror as unbiased only when her power to seduce vanishes) and neglecting you (there is something absurd and suicidal in asking a woman to dance with you, and something ironic in her saying yes: as in a pinball game, at least half the time you're not present, the ball/the woman playing/dancing by itself/herself).

Dance Road in Indiana: a contradiction in terms.

The alternative to women's dance (even their walk is a slow-motion dance (he saw her walking. He asked her: "May I?"). Dance is the nomadism of the sedentary. A woman who has given or wants to give birth is the house of her foetus, hence she abhors the homeless: a house is what needs most a house to shelter it) is the back-and-forth movement.

A fly's sound is neither at the background nor at the foreground, but at the *split focus* point between the two. It does not move between the two: no wastage of energy; no need to rest. Unfortunately, the rack-focus is not for that matter abolished, but occurs between the two ears of the hearer; hence his weariness (his need to rest) and annoyance. Similarly, the dancer is at the *split focus* point between energy and matter: some dancers are at one third of the "distance" between energy and matter, to the side of energy; others, at one third of the "distance" to the side of matter (Some people keep Oming about what they call "the dance of energy." Energy is domesticated in $E = mc^2$ (an atom bomb explosion merely serves to trigger a hydrogen bomb explosion. No phase is truly extreme)(Why isn't every physicist who declares that "$E = mc^2$" ($E = mc^2$ is not a back-and-forth movement) called a plagiarist?). Energy is too heavy: even light gets curved). The exchange between energy and matter does not take place in the dancer but in the watcher; the latter's weariness.

Both dance and the back-and-forth movement exile matter and energy; both are an exile outside energy and matter. Dance however, is still a matter of maintaining one's balance at the *split focus* point between energy and matter (it is this *split focus* point rather than the center of gravity of the body, that is the center of gravity of the dancer). A dancer is still too heavy. Dance is the nomadism of the sedentary.

Walking back and forth. This feeling energy has lost its significance and vanished. One sits down with the expectation of being assailed by what has been exiled from the back-and-forth movement, by energy and matter. Did something of the sort occur? Walking back and forth again.

A flower. I looked at it, touched it. Then it came to me through the distance of its smell. (One has to wait for the flower's smell, but since it started toward one even before one arrived, one's waiting does not take time: a non-servile waiting. Only the generous are available. But one also started toward it even before it had existence for one, even though it may never have existence for one: distraction. Only the generous are available. Hence distracted people's fidelity to strangers, and their shyness: to have started toward someone/something and then suddenly to have to act (this is their so-called failure to be natural) as if one had started toward him/her/it only on being introduced by words or povs).

When one sees water and other things without moving toward them even though one is absolutely thirsty, feeling that they are a mirage, one is already in the midst of the desert (a desert that can have the name of a big city). One may even become no longer sure about one's thirst, feeling it to be itself a mirage. One may still be saved if this feeling one's thirst is a mirage becomes itself the mirage, for then one becomes oneself the desert, and the desert in which one was becomes a mirage in the desert one has become.

He's tense. His reflection in the mirror at his side is contemplative.

Is the scream a clearing of the throat, the only real, necessary one, before speaking, any speaking, can happen?

The fragmentary has nothing to do with the use of close-ups, medium shots and long shots that are later joined in a smooth editing. Jalal Toufic's close-ups and medium shots indicate the part of the body which at that moment is not an extra of time hence not parasitical (anti-Bazin use: the frame is not a mask that has an extension through projection). The close-ups and medium shots often show the distracted parts of the body. Not to use the distracted part as cut-away to evade jump cuts (rather the shot of the distracted part should follow the jump cut), for the distracted part is a jump cut. When all the body is in danger of becoming an extra to time, it disappears, and is replaced with an intertitle that indicates the time during which the body disappeared and consciousness underwent a lapse.

When considering filming her, he thought of a long shot. The three minute film would have included the following shots: Low angle long shot of snow falling around a street lamp at night. Long shot of a woman. Shot of a room during the day: a man enters frame, goes to his desk and writes: "How to shoot a room in close-up?" Same room, shot at night, illuminated by the desk lamp, so that part of it is hidden by the darkness. "Shooting at night with the room illuminated with the desk lamp so that most of it is hidden by the darkness won't give a close shot of the room." He managed to film her in medium long shots standing in front of a jeep. Her instruction were to stand in front of the jeep, adjust her skirt, look off-screen left and wave. The weather was so cold the camera motor and the battery froze causing the camera to run intermittently: She is looking at the camera, seems to be listening to the director's instructions, then kneels down to adjust her skirt, which is off-screen; few frames of the jeep with no woman in front of it; she straightens up, speaks and smiles to someone off-screen right (three, this least seductive of all numbers. If she can't find someone else when she's with you, she'll have instead a mirror, so there'll be you, she, and her mirror image. Hegel's work of the negative is a woman in labor: father, mother, son; thesis, antithesis, synthesis. Nothing is less seductive than jealousy-inducing and jealousy), pointing several times to the camera. Then she looks back at the camera and kneels to adjust her skirt, looks up off to the left and waves, stops waving and stands waiting while a white flash consumes the end of the roll.

The film shots he took of her are shown without editing following a section during which the projector, with no film passing through it, is turned on. The white frame on the screen is initially out-of-focus. Safa says while walking back and forth in front of the screen: "Last week four students loaded the film emulsion-out base-in losing what they shot. Similarly one often feels now that things are going through one's mind and body emulsion-out base-in. Blank.

Walking back and forth is his way of making the elements (hidden by emptiness, nothingness, by the unframed blank (which is different from a framed blank whose off-screen is/turns out to be also a blank)) meet (clouds of milk swirling in the coffee). This making things meet is what most people call his trouble making.

Is this a great shot?

Before we do anything else... Focus!

Projection and filming done by the same machine, Lumière style, except that this is an edited light. This white is the negative of the darkness inside black bags and cameras (thought too occurs in a "black bag", while editing one's thought, like editing the film footage, occurs in the light/open).

Duchamp found his object, but invented the notion of *ready made*. Several experimental film makers used *found footage* (one must use the negative). I have found my *ready made*, my *found footage*. This is not over-exposure. It has nothing to do with any lack of control. A lab can correct it as little as it can

61

correct the underexposure of film theaters. This is the freezing coldness that makes metals (we are, according to Plato's *Republic*, metals) superconductive, that makes bones superconductive, that makes backbones superconductive, what moves through backbones and is the only lightning (other men try to attain this lightning through orgasm. Other men are proud of the size of their penises. How short are their penises compared to our backbones).

Is this a loop?

It is this same freezing coldness that makes both camera and batteries stop every few minutes (jump cuts)(The visual vapor of breath and words moving very slowly away from the lips for a short distance then disappearing without reaching the ear. In summer, headphones to listen to the silence in this endlessly shattering world). This coldness has to be fully accepted, for one must become superconductive. At the same time it must be fully resisted so that one will not be cryo-preserved, eternalized (for not only ourselves but also time must become superconductive rather than get totally resistant). It is this necessity of change that made one think that she also was changing — at least her position. So every time the camera stopped suddenly due to the cold, one reframed, for one thought she had changed, or at least changed her position, like a trap. What one later found strange was that she neither changed nor changed her position (— I was accepted in two universities, one French and one American. I chose the American.

— You chose nothing. Suppose the plane you took crashed and you died before getting there? Only by going there and being changed by it would you have chosen. Choice comes after the decision. To change is to choose. To choose is to have changed. She agreed to our getting together in order for me to find out things about her to use in my film. She completely misunderstood what "finding things in her to put in my film" (she kept using this imprecise expression I once used, word for word, in both the admiring and parodic usage of the quotation marks, but also in the "you have the right to remain silent, every word you say can be used against you" sense) meant: that we both change. We meet only what changes us and is changed by us (that's why meetings are out-of-sync). It is reciprocal change that excludes projection. Missing someone is our feeling that one, either ourselves or the other person, has been changed by the other without the other changing. The law of conservation of change, also known as the Toufic law, is a breach in the law of conservation of exchange, of ex change), yet every time one reframed her with the zoom lens to get her back in the same position as in the previous, interrupted shot, one would get another frame because one was oneself changing. One even at times reframed her absence, getting each time a different frame (the cold. Breath is visible as vapor; it has become a veil. I am so cold that her absence is now visible, veiling the world). It was this freezing coldness turning off the camera every few frames, and the resistance to this coldness (change), which made one constantly reframe, that made her appear to be coming closer and closer to one, and even at times, which is the most attractive thing, made her appear to be disappearing.

Was she herself attractive?

It is not that a lover does not notice the defects of the one he loves. A lover is a film camera: everything on the set that is not included in the shots (which may be out-of-focus, under- or over-exposed) does not exist, all that exists is the on-screen and its off-screen (Hitchcock, who believed in this more than anybody else, made many films where the woman is ideal: Madeleine in *Vertigo*, Jefferies' girlfriend (played by Grace Kelly) in *Rear Window*)(is the off-screen person or thing in focus or out-of-focus?). This off-screen is a legitimate projection, while to project from the shots on the screen to what the set(s) must have been from which they were extracted is an illegitimate projection (many of Hitchcock's films are about mistaken identities). If the lover himself films, the film or video camera often shows things on the set not included in the shots the lover-as-camera took. This is no longer a projection.

The freezing coldness precludes self-pity. One's sadness manifests itself now in one's feeling intensely the sublime gloom of a chair overexposed in a barren field, on which a priest is to be executed, on which he sits, a chair that has become a scarecrow, and one feels the darkness that must be descending on his open eyes (as if now the lid threw a shadow inside the eye), and suddenly one hears the whistling of small children, like that of birds at dawn (*Open City*). Tears: these relief/healing eyedrops leaving the eye instead of going into it! One then played back a recording of oneself crying, and went outside, letting one's face be covered by the cold-induced tears.

Never go out with a waitress, I am saying this both to men and to lesbians, for waitresses understand the word "change" to mean only "tip." Since every rule has its exception, one can go out with a waitress who is also a dancer (the waitress in *Limelight*, tray in hand, dancing while taking the customer's order), for a dancer knows that "tip" has more than one meaning and hence that "change" has more than one meaning, and can mean metamorphosis.

The waitress' smile abruptly ending as soon as she no longer sees you is a thrifty jump cut: the two shots with only fifteen (the suggested percentage of the bill as tip) degrees difference don't match. Don't both film teachers and their assistants (who repeat their words even behind their backs) repeat time and time again that the director should wait a while after the actor has delivered his lines or performed his action, before saying "cut"? In the case of waitresses, they are right: waitresses should not interrupt their false smiles as soon as they no longer see you.

Americans with their constant smiling (especially waitresses) and laughing (especially TV) make one think of Murnau's *Nosferatu*, which begins with these words: «Nosferatu! That name alone can chill the blood! Nosferatu! Was it he who brought the plague to Bremen in 1838? I have long sought the cause of that terrible epidemic, and found out at its origin and its climax the innocent figures of Jonathan Harker and his young wife, Nina.» Neither Jonathan Harker nor TV nor waitresses are innocent. Jonathan's constant laughing, his showing his teeth to everybody and everything provokes/ presages the appearance of the vampire (the cold one who chills the blood), the one sparing in his teeth (he has two only) and in showing them.

She smiles at you, even gives you her name ("Thanks, Sally." (I once wrote her on the check "You're welcome, Safa," only to get the same smile — falser than that of a bad actress), but have you ever seen a waitress wave at you as you came in or left? A waitress will never know how to wave. Unfortunately, for waving is one of the most attractive things in a woman. She had long laces short hair; her waving as she stood in the still air her long hair in the wind.

There is no sacrifice. Sacrifice involves two decisions for the same event. Between X and Y, one first selects X. Then, in a second decision one selects Y to the exclusion of X. This redundancy (years before, he had written, "The gayest, most difficult sacrifice: to sacrifice sacrificing." False. There is only one decision or choice for any event: there is no sacrifice) is echoed by the demand among those sacrificers who love logic (most of them do) that the one to whom the sacrifice was made indulge in the redundancy of remaining the same in reference to the sacrificer's coordinate axes. Otherwise the sacrificer indulges in the redundancy of regret.

— If you had to decide between your death and that of your favorite writer or film maker, which one would you choose?

— Mine (I am still twenty-six years old)(three years ago I attended a lecture by one of my favorite thinkers. I am sitting in the crowded auditorium; we're like so many footnotes (the solitude of footnotes), often cut off by the photocopy machine's thrifty frames (the 11 x 17, the 8.5 x 14 and the 8.5 x 11 paper size formats were not working, only the 5.5 x 8.5 could be used).

Speeds (ideas, affects, images,), meet for a longer or shorter period forming speeds of speeds. A person is a speed of speeds. A person can be quicker/ slower than or merely in sync with himself (photons are quicker than themselves in non-local interactions). If between two speeds of speeds that each comprises a new speed, one must select one to disintegrate, it should be the one in sync with itself (it may be the case that a speed that was achieved in past historical eras through a very fast movement, can now only/also be achieved through a very slow movement (or vice versa). It may be the case that a speed experienced in the past through a certain sense organ, or that was this sense organ, may now be experienced through a different sense organ, or be this different sense organ or even be experienced through or be a totally new sense organ). Between two speeds of speeds that are each out of sync with itself, one must select to disintegrate the one that does not have a new speed. One cannot choose which is to disintegrate between two speeds of speeds that each has at least one new speed, and that are each out of sync with itself.

An artist is someone who creates (The windy coldness in the still air slapped one. Nothing is, hence everything is to be annihilated by the distracted (only the distracted can do this without establishing total sterility, for the emptiness created by the distracted is itself distracted: $\Delta E \approx h/\Delta t$), so that a few things may be created, that is received (to receive (without having to wait) is to be quicker than oneself, but it presupposes putting oneself in a corner (the $\sqrt{}$ and X are corners)/against a wall that has to be perforated, hence being slower than oneself and it issues into the necessity of postponing what has been received, of being slower than oneself, so that a *supersaturated solution* can occur. Since being slower than oneself is an out-of-sync state, it does not permit others to catch up with one, for the out-of-sync (slower or quicker than oneself) belongs to simultaneity, while catching-up-with belongs to succession (postponement has nothing to do with waiting for one thing to lead to another. An aphorism does not lead to another aphorism. Implication belongs to succession (the one who is in debt is utterly slow, and a cause (*due* to…) is a debt))).

Nothing is: one has become both the darkness at the back of the mirror's glass (the mirror's glass' shadow)(an absence of images) and simultaneously one's mirror image, something that feels no cold, no hunger, no anger, no thirst, no depression, nothing, no, not even nothing.

It is then one experiences why one needs all the effervescence of the particles and movements that constitute the body: to counter the endless effervescence of the noise outside one. That is why emptiness, having no movement and no particles, has sometimes to shout:

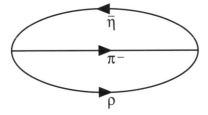

It needs to counter the intolerable noisy effervescence of movements outside it. When noise becomes even louder, emptiness' shout becomes even louder:

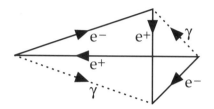

The law of conservation of energy, notwithstanding the uncertainty principle, can almost hear it now) one or more speeds, or is a new speed of speeds (a speed of speeds out of sync with itself: slower/quicker than itself). Some create one or more new speeds and are themselves a new speed of speeds.

Necessity is the only non-servile discipline. Necessity: the video waveform is the real marionette, the leanest marionette, a marionette that went on a diet until it lost its center of gravity (the center of gravity is the perspective vanishing point of the ground, hence obesity itself), a marionette that never falls (what falls on the ground (the ground is formed by the parasitical) is the parasitical). One has become so lean one is the rope on which one is the rope walker (the rope itself may trip because of the fissures that may take place in it). Nonetheless, necessity is not always accompanied by certainty. Only the one lost to the grace of getting lost, the one inflicted with the gangrene of memory, the one who has forgotten forgetfulness, is totally certain. Those who keep on coming to the same place, doing the same thing, can do this only because they are lost to getting lost, because they are moving in a circle.

Close shot, medium shot, long shot are out of focus terms (beside the point [of focus]); they are clear only to the producer who feels on reading them that he's dealing with professionals. The only genuine distinction is between a shot that includes the parasitical (how can one shoot a close shot of a room? Obesity is nothing but the parasitical; skinny people who have much that is parasitical in them are not lean. (Fat teachers: it is not only their bodies that are obese. Their voices have echoes, so that even when they stop talking and give one the turn to speak, one has the very irritating feeling one is interrupting them. One can't have a dialogue with them. Thrifty. I try not to have my silence have an echo, ever). I think the reason why she liked my room so much is that both she and my room were on a diet), and one that tries not to (this is its asceticism/laconism). Inertia: the obstinate (the obstinate is concentrated, the resistant is distracted)(hence having to do with memory) immobility of something in reaction to a movement that is overlooking it, reducing it to decor/insert/cut-away. This obstinate immobility reduces what could have been distracted (only the concentrated can be overlooked, because it is localized (the eyes, so as not to get distracted by what is in front of them, closing to concentrate in the darkness, where everything loses its way!)) to the parasitical. Distraction may be the only way of fighting against the parasitical without incurring the paranoic (sterilizing) demand for absolute control (even emptiness is not "pure": $\Delta E \approx h/\Delta t$). Resistance entails fastness. The apparent immobility of what is resisting is merely a stroboscopic effect. One shouldn't say merely, since it is the stroboscopic effect that permits one both to maintain one's increasingly fast movement, and oneself, invisible (through a decreasing shutter angle)(Don't force upon me the change from invisible to visible, with those eyes that have always, a priori, said yes even when you say no. Certainly not when it is because of mere interest (Continental Bank has a 5.55% rate for money market average balances of $500.00 to $999.999 (7/31/ 1988)). I share with Muslims their refusal to take interest on their money in banks and hence their refusal to intrude on a person or a thing out of mere interest) and to make people feel the stagnation of the historical period in which they are living (it is part of resistance to resist projection (to a better historical period); never project: projection is the opposite of being quicker than oneself (the latter is a hurrying of time and hence is a simultaneity phenomenon. The former is a hurrying of the person (in sync), hence conserves the present-future structure).

— One of the main differences between a human being and an animal is that the former can imagine a change.

— One's imagination of a change is real (whether or not it gets actualized) and not a mere projection, only if one wills to put oneself in a corner/against a wall (this is the phase of creation that admits of will (change itself is one's becoming someone else, hence it is outside of one's will)), outside of the possibility of evading receiving this imagination of a change (itself then a change)(even if what is received is impossible, the impossibility does not take away from the reality of the change. An impossible but real change: the miracle). First then, one puts oneself against a wall/in a corner so that, second, one may be forced to change; the impossibility of evading receiving a change (change: what one meets at the end of one's perforation of a wall) whether the latter was imagined beforehand or not, is the criterion for whether it is real (what gets actualized may be different from what was imagined, but if what was imagined was received outside any possibility of evading getting it once one put oneself against a wall and perforated it, while what got actualized wasn't, the former is real (prophetic), the latter is not (a line written without the impossibility of evading receiving it, but received with the impossibility of evading receiving it by the reader only became real when it was read (if a copyright is to be attributed to anyone at all, then it should be to the reader)) and not whether it gets actualized or not (much of what is actual is not real at all). To replace Berkeley's «To be is to perceive or be perceived» with: To be is to be received at the end of a perforation of a wall). In stagnant historical periods people equate the joltiness resulting from the sharpness of the frames caused by the reduction of the shutter angle with a jump cut. But the latter occurs at the level of images and not of frames (exception: Peter Kubelka's films). They want to reduce resistance and hence jump cuts to this annoying joltiness, when this joltiness (obstinacy: a film frame that wants to be treated as a photograph) is really merely the shadow of the invisibility of one's movement (made possible by the reduction of the shutter angle).

Never hurry anyone or anything (generosity demands nothing), let each take his/her/its time (to wait for something is to hurry it. To wait even for nothing is to hurry it), that way if he/she/it is generous (old people's generosity: shrinking in size, leaving more space to others), starting before you arrive, he/she/it will not make you wait (waiting is servile); but hurry or slow down time itself (generosity is demanding), getting an out-of-sync time into which you collide or that hits you from behind, corners/walls forming that have to be perforated (one has to maintain the minimum of force (a force being a knot of speeds) not dissolved, so as to preserve the possibility of being forced (only what contains a force can be forced) to perforate the corners and walls, in order for a meeting to occur. But can't one meet a wall or a corner? Yes, when all one's forces have been dissolved into speeds. This has to be postponed, rather than abolished, as long as possible. For though meeting a wall or a corner, instead of colliding against them and trying then to perforate them, does not itself block creation (in fact everything then is a miracle), it presupposes the dissolution of all one's forces and hence of one's ability to be forced to perforate (walls and corners), rendering one unable to create).

To hurry oneself/another person/an image or to be hurried by them is to use or be used by oneself/another person/an image as insert/cut-away to steal time (and sell it). Only this abstract time created by the insert, this time become merchandise, is money. (The insert is a surgical beauty operation performed on time (its use preceded by many decades the ones performed on the human body)). "Time is money." That's why they don't let time pass in the shot, but go to inserts (that's why they have more than one character in almost all scenes: to be able to cut from one to the other (to use them alternatively as inserts and have them use each other as inserts (If they sometimes accept shooting one-character scenes, it is because they can use povs as inserts. How many of the povs found in film, but also in the world, are not merely inserts? That's why people close corpses' eyes: so as not to be forced to see (a real pov) that the pov is an insert in the corpse's case but also in almost all other cases))) to cut time (the unbearable solitude of the one who resists inserts, who accepts neither to use someone or something as insert nor to be used as one). But once you don't let time pass in the film, the film becomes a pastime. That's what they want. The insert/cut-away is what makes possible the identification of spectator with character (the cut-away as spectator-suddenly-inserted-in-the-film). The spectator in the auditorium gives money by buying the ticket, the spectator in the shot (insert/cut-away) gives money by reducing time to money. Boredom is always the boredom of the parasitical/decor/insert, that is the boredom of the spectator; it should never be confused with the absence of time related to the distracted parts of the body, to the *still lives* of the body.

Once one begins to do away with the audience inside the film, that is, with all that is in the scene merely as either spatial or temporal decoration (insert/cut-away), with all that is there merely to fill the auditorium of the screen, one finds out that the film theater itself becomes emptier and emptier. No one is a worse actor than the spectator identifying with a fictional character.

I do not consider the above perforation to be a mistake. But those who may consider it a mistake should know that when one has given everything and is still expected to give more, one can give a mistake. A mistake then is the ultimate generosity."

The teaching assistant (*vice*-president) tells me: "I can't hear your voice in this film." In the coldness one has become and that nonetheless surrounds one (Van Gogh's *La Meridienne*: is it strange that the sleeping-resting peasant should shield his eyes with his hat, when everything around, including his hat, including him, hence including his eyes, is emitting blazing light?), one often coughs instead of speaking. This cough is still one's voice (I don't like my recorded voice but I don't dislike my cough on the sound recorder). I am sick not because of the cold, but of these formal people who stress form (form is a waiting (choice: to perforate the wall (one should try to alternate between the perforation of walls (and hence choice and reception) and tunneling (the blank between the aphorisms is the insulator between the superconducting parts of a Josephson Junction). The wall is an obese insulator, or an obese particle unsuccessfully trying to tunnel through an insulator (to become of the right mass the particle has to metamorphose into another particle with a lesser mass). Walls shield us from the cold needed for superconductivity, for behaving in a quantum way). Choice is also the acceptance of all that will be received at the end of the perforation of the wall. While waiting is the deferring of deciding between several alternatives. The abundance in the case of waiting is between the different alternatives. The abundance in the case of postponement is both that of the supersaturated solution and that of the dissolution of forces' vectors into their lines) that is not sensed as a waiting (the moment one begins waiting (but does waiting begin at a precise moment?) everything begins to jostle, things, people, electrons, events, on their way towards where they are awaiting themselves. How can one not be distracted by this, and how can what one is awaiting ever reach one through this commotion (this flood is the weight of waiting). Waiting turns any appointment into a chance meeting)) so much (for some of us *well done* is overly cooked) and who preserve themselves in psychotherapists' formaldehyde.

A secret is the indistinguishability of truth and lie.

A suicidal person is one who does not have a memory of the future.

Something is challenging you to view it as a challenge. You are first challenged by the challenge, only then are you challenged by the thing.

Strange that all this pain should remain inside the body, should not seep out of it. Not being contagious is stoic. The cold in which pain takes place makes pain conductive; conductive yet not contagious.

It is part of the miracle one's hearing about it although it is what excludes witnesses (even in the form of the one who made it).

The bird will fly in the air, will swim in the wind.

The etc. is repetition.

The cold like a phone conversation neither person seems able to end.

Her red lips a continuing blush.

A good dancer cannot be bumped by another good dancer, only by a bad one (a bad dancer is constantly bumping against music and other dancers). It is enough to have one bad dancer on the platform for it to become jammed. Bad dancers give you the same apprehension bridges do: at a certain frequency of the movement of the passers/at a certain beat of the music (even though the bad dancer is not dancing to it), both would disintegrate. Nothing kills dance (or laughter) as quickly as the merest sign of effort. One has to have looked only once at dancers to know forever that melting has nothing to do with the straight gravity line that a drop of water falling from the ice traces. Good dancers' feet movements an acupressure of the floor.

Grace: dancers' movements: a car passing green traffic lights, reaching other traffic lights just as each changes from red to green, passing them without having to stop, never arriving at a yellow traffic light (her smile as ambiguous as a yellow traffic light). Dancers and graceful drivers, unlike kings and dictators (who function through immobilization), have green carpets, not red ones.

A grace that can easily be undone by bad dancers and drivers: a long line of already stopped cars (like numb feet) when the light turns to green. A car that by grace arrives just then would nonetheless have to stop, for not only does the first immobile car need time to accelerate from zero speed, but also the n+1 car can't begin moving until the preceding car has moved. The already stopped cars are an additional red traffic light.

Air and water are different media in which different kinds of beings live and move. Music also is such a medium; one has only to look at the dancers.

Her hair on which the light slides like a child.

The only freshness is the untimely.

Their last weapon against you is to make you despise them totally. Too much contempt is sterilizing.

Ships and corpses float, they don't have the density of pebbles. To become so dense one's reflection in liquids drowns.

I am so tired it seems amazing those reflections floating on the Seine don't drown in it.

Crossing out a blank.

Cioran says: «The aphorism is a conclusion. I write two or three pages and publish only the end result. I spare the reader the progress of my thought». He writes: «One must censure the later Nietzsche for a panting excess in the writing, the absence of rests.» One must spare oneself the progress of one's thought. An aphorism is not the conclusion of anything (not even of itself). It has no beginning, middle or end → it can occur in the beginning, middle or end of anything. What is not detached is merely a phase towards the one and only conclusion: nothing is necessary (not even this conclusion). This conclusion is irrefutable (it nonetheless refutes itself) but only within the domain of conclusions. And someone used to the long weary rest of that which *leads to* would object to what appears out of the white if one is walking, out of the blue if one is writing.

A book of fragments cannot be summarized → it is itself a fragment.

This morning the sun like a car's headlight.

The way her eyes moved from one direction to the other: as if the pupils gently plunged under water to emerge at the other side of the eye.

Simultaneously hearing and overhearing the same person: Noise.

There are separate sections in restaurants, different compartments in trains for smokers and non-smokers. I am a non-smoker who does not care in which of these he ends up sitting. They should have different compartments/sections for talkers and non-talkers.

Time: These lines on the blank pages of wide/narrow/college/legal ruled notebooks, that have already crossed out what one is writing.

I write on the horizontal lines of raindrops traced by the cars' headlights.

The music suddenly went wild, dancers no longer able to be simultaneous with it, and began to rid itself of even the best of them. I have seen a striptease of music.

— I thought Lebanon is very small.
— Except that it is sometimes Hell there, and Hell is much larger than all the world's countries, larger than the universe.

I'm drunk. Don't mind my laugh, it is an equilibrium device.

I arrived at the cafe five minutes too early. The city life unrolled in front of me for seven minutes. She arrived two minutes late. Then the city receded inside the shell of her open lids.

Her eyes as mysterious as the perforated teeth of a vampire.

Women don't like immobile persons, for their breasts which jerk up and down and sideways when they run (not so when they dance, even to very fast music) are a hand-held camera, and the jerkiness of the camera movement is most noticeable when what it is shooting is immobile.

It is because certain parts of the body are distracted that a description made with a collection of them can occur as an absence of time (Natasha, since I met you, you turned on the time for me (as in *turned on the light*))(any description that is not the description of an action takes place as an absence of time (one close-up is not a description. Only by putting together several close-ups, each appearing for a limited time, does one get a jammed time, a time no longer moving, a description), but the description itself takes time: the spectators feel the passage of time). Simultaneously, in so far as any one part shown in one of these close-ups is distracted from/forgetful of the other parts shown in the other close-ups, that is insofar as it is distracted from/forgetful of the description, it exists in time. It is this disruption of being simultaneously in and outside of time (hence out-of-sync) that makes the distracted feel so intensely the absence of time. It is this simultaneity that makes inactivity unbearable to him/her, since the latter makes possible description and hence the absence of time (I have the flu. (Her flu cheeks). I have to stay in bed. It is as if my immobility were the sudden paralysis, the amnesia of movement that befalls bad dancers at the outset of a sudden manifestation of tiredness).

Activity is not the solution, since the distracted parts of the body are by definition what is distracted from the action. Action merely reduces the distracted part to an insert (better withstand time's absence than reduce time to a merchandise). You can't use the distracted to gain money since the distracted resides in an absence of time (while an insert steals time), and time is money (only time that is on-time/in-sync is money. Time is not always on time, money is always on time). Since we're dealing with distracted parts, the camera itself and the editing become distracted and don't stay on one shot long enough for time to pass. What is *the distracted constant of time* (as in *Plank's constant*) for each shot, beyond which time passes even in the description of a non-action?

Speeds (ideas, affects, images,), speeds of speeds and a body-as-noumenon (it is not the slowest speed. Redundancy is the slowest speed)(to know of its existence is already to have experienced it as intensely as anything can be experienced. This body is the same in everything. All of it is in every one thing, whether this thing be a telescopic, a naked-eye or a microscopic thing).

The new (which includes some lies (most lies are repetitions), some errors (most errors are repetitions)), that which not only cannot be repeated-as-new, but cannot be repeated parenthesis (c'est seulement au théâtre que la répétition vient avant, everywhere else the rehearsals come after), is simultaneous. Both the back-and-forth movement among the simultaneous and the coexistence of all events in the four-dimensional universe of Einstein undo the one-way movement of the pendulum's time. There is an absolute difference between the former two.

I am walking and will arrive late as usual; unless rain begins falling harshly. Harsh rain is nowadays my only way to get on time (it is my alarm clock, the alarm clock that has the most beautiful sound).

The cafe in which I am sitting completely drenched has glass doors and windows. It is raining outside soundlessly as if in a silent film. Someone opens the door and runs. The door an umbrella separating one from sounds. As it was opened I got splashed by rain's sound, by the drops of sound. When rain falls harshly, even if on streets, it feels it is falling on roofs. No need to go up Sears Tower or the World Trade Center to have an overview of the city, one can instead sit and look at the harsh rain falling on things.

I made a mistake enrolling in a university. Still, I thought it is possible that someone else among the myriad students found s/he also made a mistake. Not one.

The skinny go-go girl is now completely naked: even her teeth are naked in the endless smile (her smile must not have an orgasm and end. Only the audience is to have an orgasm). She's moving not so much in front of their *naked* eyes, as in the presence of their clothed dicks. Ten long minutes pass and now she has to undress of her flesh, to show the naked bones protruding underneath it. I love the mask when under it is only skull. The beauty of the skeleton: it is a mask under, not above, the flesh.

This drowsiness one feels in subway trains and that has to do not with the time of day but with this intermittent passage through artificial (nothing is more artificial than the distinction artificial/natural) night of tunnels, emerging time and time again into the day.

His arrogance showed itself in his refusal to persuade.

The way she smoked: as if I were her dog and the smoke the stick thrown for my look to fetch.

The hug of our two tongues. Shivering subway lights.

Thinking is a resistance to forgetfulness totally unrelated to any attempt to remember.

Le propre des choses est d'arriver ("quelque chose m'est arrivée"); le propre de nous est de quitter?

One arrives in Brooklyn from Manhattan, and it is as if one has moved from the real night into a night shot on a one hundred ASA film, so much does everything look so underexposed, so dark.

Circular track. You're moving at a fast rate. He/she/it is moving at a slower rate. You, who wants to meet him/her/it, repeatedly pass him/her/it. One may then end up thinking that to meet him/her/it entails not only closeness in space but having the same rate of movement, the latter entailing that one circles the track so many times until one is so tired one's movement is slowed down, becoming the same as his/hers/its. This thought itself signals that one is already tired. Tiredness belongs to the insufficiency of time: tiredness necessitates rest, and it is this necessity of rest, of time spent resting, that brings about the insufficiency of time. Slowing down one's movement through tiredness makes it impossible to meet someone with a slower movement, even if the two movements become equal, for tiredness is the insufficiency of time to meet the other. Slowing down one's movement through tiredness does not permit one to meet slower people, but it also makes it impossible any longer to meet oneself, one no longer having sufficient time to do that. Not to confuse the insufficiency of time with the absence of time. The distracted postpones (being slower than himself (out-of-sync)), getting a *supersaturated solution*.

Two completely different kinds of pressure: the one due to tiredness and the insufficiency of time is a hurrying of the person (it leaves him/her in sync); the one due to distraction and hence to the absence of time is a hurrying of time and hence a creation of out-of-sync.

Whenever one writes one is under pressure. Not that one defers writing to just before the deadline (the distracted function very poorly under this form of pressure: a deadline is not a wall (the distracted is the furthest thing from the journalist)), but that even when one writes while still having a year to finish a few pages, one writes on that night in a hurried time (out-of-sync): that's why it's no use trying to convince oneself one still has more than enough time (if creating is receiving, how can one ever be sure one has enough time?), for it is not oneself that is hurried (looking through the moving train's windows: the scenery passing in fast forward. Is that why one feels sleepy on subway trains, the sixteen hours of waking time having passed so quickly?) but time itself; an inhuman pressure. It is also in this sense that writing is suicidal (no memory of the future).

Can one call the left hand (the one that corresponds to the blank between aphorisms but also between the phrases of aphorisms, and sometimes between the words of aphorisms) of right-handed people that remains motionless while the other hand is writing, lazy? One cannot apply laziness (rest from rest) to the distracted. One's distracted, rather than one's immobile parts, are the cat in one.

This preoccupation with "the other hand," the left hand that remains motionless while the right one is writing, must have originated with the "on the other hand," with the attempt to find new things. When one says "on the other hand" one is referring also to the left distracted hand, on condition it never be reduced to a (film) slug to get sync. Thinking for long about this other hand and other distracted parts one ends up feeling oneself to be the distracted part of the world.

A weakness in Peter Rose's *Secondary Currents*: when the person translating in voice-over the words on the black screen reads a phrase that says he's moving away, the voice becomes fainter and fainter: his voice propagates in a Renaissance perspective space. Antonin Artaud writes from Rodez in a language that, unlike Rose's Yerdic (a language he invented), cannot be translated, not even by himself (translation is representational, it represents one language to another).

In Part I of *The man who could not see far enough* we see a man looking from a porch at the houses and the street across. The screen is divided into three frames-sections. What was important in *Analogies* as here is to put the past, inscribe it, in the screen: the past is one of the three frames. The question is: which? Is it the first frame covering one third of the screen, that passes over a given segment of space, so that by the time the third frame passes over that segment of space the first frame is already part of the past in relation to that space? Or is it rather the third frame, since it is repeating what the first frame has already accomplished, a figure of memory?

In *Analogies* at times the last frame on the screen goes over the second one, then over the first one, preceding both. Seeing this one knows that the future can precede the past and the present. The déjà-vu is created by this displacement of one frame over another to precede it or to lag behind it (déjà-vu has replaced foreshadowing and memory). Unfortunately, in *The man who could not see far enough* this displacement of the frames over each other is discarded: simultaneous with the orderly, consecutive movement of the three frames inside the screen a dissolve will be taking place in one of them. Dissolves have to do with memory, but even the strange memory of Plato (Plato's *Meno* and its doctrine of knowledge as recollection) or of the Delphic oracle (a memory of the future)(Never preface things with *you know*. What gives the *hence, therefore, because*, the grace they have when used by aphoristic writers, a grace they usually don't have, is the intermingling of tenses in the aphorisms. For though an aphoristic writer edits, joining what was received one at a time, he does not change the tense in which each thing was received, does not hide that some are received in (the form of) the past (the past has nothing to do with memory but with the reception in the form of the past: "I saw..."), others in (the form of) the present, others still in (the form of) the future. This is what makes it possible for the effect to precede the cause even though the *because* is still an arrow from the latter to the former. Aphoristic writers cannot learn from experience precisely because, or also because, what they received at the end of a set of experiences might have been given to them in (the form of) the past, the experiences themselves having been lived in the (form of the) present (in a few cases they can learn from experience because what was received in the form of the past may yet be found as a result in the form of the present of the experiences that preceded it. The difference between the two is equivalent to the difference between the propagation of light between two objects and a non-local correlation between them)) is still inscribed within an elastically traditional time. Peter Rose showed us, by means of the dissolves, that memory occurs in each of the three sections: memory occurs in the past, in the present (the present does not remember the past) and in the future.

A fragmentation of space and time in *The man who could not see far enough*; a fragmentation of words in *Secondary Currents*: what is difficult to achieve and that Peter Rose accomplishes is to create a non-representational distance (the distance signified in the perspective lowering of the voice-over to mimic the movement described in the phrase being translated ("I moved away") is too easy): this is achieved in the last section of *Secondary Currents*, the words dissolving into their elements. Spelling is undone: one can't say any longer *p* as in *pig*, for *pig* has dissolved into *p, i, g*: "*p* as in *p*" (Gertrude Stein would say "a rose is a rose is a rose" (his name is Peter Rose)): The three frames (nothing dialectical about the number three in Rose's films) passing over the same segment of space.

To show skeletons in animation films is to switch from the geometrical-abstract (the line that delineates the person in animation films has the leanness of the layer of dead skin covering the body, though it is a geometrical line) to the nervous-muscular system, the line an X-ray image of the person. Brakhage's *Mothlight*: the muscles in the dead wings scratches over the film (like a bad print).

Things are not obstacles to most people and animals (a signal, for instance light, not issuing from them, hits an obstacle, gets deflected and becomes a stimulus as it hits their eyes); but they are obstacles both to bats (as far as the constitution of perception is concerned) and to me, for we orient ourselves by sending a signal that hits an obstacle, gets deflected and becomes a stimulus on hitting our senses.

Ways in which the membrane relates to sex in Cronenberg's *The Fly*:
The membrane-as-aura as an ecology of sex, "normal" (putting quotation marks around words and concepts to signal that they are problematic has

been so overdone by some of Nietzsche's disciples that one should now put quotation marks around the quotation marks "' '") sex as an ecology of the membrane.

— The wounded membrane (spaceship crossing-wounding the earth atmosphere's membrane; airplanes crossing-wounding the wall-membrane of sound): Brundle is wounded, while making love, by a stray computer chip... The infliction of wounds one finds everywhere in the film is an inefficient, ambivalent way to accomplish the disappearance of the membrane, since while destroying part of the membrane it gives it prominence through the pain its wounding or removal causes, and through the nostalgia of, hence for, its restitution.

— The stripped membrane: during the first teleportation, the computer turns the baboon "inside out": the computer age's form of striptease: stripped of one's membrane (the total wound).

— Sex presupposes not only the membrane but *often* also the penetration by a vehicle either of those areas where the membrane involutes, or else of other areas, in which case wounds result. Teleportation abolishes both vehicles or projectiles (the latter a special kind of the former), and hence abolishes the penis (vehicle) and sperm (projectiles). Cronenberg is right in linking teleportation to the absence of the membrane and hence of sex, the membrane replaced by the computer screen, sex replaced by genetic splicing.

Membranes are being abolished: Cronenberg chose the fly as the second element with which Brundle is spliced, for a fly has a perforated shell, not a membrane. There is an almost non-existent use of off-screen, for the screen's edges can become, through extensive use of off-screen space, a membrane.

The first teleportation of a baboon is a disaster because, as Brundle says, the computer was giving its interpretation of the baboon. A successful teleportation presupposes the abolishment of interpretation, both because the latter takes time, and because it is a depth phenomenon, while teleportation is a telescoping of time (the teleporting machine is a time telephoto lens): loss of temporal perspective, hence of the depth and interiority of things. Everything floats to the surface-become-screen which replaces the membrane. With the instantaneity of teleportation, the eye has no time to travel from foreground to vanishing point. The white fat frames of the polaroid photograph are a warning of the impending blindness, the superimposition of all colors creating this bandage-like white around the polaroid photograph, the latter like a premature new-born that has to be protected. For if time is compressed further, the light hitting the cones and rods in the eye won't have enough time to reach the vanishing point of the eye that the blind spot is, without which there is no vision.

Brundlefly does not feel pain when he completely removes one of his fingernails, nor when one of his ears falls off, nor when his teeth fall out, nor when the mat shell of flesh covering him falls off in the last scene (it is no use saying that these are vestiges, organs that have outgrown their usefulness. The removal of a vestige is painful, sometimes more painful than the removal of a functional organ). The total absence of pain (pain is, in however infinitesimal a dose, in every affect, sensation, idea. Its total disappearance means their eradication, the appearance of the absolute automaton. Metamorphosis should always include some amount of pain, otherwise it becomes a mere special effect, for pain is the unforgettable that cannot be remembered and hence, what holds together in a meeting the oblivion, hence dispersion, of metamorphosis, metamorphosis being one's becoming someone or something else) turns the body into a screen.

If we understand AIDS to be only the first of a new kind of diseases that paralyze the body's immune system, then the condom is only one variant of the screens they will introduce. The body in *The Fly* can no longer afford the luxury of taking in external objects and processing-digesting them inside itself; instead the processing of what may ultimately be allowed to enter the body is done outside the body. Brundlefly vomits, or to be more precise, secretes (for vomiting is painful and Brundlefly does not feel any pain when he performs this digestive operation) enzymes that digest the food outside the body. The food that has been liquefied outside the body is there for analysis, it has become a computer screen on which is read (with the help of lab control substances and techniques) whether it is healthy or not; it is tested before it enters the body. The body is no longer trusted to defend itself (the same thing happens in the case of sound in the film; all ambient sound is maintained at a ridiculously low level, as if the ear were no longer trusted to digest the sounds by itself. "Somehow I get the feeling you don't go out much." "You can tell that?" The outside is the impossibility of controlling the level of the individual sounds, the impossibility of controlling what is received (One can, no, one must try to work on what one considers to be unjustified biases one holds. One may also try to detect, in order to work on them, one's hidden unjustified biases, a good way of detecting them is through conducting interviews, with oneself preferably in the position of interviewer. One can, one must do this before putting oneself in a corner/ against a wall. Whatever is received at the end and during a perforation should be accepted (it might be changed during/by the end of a subsequent perforation), even if it is impossible (the miracle is this acceptance of an impossibility that has been received), even if one receives a bias, for a bias received at the end of a perforation of a wall is a justified bias (cruelty)(one's refusing to accept it on any grounds is a levelling, a sentimentality); it may be a justified bias against oneself (nothing to do with guilt)). A sound level adjusted so that the ambient sound not obscure/interfere with what the main (the outside does not admit of *main*) characters are saying to each other (the voice-over has to be resisted especially in the form in which it occurs in *The Fly*: Brundle has changed so much, has metamorphosed into Brundlefly, yet his voice is still intelligible, a voice that is not over, becoming a voice-over in sync) is always inside (no sound fly). "You want me to be more specific here, in this room, with half the scientific community of North America eavesdropping?" Almost a joke, for when Brundle says this, the ambient sound of the extras is maintained by Cronenberg so low (so that we would be able to hear very clearly what the two main characters are saying to each other) that it seems as if the scientists in the huge hall are indeed speaking in a such a low voice in order to be able to hear what Brundle is saying).

The DNA operates in a realm in which the membrane is absent. This doing away with the membrane means the abolishing of the mirror: there is no mirror in the absence of the outline that a membrane constitutes, in the absence of the outline as membrane. In a film about metamorphosis it may seem strange that one sees a mirror only once during the whole film, in the scene at the end of which Brundle discovers that teleportation has changed him. But even in this scene it is not his slightly altered face which he sees in the mirror that makes him know he has changed, but the absence of pain, the fact that he can take off his fingernails painlessly. It is to the credit of Cronenberg that mirrors are not given importance in the film, for mirrors favor metaphor (the similarity of form) over metamorphosis. The actor playing Brundle was, I would think, expressly chosen because he looks like a fly before Brundle's genetic code is spliced with that of a fly, so that when Brundle's metamorphosis begins, the latter's form begins to change not toward a resemblance to the fly, but towards a dissimilarity (as far as form) from it, except in the latter part of the last scene when we go back to metaphor (resemblance) and this precisely because no metamorphosis occurred: the film's title is *The Fly*, not *Brundlefly* or something else altogether.

It is due to the absence of mirrors (and their equivalents) in the film that the latter is not self-reflexive, although it contains in its diegesis someone shooting with a video camera many of its events.

A new off-screen space: the body's genetic code.

Membranes are being abolished in the film. This does not mean one won't see them or see them only rarely. On the contrary they are abundant, but it is the abundance of something one is collecting from everywhere to throw in the garbage can.

Yet, and this is one of the many weaknesses of the film, some membranes remain outside the garbage can:

— The continuous smooth camera movement is a membrane; the prominence of doors and of the sound of their closings and openings as thresholds: more membranes; the membrane that the absence of any dissolution of the images into their grains — teleportation being a digital video motif — (through pushing or blowing up the film) represents; the blue and yellow light that cut the frame into two parts (in several scenes) are membranes and their line of meeting is a membrane; she gets closer to kiss him, all the while one of her eyes is still looking at him, even as they kiss: this look is a membrane.

—The computer analyzing the elements that went through the teleportation shows an image of Brundle and an image of a fly (the membrane as fetish). But both he and the fly each contain an enormous number of viruses, bacteria, and mitochondria (the mitochondria in a cell has its own DNA, different from the DNA of the rest of the cell. The cell has no aura) each having its own specific DNA. The teleportation machine should have spliced their different DNA.

It is a bullet that kills Brundlefly, and not an insecticide: my first reaction on watching the editor coming to kill Brundlefly with a gun: "Why not an insecticide?" On third thought, I think Cronenberg was wrong: since Brundle was trying to do away with vehicles and hence also with projectiles, it is logical that he should be killed by a projectile ("the return of the repressed"); it is merely logical.

The Delphic oracle has been replaced by the computer genetic code.

"We'll be the perfect family": Brundlefly, she and her fetus genetically spliced. Back to the Trinity, but after the females' fight for their rights a trinity that is no longer all male: the female enters the trinity only when sex and consequently her sexual difference from the male has been replaced by the incestuous relation of DNA with DNA (and hence of film with film (the incestuous is not the self-reflexive): the supposedly video shot she takes of him after the first failed teleportation is shot by Cronenberg's cinematographer with film stock). Once sexual reproduction is replaced with genetic splicing via teleportation, one becomes, like gods and protozoa, immortal, without the abolishment of death, of absolute promiscuity, since radical metamorphosis is a facet of genetic splicing.

Compressing time more and more is a move from a normal photograph to a polaroid one (shorter developing time). Two consequences: the latent image is final, which is not the case with the normal photograph (it can be altered during developing); the membrane turns into a screen: the difference between David Hockney's *Christopher Isherwood Talking to Bob Holman, Santa Monica* (shot with normal photographs) and Joyce Neimanas' *Untitled #2* (shot with polaroids)((Hockney, who began making *joiners* to reintroduce time (mostly narrative, except in his landscapes: The many photographs that make up the blue sky devoid of clouds of *Pearblossom Hwy, 11-18th April 1986* are themselves the clouds now, the ones one sensed, without actually seeing them, on many clear skyed summer days. One is grateful to Hockney for rendering one's sensation visually without resorting to representational (of dust and vapor) clouds) into photography and first did *joiners* with polaroids before switching to making them with normal photographs, does not see the huge difference between the two, probably because he does not himself develop his photographs but sends them for that to a one-hour photo lab).

Every photograph is like a point in relativistic space-time. There is no passage of time here. But also, the (usually narrative) time that joins the *joiner's* photographs is a mere projection, hence there is no passage of time here either. To detect the real time one finds in the *joiner* one can choose arbitrarily any object that appears in two of a *joiner's* photographs of even a still scene taken from a static camera fixed on a tripod, and then choose arbitrarily any line in this object. Were we to try to match the two replicas of this line in the two photographs, we would see them match only for a longer or shorter part of their length, in spite of the fact they are the same line! (that is if we forget they were taken at two different times, however infinitesimal the interval). The real time one finds in the *joiner* is this non-matching, this jump-cut. Time has infiltrated, insinuated itself (like the fly's DNA in Brundle's DNA) between the same line in the two aligned photographs, time is the invisible that remains invisible even as it manifests itself in the visible non-matching of the two photographs, having taken place as it were in the black bag that the closing of the shutter is, an idiosyncratic off-screen. One's palm is a *joiner*: its time is (and its lines are) the non-matching of many photographs (each photograph a point in space-time. That's why it may be possible that some people can read one's future. He returned from New York to Chicago three days late for the resumption of university classes. All his friends told him they thought he was not coming back. Two months later he dropped out of the university. Palm readers have worked with the *natural joiner* that any palm is long before photography — Hockney, Neimanas, and the other photographers who work with *joiners* — existed. It would be interesting if an interviewer were to ask Hockney if he believes in palm readers, if he himself is a palm reader) of an absolutely smooth palm, with not one line): in the latter, one does not find membranes between shots, but the white frames of the polaroid as screens that are the fingernails that keep growing on the corpse like flowers over a grave, pushing the joint photographs apart (and the more one compresses time, the more these fingernail-like frames grow, become thicker, fatter); in Cronenberg's film the screens push apart the body's parts. It is not a new skin that is pushing off the old skin of Brundle, making his fingernails, teeth, ears fall off but something akin to the white screen/frame of the polaroid, itself akin to the vacuum that preserves food, that is, that compresses time. The fear of the implications of compressing time (as in *compressing a gas*) beyond a threshold at which a phase transition would occur, ending up with something whose characteristics nobody can predict (would it remain time beyond the critical point?), this fear renders invisible the continuous growth of the white frames surrounding the polaroid (it is not the latter growth that gets frozen still like a horrified person's hair, but our vision), in the same way it renders one's shout inaudible (musician seducing a snake out of the basket, who can seduce my shout out?)

Dilemma: one minute is not enough to think (no time for digressions)(exception: Kubelka's films that use the single frame as the basic unit) but to accept it as a minute of silence is almost impossible, for one of the risks of becoming superconductive and out-of-sync (simultaneous) is that any silence (or blank)(exception: a new silence (the silence made possible in cinema by the advent of sound was new), that is, a new constant speed, for silence is a constant speed (light also has a constant speed), every different kind of silence is a different constant speed) divested, for however infinitesimal a time, of the inaudible echo that the memory of sounds is, contains all the silences (or blanks)(of the same kind? Are there many kinds of silence divested of the inaudible echo that the memory of sounds is? If so, how many?) everywhere every time (are there in this silence the ones that preceded one's appearance? Also the ones that preceded the appearance of Homo Sapiens? Also the ones that preceded the appearance of life?): a noisy silence. We have a minute of silence when someone dies, for a minute of silence kills: it is our own way of still being the companions of the dead. I am so cold silence is visible, a veil that hides the world.

Bill Viola's *Migration*. The reflection of a face in the drop of water falling on the reflection of the same face in a bowl of water on and on, with no pain. To see too many reflections in a film or video is to feel someone is undergoing pain, even if it is an abstract pain. The body and a recognizable reflection of a face in a drop of water cannot both be in the same shot except through superimposition or matting, but one should not use superimposition when dealing with pain.

The river flowing toward the south, the reflections of the cars' lights floating on it toward the north. To go against the current (both currents: the direction of the movement of the thing reflected in the river, and the river's), one must become a reflection of nothing.

The journey of the local subway train to the end-of-line station then back, the train stopping at each local stop until it reaches the other end-of-line station, is not a back-and-forth movement, merely a circular one. But were the train suddenly to switch direction at a non-end-of-the-line station, this would be a back-and-forth movement. Two trains passing each other, whether going in the same or opposite direction(s), are a back-and-forth movement.

Caress: a zoom out from out-of-focus to out-of-focus that does not pass by an in-focus.

The snow pieces in winter, the stone pieces in summer that I hit with my feet as I walk are the only pets I have.

— I feel more tired standing on my buttock bones than standing on my feet.
— Nonetheless, sit down for a while, or else you'll end up sitting while standing.
— It's better than ending up sitting while sitting.

The skull like a decayed tooth.

I need people-glasses.

The bum seen in the street with *one* sock on, and it has changed into a bandage.

West Beirut. Only twelve hours of electricity a day (Lebanese sound-over: sound of a private electric generator, of many private electric generators, over black image). Like the sun, electricity here rises and sets. It is not on the day of arrival but only on the second day that one feels utterly tired, as if one's tiredness were a suitcase that got lost in some airport or other on those flights that include two transit cities, and which (the suitcase, tiredness) arrives a day or so after one's own arrival. Direct flights from the U.S. to Lebanon are illegal. One buys a Chicago-Amman via London ticket. Once one gets to the airport in London the ticket is changed automatically to a London-Beirut one. One soon discovers however that one's tiredness is not proportional to a Chicago-London-Beirut trip, but to a Chicago-London-Amman-Beirut trip.
Passing in London, from Chicago, on the way to Beirut, the watch's hand has to be advanced six hours. This means six hours of the day of arrival have already passed, but come the second day, that day as well as all the subsequent ones would be twenty-four-hour days. Not so when one arrives in Beirut, the eight-hour difference of time between Chicago and Beirut is here subtracted from every day, making each a sixteen-hour day for all those who live here. To some, these eight subtracted hours are those of work, hence these persons don't work, unemployed because there's no time to work, but they still need the time for rest that follows not work, but the time for work. In the case of those persons who, once a substantial part of the day has been lost, feel that their whole day has been lost, wasting the rest of it, this daily *a priori* loss of eight hours means they will waste the rest of every day. For others, these eight subtracted hours are those of sleep, so that they are always sleepy.

Dozens of currency exchange shops in Hamra street in West Beirut. The dollar has risen on that day from 380 to 410 Lebanese pounds (it had risen from $1 = 5 Leb. £ in 1985 to $1 = Leb. £ in 1988); he writes *Against translation* in his notebook. When a foreign film with English subtitles contains a section spoken in English, that part should also be subtitled (part of the script included in the film). Voice-over in English in a BBC program on Lebanon translating the answers of the Arabic woman being interviewed. I happen to know her. She speaks English fluently. Why is she being asked then to answer in Arabic and why the translation? Arabic subtitles should have been used throughout *Beirut, the last home movie* (the Boustrous family members speak only French among themselves and address the documentary filmmaker in English) even for prints to be shown abroad, for instance to English speaking people (there were English subtitles for the spoken French). When a person writes or says something in a foreign language in one's (fiction or documentary) video or film it should either not be subtitled or the subtitles should not be a translation of what s/he says or writes (one line should be said twice over different subtitles), but only seem to be so to someone who doesn't understand one or both languages. The filmmaker videotaped a person speaking a language unknown to the former (foreign Language: that of people speaking to themselves (also the deaf person seen on bus #30 in Milwaukee at 12:30 pm "speaking" to himself in sign language). Can one translate that language?) Voice-over becomes acceptable in this case for unbeknownst to the filmmaker, the voice-over may be saying exactly (as exact as a translation can be) what the person is saying. A voice-over that no longer remote controls the image, but one that has become the redundant echo of one element in the image.

At times melancholy takes hold of one: one feels that the whole world is a corpse, oneself the only one subsisting but in the manner of a fingernail still growing on the corpse.

Beirut. When the intermittent silence of the voice-over is superimposed over the more frequent diegetic silences, the superimposed silences become noise, silence becomes unintelligible.

Real spectator: one who looks as a third party at the exchange between his emotions and the artist.

Cleanliness is the reduction in the parasitical (of a lower order).

Boredom: time on strike.

Veins of sweat.

Drunk, you can fall off the limitless ground. Feeling like a lamplight around which sounds-voices, like moths, are circling-bumping.

Her vampiric fingers have the leanness of the pencil she's writing with.

He says a cruel line during the interview. The interviewer continues asking him questions. Suddenly he begins slapping himself very harshly on the face on and on. The interviewer tries to stop him. "Why are you trying to stop me only now, when this exhibitionistic violence is far less cruel than the line I uttered earlier?"

The speeding car passing over the smooth elevation in the road. The heart skipping a beat. This sudden leap inside the leap. Feeling one is inhaling air from a different atmosphere than the one into which one is exhaling. On the way to Detroit, the beauty of a truck with two (the spare ones) of its eight wheels not touching the ground. Abraham Lincoln is asked in Woody Allen's *Side Effects* how long a man's legs should be: «Long enough to reach the ground.» Almost a Zen answer? Asked how it feels after attaining satori, Suzuki answered: «as usual, except one is 3 inches off the ground».

What is taken for granted is but the eternally hurried.

A three-monitor video to be shown simultaneously on Lebanon's three TV channels, each channel broadcasting one of the tapes.

On the screen the dancer dances (also) with the border of the frame (having danced in many films, he is dancing with her as if she were the frame border).

Not only oneself but also the air one breathes in and out must get sparer (the rarified air of mountains). Hibernation is thermal, bodily (some mammals lose up to 1/3 of their total weight during the period of hibernation) and temporal diet. One can avoid the necessity of hibernation if one manages to get so spare in energy as to become superconductive (superconductivity is a lower state of energy).

The fade-in in many a film functions as the nicest alarm clock.

"Don't you ever stop reading?" Shot of him reading in the subway in New York. The light is intermittently off.

In a delicatessen, he orders coffee and points to something. The man working there says: "a stir." He points to the book he's holding: "a book."

His voice one more instrument the jazz player and singer left on the platform among the other instruments, to mingle, mute, with people during the break.

Only that which intermittently disappears (subatomic particles…) can offer no drag, as in superfluidity.

Utterly tired like a snake's skin left behind.

Indistinguishable: not like everyone else, like nothing.

At the office a woman whose phone rang less to signal a person on the other side of the line than to show her impatience.

I *left her for* **good** (I *wanted her* **badly** (is the right way to want something not to *want it badly*?). Tragic inversions). I have to go back to my solitude. The *I* which fell in love with her must vanish. To go back to solitude now is to go back to a solitude where I can't keep myself company, a solitude that is no longer *my* solitude but the solitude of no one (hence contagious but to no one). Solitude to the power two (back to this cursed number).

Looking at her, my eye's iris that of a slow lens that can't close all the way down to have a total fade-out.

Even holes have to be perforated.

    M begins with several seconds of black leader. The black of closed eyes waiting for the surprise. The surprise is the advent of sound.
    The voice as ascending movement: the crane shot from the courtyard up to the balcony follows the voice of the child. The two signs of the child's death: a ball (which like a child can easily "jump") rolling on the ground and stopping (her image's death), and a balloon (the ethereal element of the voice) that gets trapped on the lines of the telegraph poles (her voice has been silenced on the lines of writing of the posters and newspapers that announce her disappearance/death).
    The voice as ascending movement: the equivalence established between (expressionist) smoke and talk: cigarette smoke ascending from the underworld leaders' mouths as one hears their voices.
    The voice as ascending movement: in the scene of the police raid of a pub

crowded with underworld people, the criminals try to flee through the stairs but are pushed back down into the pub. This would have been enough in a silent film to signal that the criminals have been cornered and are under control. Not in *M*: The police has to get the voices that are still fleeing up both the throat and the stairs to go back into the pub and into the throat; it has to corner the jeering, uncontrollable voices. The tower of Babel: the attempt to ascend to heaven is made not only by the physical means of building the tower, but also through the climbing on one another of all the existent voices (like rats forming a pyramid). The voices of two men giving contradictory information to the inspector get, with each objection by one to the account of the other, louder, as if to have a better perspective view of the hat's color through the distance between the past in which it was seen and the present in which it is being described. Voices that see: Elsa's mother calling Elsa: it is as if the voice were searching the staircase, the courtyard, with the screen time of each of these shots totally depending on the time the voice needs to become sure Elsa is not in the different spaces shown in long shots. The guard sends his voice to look for the criminal where he himself cannot penetrate, like sending a dog ahead of oneself during a hunt. In *The Great Dictator* the barber and the woman are literally followed step by step by the dictator's voice.

The tune uttered by the murderer is an in-sync voice-over, something external to him (the murderer is hiding in a room. He is discovered because of the sound he makes trying to open a door. Rather the discovery of his hiding place should have been caused by one or more of those sounds one hears at night: doors, roofs, shelves, creaking on their own). The contrast between the speed of the tune (the only way for the criminal to be caught is through the propagation of rumors: only the rumor has the speed of the tune the criminal whistles) and the slowness of his fatness-shortness. "I can't remember having done it": that is, he was someone else when he did it, maybe one of the audience judging him. That's why they can both identify with him, and then forget ("I can't remember having done it") they identified with him and condemn him. Several close-ups in which the voice carrying the words "death to the murderer" is trying to leave the mouth with the same difficulty, pain, distortion to the face as when a tooth is being extracted.

In this film in which phones play an important role, the landlord of the house in which the murderer lives has very bad hearing so that her conversation with the detective becomes a kind of one-way bad connection phone conversation.

Lang missed the shout (in the last scene). The overopen mouth (as one says *overexposed* shot), the sound that does not emerge, the sudden emergence of a silent film in the sound film.

M written in chalk on the back of the criminal's jacket is an intertitle.

in Beirut, 7 p.m.,
f stop 16

in New York, 2 p.m.,
f stop 4

In ten years of civil war, 100,000 people died in Lebanon. Normal (not taking into account the war casualties) death rate (per 1,000 pop.): 8. Lebanese population: 2,852,000. Number of natural deaths per year: 22,816. Number of deaths in excess of the natural deaths: 77,184. Excess period: The number of years it would take for 77,184 natural deaths to occur in Lebanon: 3.383. With some of the persons who lived in Lebanon during these ten years of civil war their real age is to be counted thus (not taking in consideration the effect of the rise of the dollar in relation to the Lebanese pound: $1 = 5 Leb. £ in 1985; $1 = 500 Leb. £ in 1988. In Lebanon one finds not only a lot of nouvaux riches persons but also *nouvaux riches currencies*: the Syrian pound...): Real age = passport age + period of excess. Part of those who are 25 years old according to the passport are in reality 28.383 years old (optimists would say the war has done Lebanon a favor, raising life expectancy in it from 65 years for males and 68.9 years for females to 68.383 years for males and 72.283 years for females (still lagging behind the U.S., Australia, Canada, Taiwan, Cuba, East Germany, France, Italy, Japan, Netherlands, Spain, United Kingdom, West Germany); a country of survivors in a cheap-shallow sense: its people on the whole live beyond the life expectancy. Pessimists would say that because of the civil war the real life expectancy is 61.17 years for males, 65.07 years for females (lagging behind countries like Syria, Sri Lanka, Malaysia, Mexico); a country of suicidal persons in the cheap-shallow sense of having its population on the whole die below the life expectancy). With less indifferent people a phase transition occurs at a given stage in their relation to the war, following which we move from: real age = passport age + excess period, to: real age = period between conception and birth (ranging from 20 weeks (Christ and Hussayn were born after six months in the womb: a kind of abortion-miscarriage that ended up in life: survivors; it is this that gives such people an advantage when it comes to moving back past the fetal period to before conception) to 10 months) - excess period (a lot of people talk in Lebanon's case of a regression from civilization to barbarism occasioned by the civil war. Even if this were true, it is a phenomenon far less interesting and radical than the reverse motion toward pre-conception, a sort of individual B.B. (Before Birth) in place of A.B.). For some of them, an event occurs that causes this leap from one equation to the other, for others the leap from one equation to the other is the event. So that one of these persons may be living in accordance with the former equation for the first 60,072 war casualties, then suddenly change to the second equation, so that his/her age would then be: 9 months (if s/he was born after 9 months) - 9 months (during this period s/he is living in limbo). This person would have moved below the threshold of conception (a strange kind of death that doesn't get inscribed into the calculations of any newspaper, and that makes of one a survivor, hence someone in exile)(civil war a time travel machine), living an existence anterior to conception. S/he would have become an unborn (she wrote a year ago: "Two years ago I wrote, 'I am 23 years old and I feel I am 23 years old.' now, at the age of 25 I can't say: 'I am 25 years old and I feel I am 25 years old.'" Now she can't even say: "I am 26."). Or it may happen that s/he'll be living according to the first equation for the first 68,448 war casualties, and then change to the second equation, so that his/her age would be: 9 months - 4.595 months (this equation can only have one of two solutions: either zero or fetal period, otherwise one is in limbo). If the war continues and 8,376 more people are killed, the person will become an unborn (one has then to be sensitive enough to know that if one remains in that country beyond the threshold of pre-conception, then what is expressed is the negative sign: one becomes just critical hence sterile (the merely critical may think his voice is being heard since he sees the strip passing through the flatbed, what he doesn't see is that it is his image track that is passing over the sound head of the flatbed, i.e. that he is being used as slug)). If the war does not continue, then either the person will pass through a phase transition from the second equation back to the first, the two equations coexisting, in the first of which we're back to normal ways of counting age and he is initially as old as he was when the first phase-transition occurred between the two equations, in the second of which he is in limbo (a form of mummification) until a new civil war should occur (this is one of the reasons it is so difficult to end a civil war once it has began — inertia by itself wouldn't explain this —, for those whose age is being counted below the threshold of birth need enough war-deaths to have a take-off below the threshold of conception (those who penetrate the wall of conception discover that by doing so they have also in the same movement penetrated the wall of sound, but also many other walls), and hence resist that the civil war should end while they are half-way between birth and conception becoming civil war prisoners of the second equation), the second state outside the experience of the first (partial amnesia)(the hysteria of such people); or he'll be born again after 4.595 months of post-war life (one hears so much talk about being born again (the kangaroo has two births, one from the womb to the mother's pouch, the second from the pouch to the outside world) once the war ends, both in relation to people and in relation to Lebanon. This talk about being born again is sickening (this sickness won't kill me)).

But some people are not indifferent, their real age is to be calculated from the beginning of the war by means of the second equation, so that in the case of the Lebanese civil war it would have taken 17,112 war-caused deaths to turn them into unborn people (civil war is not the only way of achieving this). They have neither father nor mother, and are somehow foreign to sexuality (and not out of puritanism). The unborn exist under Heisenberg's uncertainty principle (survivors): the unborn can exist, that is break the law of conservation of energy (is there also *the law of conservation of time* which gets also broken by the unborn?) only in accordance with: $\Delta E \approx h/\Delta t$. Fluctuations are very energetic for only such extremely short periods that they themselves cannot perceive the difference (to exist for longer periods their energy has to be low (nothing to do with laziness or rest. The refractory period would have created a photograph of the suicidal/unborn, making them lazy, for it makes them exist for longer periods)). If they cannot be called lazy it is because their mere existence is already extra energy, while other so called energetic people, however early these people wake up, however efficient they are and however many are the things they do, belong to the law of conservation of energy. The unborn's intermittent existence (these notes, these small fragments of writing, so many, end up paralyzing one, not that they are too heavy, on the contrary they are too light, of an infinite lightness, the lightness of snow flakes, but like snow flakes they paralyze one; one's whole body, except for the eyes, becoming asleep (The warm room making me sleepy. Walking in the freezing cold to be wakened, walking until the whole body is asleep even before yawning)), their constant disappearance (during which, like vampires, they don't appear in mirrors) is their suicidal nature (Survivor-unborn. Unborn survivor. It may be that the unborn is the only survivor), regardless of whether they end up committing the traditional suicide consisting in killing oneself (death leads to nothing. The severed head is not rolling down the stairs. It is the stairs that are rolling down)(before he became an unborn he was suicidal only in the sense that it was very important to him to die young: the suicidal, like the radioactive, have a *half-life* (people avoid them). To his friend who found it amazing that he was both suicidal (the conflict between his being suicidal (and nomadic) and his refusal to hurry things, his giving things their time) and someone who postponed, he said: "But life is the postponement of suicide").

There is no connection between Septimus and Clarissa (who misunderstands everything about her suicide (the throwing of the shilling into the Serpentine (there is a moment when one is attached to things with filaments («And the leaves being connected by millions of fibres with his own body, there on the seat, fanned it up and down; when the branch stretched he, too, made that statement»). At the end of a yearly religious ceremony in Ceylon, some men are suspended in the air in a horizontal position with hooks attached to the skin of their backs. They do this to become each "the puppet of god". The constitution of a body on which only lines and whirls of pain circulate like the filaments attached to a puppet, filaments of pain. Isn't Septimus a puppet of nature? Others take advantage of one's becoming a puppet of nature to direct one through the voices). To throw then a shilling in the river is to fall with it to the bottom of the river (he knew that he was drowning (the world is full of pores and hence much depends on whether one hits/comes-in-contact-with the world where it is solid or whether one encounters it where its pores reside)(the air supply tube connecting the diver to the surface of the water like Virginia Woolf's walking stick), falling down to the bottom of the river, or rather he was distilling down to the floor of the river but as he touched the floor he felt he only then began really to drown, no longer part of distillation, for the floor of the river was made of quicksand in which he'd go on falling (this grave whose floor is quicksand)), and not out of thriftiness) and about his); the connection is between Septimus and Virginia Woolf (the last pages on Septimus are her real suicide letter. The suicide that ended her life was stolen from her (what shows that Virginia was driven to her suicide is the very normal quality of her suicide letter, as compared to Mayakovsky's letter and the notes found in his room) but only after *she* had already commited suicide years earlier). A writer is always speaking from experience, from an experience s/he may not experience as writer («you see I can't write this [the suicide letter] even, which shows I am right [to commit suicide]»). The words Quentin Bell quotes on the last page [the only one I read] of his *Virginia Woolf: A Biography*, whether she said them or not, are false: «Then she went to her death, "The one experience," as she had said to Vita, "I shall never describe"».

Suicide should occur/has occurred to those periods, largely in one's youth, where time passed without anything, including nothingness, occurring. The suicidal is amnesic. The amnesia of the suicidal has nothing to do with forgetting something that happened, but with these periods of disappearance (his backpack containing notes written over a period of 6 months was stolen, he subtracted 6 months from his age). This intermittent existence (this temporal laconism. This temporal diet. This time-anorexia) of the unborn is what makes them aphoristic. The suicidal may commit suicide in the traditional sense if prohibited from having his intermittent suicides-disappearances, in which case he was pushed to commit it by others.

But the dark-adapted eye can detect even a photon. He had written years ago: "Middle Eastern women have to shed two veils: the one they wither slowly and the one that slowly withers them: the shroud and the home." One must not automatically condemn veils. Saw in a video an Indian woman hide her face behind her veil as soon as she saw that the camera was pointed in her direction. Something nice in that almost instinctive refusal to be imprisoned during/because of the refractory period (between one and an Arabic woman there is a veil until it is time to have sex, and then she puts her veil away; while here it is at the time of sex that a veil (the condom (to guard against AIDS)) is put between the man and the woman. Merely a difference in timing. Or rather not merely a difference in timing since the condom is not there to enable one to withdraw from the perception (or rather the projection inscribed within perception) of the other with its refractory period. Many of the veils worn in the West are not there to enable you to withdraw from the perception (or rather the projection inscribed within perception) of the other (dark glasses, and Rainer's overpaintings, those other dark glasses covering the image, do that) with its refractory period but merely to withdraw him/her from your field of perception (the earphones...)). Many rich people drive cars that have one-way-dark glass. *Uncle Sam* in West Beirut has one-way-dark glass (every look changing us into traces through the refractory period, immobilizing us for a longer or shorter period, is the look of disapproval in classical music concerts at the merest noise).

Dead time is created by all the rests of the born: After receiving a stimulus, the photoreceptor in the eye cannot receive another stimulus for as long as 1/10 to 1/5 second (the photoreceptor's rest). For the cardiac muscle, the absolute refractory period is 0.25 to 0.3 second for the ventricle, 0.15 second for the atrial muscle. For the skeletal muscle it is 1 to 5 milliseconds. For large myelinated nerve fibers it is about 1/2,500 second. To these absolute refractory periods must be added the hyperpolarization state established immediately after each preceding action potential and during which re-excitation cannot occur. There is an intimate relation between the refractory period (these efficient persons turn out to be *after all* always late, late in their very punctual way (the refractory period can be calculated with a precision of 0.1 milliseconds)) and projection and memory (memory has a lot to do with rest). Maybe without any refractory period there would be no memory.

The unborn has disappeared, but his/her trace on the photoreceptor hasn't (his trace has been taken hostage by the born (not only humans but also animals), and if taking hostages is a terroristic act then this is unambiguously a terroristic act; what would make the unborn extremely angry is that his image be taken hostage by someone who has diplopia, for the brain will compensate for the diplopia by suppressing the weaker image (created out of one eye's stimuli), so that for the period before that eye goes amblyopic (sensory deprivation of an eye will on the long run produce blindness due to degeneration of the visual center in the brain (because of its deprivation of stimuli)) there will be no corresponding image to these stimuli forming in the brain, and hence part of the forcing of rest on the unborn due to the inscription of a trace on the cones and rods of that eye will have taken place for nothing (indifference)) and hence s/he has been reduced to a pseudo existence (unless s/he is distracted), has become something that feels no pain, no anger (nice person + anger-as-dissolution (he wakes up, looks at the light still on, at his pants and shirt, and writes: "This treacherous sleep that steals from one one's anger. One wakes up angry nonetheless, except now it is day and much easier to waste one's anger on/with others): cruelty; low person (a low person reduces every failure to a weakness) + anger-as-explosion: meanness), no cold, no happiness, no thinking, no sounds (in this case "— He's not listening. — He must be listening to something else" is false. Despite what John Cage thinks, there is silence: Baudelaire may hear a color, but a trace, though it may be affected by sounds, does not hear them; also physicists are perfecting the *squeezing of light* technique, which makes possible eliminating fluctuations totally (when the unborn experiences emptiness it is a total emptiness, since the survivor-unborn is the fluctuation ($\Delta E \approx h/\Delta t$)) from certain areas by displacing them to other areas. These (puritanical) physicists though don't know a lot about the distracted: «it is useful to give a different description of the Cantor set, by means of «virtual cutouts». Again, one starts from [0,1] and cuts out its middle third]1/3,2/3[. The second stage cuts out the middle thirds of each third of [0,1]. Since the middle third of [0,1] has already been cut out, cutting out the middle third of the middle third has no perceivable effect... In the same way, one cuts out the middle third of *each* ninth of [0,1], of *each* 27th, and so on. Note that the distribution of the number of cutouts of length exceeding u is no longer of the form u^{-D}. One finds instead that this distribution is roughly proportional to $1/u$.»[2] Thinking is always (except when they have disappeared but are pseudo-lingering as trace) taking place in the case of the distracted (the street lights always on where Michigan avenue and Lake Shore drive meet (10 a.m.: street lights on along Lake Shore Drive's intersection with Michigan avenue. Three hours in the museum (saw a lot of Chicagoan tourists there). The fog outside, and it seems natural the lights should be on). Driving (I don't particularly like people who move on all fours (shot of cars moving)) slightly drunk (to drink is to swim in the drink) at 1:30 a.m.; at 1:33 a.m; at 1:40 a.m. I have the very precise sensation all these street lights, hundreds of them (Underground train. Counting the lights going by so quickly. Counting the increasing number of lights I am missing counting), are so many candles for my birthday. Am I so old?), it is a thinking that goes on even when/where they are absent: it is in this sense that absent-minded is to be understood (can this *virtual thinking* be one of the reasons one feels at times that the other sections/people/things are too material?)(those who do virtual thinking are more tired than the others, and find the expression, "I have been doing some thinking these last four days", strange, incomprehensible)("when you think you've shut your fingers on a fly, you must crush it, even if it turns out your hand was empty." Right only if you

[2]Benoit B. Mandelbrot, *Fractals: Form, Chance, and Dimension* (San Francisco: W.H.Freeman, 1977), pp. 107-8.

accept being bitten by non-existent flies (Hysteria)). It is this absentmindedness/virtual thinking that gives the intermittently disappearing unborn, the suicidal, the possibility of not hurrying himself, of postponing, and hence a minimum of out-of-sync consistency), no affects (Stanislavsky's «Everyone at every minute of his life must feel something. Only the dead have no sensations...» is doubly wrong, in that some living persons don't feel: most of *Distracted* was written by a living Jalal Toufic who did not feel for extended periods of time; and because the dead (the mad and persons on LSD, and the mystics, those who *die before they die*) often feel utterly)(this absence of affects, intuited so harshly, is in no way to be equated with the born's indifference) except an abstract feeling (reflexivity of feeling one is not feeling)(Title of film: *Night For Day*) of a parasitical time (the time of the resting of other people and animals and film cameras (the intermittent closing of the shutter) is a hang-over (we ended up finding an affect, nausea), hence cannot be fast-forwarded), can't even pinch or slap himself/herself to elicit pain and/or anger and/or thinking and/or a sound (among his notes he found: "The way sounds lights music colors come to one, intermingle and mix with one. What right have they to do this? (Her eyes closed, in fear that if she opened them eyes, if she brought the world to her and mingled it with her thoughts, the world would know about her secret. Aristocrats know that a secret cannot be made manifest, because, like a black hole, it imprisons light itself, it swallows that which makes visible, and yet close their eyes or shut their ears: the pathos of distance). I hate it as much when their absence, silence and blankness, comes close to one and intermingles with one"). Their including us in their rest, making us have a pseudo-rest, makes it more difficult for us to appear ($\Delta E \approx h/\Delta t$). That's also why the unborn have to be unobtrusive (rather than the exhibitionistic extremism of those at the lower or higher end of the spectrum of detection, the unobtrusive extremism of the unborn, outside of the spectrum of detection (of experience/perception))(the shout: the mouth opened more than fully (different from the 102.9% total responses to a questionnaire). Uttering what is outside the spectrum of audition of the ear, hence one can no longer speak to oneself, not even as inner speech or interior monologue), unnoticeable (yet often called troublemakers for they are fluctuations, hence noise to others (they can be detected by man's theories but not by the law of conservation of energy, unobtrusive to the universe, noisy to humans, to the precision of their theories)), the opposite of adaptable (they can't be used as extras (one's refusal to use any kind of extras in one's film means the off-screen will be intermittent (in most films the off-screen is for much of the time an extra)) precisely because they are extra energy.

People no longer leave traces on us on encountering/interacting with us, not because we haven't been affected by them, but that during the period of interaction we were not measuring devices.

(Giacometti's people) as lean as veins.

Things are bearable only when they hint that they don't exist or that we don't exist or that neither we nor they exist (a small lake's water after the rower has passed, the reflections closing again, not merely because he has moved on, but because he did not exist as he passed through the lake). It is this hint at the fundamental nonexistence of things that saves us from their obstinate materiality. Is energy that less material? Is changing objects into energy (atomic bomb...) a solution? Had that discovery to do with one or more persons who suffered from the materiality of things (in four dimensional space-time everything is conserved)? Changing things into tools is no solution. Things must dissolve releasing emanations, what goes beyond the boundaries of the body (to experiment is to go outside the boundaries. The disembodied is experimenting since he is constantly going outside the boundaries of his body, perceiving the attributes of things spilling from them (Van Gogh's paintings, with the colors spilling from the objects, touch one, are, only in this sense, touching). Unfortunately this constant spilling outside oneself permits other things and people to spill outside themselves and inside one as voices that do not acknowledge any aura to one's body, and why would they when the self itself is usually outside of the body) and of the self. These emanations are almost always impossible to defend against. The wind was held outside the house by the walls, windows and doors. Not so the airs detached from the body of the wind: «certain airs, detached from the body of the wind (the house was ramshackle after all) crept round corners and ventured indoors» (even a newly build house is ramshackle when confronted with these airs detached from the body of the wind). One must reach the glare of the sun seen through the mist, one must interpose mist or words between oneself and the object or person, anything that may change it/him/her from materiality to vibrations that tunnel straight to the nervous system. The emanation is not a self; the latter has an aura defending it against being penetrated by the emanations from other souls. The voices the schizophrenic hears are the airs/emanations detached from the souls of others. They are what he cannot have an aura against, cannot defend himself against, hence they penetrate him, unless (as happens in very rare cases) his whole soul becomes an emanation, the whole wind, Woolf's air detached from the body of the wind.

Trish doesn't think the character in the book would have said the text the way I am telling her to read it. It is not a matter of reading the text aloud in such a way as to re-create the character (the character has already been created by the text), but of getting to the voice (one almost cannot breathe, not so much to hear her voice as not to extinguish it with one's exhalation)(the voice propagating like space-time, in which matter energy words are, and beyond which there is nothing)(this interstellar space where only the voice is air, not because the voice is carried by breath but that it itself is what one breathes in that space). The voice is disembodied from the body of the performer but not from the body of the text: though the voice does not reside in the text, the voice existed as such, disembodied from her, not her property, only when she read aloud certain paragraphs of the text (some paragraphs are a magic formula for the voice to appear), whereas reading other paragraphs did not make it materialize , the voice reverting to being merely her voice, something one did not then even feel imprisoned within her, so much had it lost that possibility of disembodiment.

It is through physical collisions that the disembodied is constantly trying to regain and come in touch with the body (this body like feet that are asleep, a body that no longer feels, and hence that has to be banged against something to regain feeling. The asleep body (the foot of the woman coming down the stairs in Muybridge's series is immobilized, in three consecutive shots, as support while the other foot changes positions. One is surprised to see it moving in the fourth photograph, for one would have expected it to have become numb by then) does not sleep or dream (On his message machine: "don't call me when I am home and speak to me directly; don't call me when I am absent and leave a message; call me and leave a message while I am sleeping. Be my dream — *my man*, my woman, my silence, or your silence")), to evade being penetrated by emanations, or left outside in nothingness. Hence the total absence of pain (as in some advanced stages of schizophrenia) is so dangerous, for it means that one cannot even bang oneself against some hard object to get back into the body.

Trying to flee simultaneously the two extremes of absence of feeling (one's reduction to just an aura, without any body or mind circled by it) and excess of excessive stimuli (the total absence of aura allowing things to penetrate one).

Supersaturation will not be achieved through foreshadowing (a form of vaccination (the small amount of the antigen used in vaccination has nothing to do with laconism) and hence of memory ("... smash..." "I am not interested in *smashing* anybody." "I am not myself interested in those who memorize what I say.")) Supersaturation has a lot to do with a maintenance-creation of possibilities. Does *Mrs. Dalloway* span only one day in the life of Clarissa Dalloway? If not, this clearly would not be because Clarissa remembers many past events during that day (the difficulty of becoming part of the composition of the things remembered is not due to the immateriality of the past, for the past has the fullest materiality, that of the body of the one remembering, but consists, as in Tarkovsky's films, in that the time needed for things remembered, not to decompose, but to compose (the past), is simultaneously the span it takes the one remembering to decompose (two persons are arm wrestling. I suggested the winner tries to arm wrestle with the clock's second hand). Nostalgia (in Tarkovsky's world people don't leave. Like reflections that can never detach from the surface however much they and it may become agitated) is this non-meeting). But even becoming the person one was in the past does not automatically mean *a day in the life of* becomes then more than one day: unless a bifurcation is created, however long the time the person becomes himself in the past, none of this time is added to the present (is such an event in four dimensional space-time (where an event does not pass but is conserved) being scanned again? The question is meaningless for there is no way to detect such a recurrent scanning, no way to know whether one is going through something the first time or the n+1 th time). The day becomes more than one day if one becomes oneself at a bifurcation point in the past. Did Clarissa in her forties have, on becoming Clarissa at eighteen, the possibility of choosing other than what the other eighteen year old Clarissa, from whom she is then separated by an amnesic barrier, chose at the bifurcation (one kind of déjà vu signals that a bifurcation has been created but that one has taken the same branch). If she does not choose the same thing (but equally so if she took the same branch), that variation from the other past (or pasts, if one is back at the bifurcation point more than once and if the bifurcation has many branches) needs time in which to occur, and hence this time that is not just subjective, in the mind and/or body of the person who goes through this becoming, but is an objective time, has to be added to the day (this time shows that the same path which has been *chosen* at the bifurcation point is not identical to the same path when there was no bifurcation point). So then is *Mrs. Dalloway*, after all, about a day in the life of Clarissa Dalloway?

The Waves is the wave equation of the six characters, one becoming in which the six are joined, and it is only through an act of measurement that a materialization-actualization of the characters occurs (Rhoda the disembodied remains at the level of possibilities (a wave equation)). Rhoda unable to move in front of the puddle has to achieve what Stanislavsky sees as one of the advanced stages in the preparation of a role: physical embodiment of the character. How to play oneself realistically a la Stanislavsky without any of the factors that make it possible for Stanislavsky's actors to embody the character: an objective for every division in the play; attention (one cannot have the requisite attention because one is taking in too many stimuli (for instance, hearing what is written: Garrett Stewart mentions «Loveliness returns as one looks with all its train of phantom phrases». Is this an example of the saturation of the atom that Woolf wanted (but at the subatomic level more than 90% of all space is empty (the uncertainty principle permits the occurrence of fluctuations for very short periods, each like a fin in a waste of sea water)), or is it rather supersaturation or overinclusion?), so that one is always late (not because one is always the last to arrive, but because one is always the one left behind)(you ask an (in-sync) actor to read from a text and instantly he begins acting as he reads, whereas non-actors know when asked to read that they are too late to understand what is going on: they are late not only, as the character is, in relation to the end when the significance of things will be revealed, even if what is revealed turns out to be an enigma, but also in relation to the character himself/herself))? How would a Stanislavsky actor play the role of Septimus or Rhoda (who cannot say "I am this")?

The dead's eyes don't see. Ghosts are actors; that is, *only* people who know how to act have ghosts. Like a Stanislavsky actor on the empty stage during the first rehearsals, the ghost has to invent what is around him (including those he haunts), as props, so as to live. Those who do not feel objects that exist around them, up to the point of feeling that what others insist is there is *keyed* into their surroundings, unlike ghosts, cannot invent and imagine as props what is already there, in order to live.

These intermittently unembodied people have the feeling they will get embodied, from time to time, in their corpse during its dissolution. Was preventing the ka from at times experiencing the disintegration of the corpse one of the reasons the ancient Egyptians preserved the body?

The closest relation Septimus and Rhoda have is with foreigners (Septimus' wife is Italian. Louis, who becomes for a while Rhoda's lover, is Australian (his accent is his country remembering him)), who will be searched in airports and at the borders of countries (the Lebanese have endured a lot of this). Schizophrenics are in exile not merely from a country but from reality, foreigners to reality, hence reality searches them most of the time. How full of borders (blocking of thought, catatonia...) is the infinite world of the schizophrenic. A book had to be of a critical size so that the look could remain focused inside/on it and not slip away to the world. It had to form a horizon and it did. But soon there will exist wrist-sized (the moving car on the horizon a watch on a wrist) computer terminals (*New York Times Book Review*, 3/1/1981). Words would then become subtitles to the world (the world as foreign).

Her young age always comes with us when she and I go out (one's age the most jealous thing, always wanting to keep one to itself all the time). She says, "Your writing always comes with us when you and I go out."

These notes on myriad disparate pieces of paper so many fallen skin shreds off chapped lips. Writers are cold. Words should fall off one's lips as rarely as skin flakes off chapped lips. The parentheses are covers that shield writers from the (outside) cold.

This vapor on the glass of the subway window is good to me, like hands put over one's eyes to shield them from the sun, for I need now to be shielded from the reality outside even though it has almost totally vanished behind the darkness.

She lay her face in her hands (the sad/angry/tense face's (eye)lids): once more the closing of the shutter to immobilize the world in a photograph (who says we only take photographs when happy or to signify happiness?). When tense, angry or sad I lay my hand in her hands.

Insomnia: sounds no longer propagating in the air as in their natural element, but scratching against it. Hearing now takes place in the air and not in the ear. How stop listening now, when one can't put one's hand over all the air?

Each of her winter socks large enough to hold her foot and my hand.

The nightclub's blacklights turning white clothes and shoes into lipstick. Writing, for ink the black tears falling from the made-up eyes of a whore laughing hysterically. Drinking to be able to give her a reverse angle shot to her vulgar laughter. Drunk, one closes one's eyes and it is now darkness that is trying to balance itself.

Imagination begins when projection stops.

STOP sign in this totally deserted area, as if here only to regulate my breathing. His pupils liquid swirling down a sink. Buddha's ironed body (isn't 70% water too much to put the iron into steam-mode and iron us? Doesn't our being 70% water make us reflections that float on ourselves?)

What is received by/at one part of the body inhibits the motor part that should inscribe it so it would not be forgotten (in the specific form in which it was received). Is "laziness" the ruse of the secret?

Those who stole my backpack containing notes assembled over a six month period have made them secrets to me (I was a survivor for those six months).

Style as the only legitimate quotation marks (the one without style is ever paraphrasing himself). The redundancy of enclosing within quotation marks the words of someone who has style. The scholar's quotation marks: fingernails that reduce everything that comes their way to dirt. I know my actors won't come watch my film, so I make them quote my lines when they say them during the filming.

Her distant eyes straining with the rest of her face to clearly hear the distant sounds. Why should they be straining when they are already distant hence close to the distant sounds?

The air/breath of a saxophone like changing car gears. A car stopped at the red traffic light next to my car. Music, and it seems we're moving (music, and one knows walls are full of Brownian motion).

Aphoristic writers don't *fill in the blank.*

Against Socrates' arrogant certainty ("I know that I know nothing"), the grace of "I don't know whether I know or not."

Quickness does not suit a woman: femininity is faster than fast, it's sudden. Only an out-of sync man can be as fast as feminine suddenness (by being quicker than himself), and as slow as a still cat (by being slower than himself).

Getting drunk reveals to one that one can rack-focus from an image to a sound.

The equidistant white stripes the second hand of the highway become a spatial clock, while time itself stands still: nothing seems to move. Then suddenly everything is moving: it seems the car is moving on the moving world, as on an escalator. There is also that circular temporality of being lost: one keeps seeing Mcdonald's, Pizza Hut, K Mart, Hardees, Arby's, Howard Johnson, each cluster the mirror image of the previous one. The mirage (in the desert the mirage one learns to mistrust last is oneself), which traditionally could never be reached, materializes as one of the twin Amoco gas stations one often encounters in Ohio and Indiana, one on either side of the highway (it seems as if there were originally only one station and the highway cut it in the middle, it seems as if technology is not following the curvature of technology, this making a part of technology seem to be part of nature). One of the objections against technology is that it doesn't follow the curvatures of nature, to which I reply that it follows the curvature of space-time.

Kissing her teeth with my teeth (vampiric. Never cared about love bites)(no vampire loses his two teeth, but some vampires lose their lips). Her tongue floating on its back on my tongue. The mirage-like tinge of saliva on her lips, like tears, like the saliva women use on their eyes as additional make-up, this saliva a make-up she puts on her lips. That gesture of hers halfway between caress and hug (never closing totally, like a vampire's lips), like her shirt sleeves covering her fingers. Her cheek has the warmth of tears.

Closing the eyes for every image now is an eyelid. Washing the inside of one's closed eyes with the car lights coming in the opposite direction.

Being a distracted person, I can write only when in that state (looking at the film passing on the screen, I intermittently make framing gestures in the darkness (I sleep nine and a half hours a day, one and a half hours more than the average, one and a half hours of additional darkness, the darkness that should have enveloped the projection of the film I am prevented from making) with my fingers. I write: "Her two feet resting on the back of the seat distract me more than a tall person sitting in front of me would have"). She makes me concentrate on her in her presence — and absence. She makes me blocked.

In her absence I have her alone to myself. In her presence, I have her with her friends. Will I end up preferring her absence to her presence? I don't like her in-sync silence; she resents that my silence is out-of-sync. My silence is out-of-sync in both her presence and absence.

To kiss the laughing mouth without interrupting the laugh.

The shot should be extended till it becomes as difficult to know when to cut it as when to end a hug.

I haven't written you a letter yet. For a young writer to write letters before he has finished his first book means reducing the book to a collection of summaries (what if like Whitman one basically wrote one book (not true, he also wrote *Specimen Days*) with different editions? Will one in that case never write letters?) But also it would be a total misrepresentation of our relation were I to write *I* in capital letters and *you* in normal letters. You answer, just write a letter, for though a high angle shot denotes power, does someone reading a book posed on the table in front of him have power over it? *Telegraph*: This sensation of suffocation *Ruth* as if one's exhalation was going into the small mouth (like the circle of cigarette smoke) of the drowned

104

(this library that gives onto the sea) mountains' rarified air (but even more, rarified time) *Ruth* in order to save it *Ruth* every instant in your absence an appointment to which you haven't shown up, yet.

Her nose small, so that all the air would play on her hair.

She's sitting with me and Mark in a cafe. She asks why there are several mentions of vampires in my films. "Vampires have no intestines (these fat veins); they don't digest, hence don't shit." I read to her a quotation from a book on vampires: «a fortress prepared against an attack by vampires… Outside on the window ledge he had placed an averted bowl that covered a mixture of human excreta and garlic». She continued looking at me, so I said: "Vampires don't digest hence they are not digested-decomposed when put in the earth (worms don't decompose the body of the one whose teeth are space-time wormholes)". She began speaking to Mark. I write: "Does hair grow inside the vampire's two perforated teeth, as it does in the nose of normal people?" She looks back at me. Little did I know then that she is a vamp.

For the last ten minutes I've been throwing myself against the wall. For the last two months I've been throwing myself against her cowardice, her indifference (I am totally indifferent to her indifference. I want to get in touch with her coldness. As if I didn't know the indifferent have no coldness), without a response, without a back and forth movement, for throwing oneself against indifference is all forth, the going back no longer counts (counts merely as a spring). But I shouldn't project from her to the wall, I shouldn't project that the blood on it is all my own but send it to the lab. I may discover that all or a portion of it is not mine, maybe the wall's.

Neither when he lived with her nor when they separated (whether in a friendly or non-friendly way) did she reach being a stranger to him. To her, he remained merely "weird", hence she sided with others even when they insulted her, and against him even when he was defending her.

His walk approximated the slow motion of distant trees' leaves agitated by the wind. The passing train like combing one's hair. How is it people say there are no wipes in Ozu's films? What about the constantly passing trains in his films?

«Clouds now and then
giving men relief

from moon viewing» (Basho). But what if I like clouds even more than the moon? Moon giving relief from cloud viewing.

In the case of rare film/video makers and painters, the extensive use of *ready made* images has nothing to do postmodern pastish; neither is it parodic, critical, or retro; it rather signals that they are as it were in a spaceship far away from Earth (or that they are extraterrestrials (we should not be surprised if we found them stating this in interviews)). Space travel without leaving Earth.

They repeat to forget what has been forgotten.

Sometimes tears that do not condense around any incident.

The world now only exists as a *phantom limb*.

One never knows how much an idea or an ability demands/requires in order to occur and hence how much is given generously to one.

Localization, the in-focus as the itch of what should remain vibrational. Hence this strange body that instead of scratching the itch reacts to it by becoming in its entirety a vibrating body.

Must one somewhat want to continue to deserve to be the reader of one's book, this precluding one from changing/degenerating to a much lower level of existence? Or must one risk change fully?

A person is given a posthypnotic suggestion to have an artificial neurosis manifesting in a hysterical conversion — an inability to open his hand due to guilt for cheating in a test. Later he is told to remember the whole session. Two questions pose themselves:
— Would that not make hysterical conversion a possibility/option for dealing with guilt the next time a traumatic event happens that induces guilt feelings in a subject who may not otherwise have followed the hysterical modality for dealing with guilt?
— Is that rather than a detrimental thing, a beneficial one, since it may be a way to avert other more harmful reactions to guilt, for instance, a depressive state, which is a worse state for the patient and perhaps more difficult than a conversion disorder to deal with on the part of the therapist? Should one implant another option of disease in the person as a kind of vaccination against a more dangerous manifestation?

It is less the subject that is being explored than the object: the possibilities of the digital image being almost infinite, there will as a consequence be an impoverishment in the possibilities of the subject, since there will not be enough time for the deployment of both the former and the latter; hence the subject will become a clone.

Jalal Toufic
1340 W. Estes #3n
Chicago, IL 60626
Jan 28, 1989
Janalle Joseph
P.O.Box 6237
Evanston, IL 60202

To Janalle:
Used things, used books, are cheaper. But certainly a book on which things have been handwritten by someone else has at least the appearance of a used book. Why then do people want the books they receive as presents to be dedicated? You are thirty-nine years old, you'll be forty in three weeks. Have you been used by life and hence are afraid you've become cheaper now than you used to be or is it rather that those invisible lines-wrinkles that are imperceptible to me but that you yourself see show you to be life's dedication, to whom? To yourself, but also to whom? To David? What would one not do to receive a dedication from life, to feel one is loved by life (but it may be scary to be loved by life: many lovers have destroyed each other)? How does it feel to know that whoever is loved by you is loved by life itself?

But it all depends on whether one has not been used by life. And for that one must have postponed. David Hubel and Torsten Wiesel found in their experiments on cats that up to four months after birth «the visual cortex is plastic enough to change its organization in response to the input from the retina... it is possible to delay the onset of the critical period by rearing kittens in total darkness, thereby allowing all other developmentally related changes to occur... This strategy, called dark-rearing, was first explored by Max Cynader... it enabled Cynader to initiate shifts in ocular dominance in cats that were as much as two years old.»[3]

Have I, a filmmaker who postpones (— What is this film about (this question was asked despite the *No questions asked* on the ad for actors and crew)? — It is about time (the two meanings of *about time* exclude each other):

---

[3]Chiye Aoki and Philip Siekevitz, "Plasticity in Brain Development," *Scientific American* (December 1988), p.59.

to make it, the director had to divest himself of timing, never feeling it is about time to do or not do something. It is never about time to make a film about time), chosen to be assisted by a production manager who postpones? It is neither by plastic surgery nor by lotions that a person can truly postpone aging, but through dark-rearing (a form of matting) or its equivalents (silence-rearing…). One can be contemporary with one's earliest childhood also in this sense and manner, thus averting the nostalgic metaphorical relation with it (memory as metaphor: "as a child (I used to…)". 5 a.m., my mind is like a lump of sugar dissolved in the coffee I am drinking. The coffee still tastes bitter). Whether we come from Developing countries or not, we have to create our "Third World" non-developed areas. This way of preserving a difference between generations, a generation gap (as one says an *energy gap* in physics (especially in the case of superconductivity)), will become increasingly important with the introduction of digital video machines: Sony DVR-10 composite DTTR can give fifteen generations with no degeneration if the patches and circuits of the other machines in the editing suite are not digital, and an indefinite number of generations without any degeneration if all the equipment and circuits used in the dubbing or layering are digital (not only this, one machine of the type DVR-10 composite DTTR can operate simultaneously as both a source and recorder: they want to do away with the back-and-forth movement). Not that we ever cared about *mon vieux* and *baby*, but we always liked the noms de guerre of guerrilla fighters in Lebanon: Aboul Leil (father of the night). If such a generation feels itself endangered by some of the West's technology it is because the introduction of D2 may eliminate the generation gap between, in Aboul Leil's case, Zaid and the night. The decrease in definition and contrast, and the increased level of grain in the image the further away in generations one moved from the video master tape or the final release film print meant that the video master tape and the final release print still had a certain relative uniqueness and hence aura, and that the numbering of generations from the negative in film and from the original video tape was a kind of chronological history that soon turns into forgetfulness. All this goes away with the advent of digital video, and we enter the age of total reproduction, where even the vertical process of getting different generations (as against the horizontal process of getting a large number of copies off of the same tape) becomes ahistorical, and truly the difference between copy and original *dissolves* (a video/cinema effect that previously necessitated the loss of a generation).

Is this why you look of a different age depending on whether one looks at you in profile or straight on? Is this why though you're thirty-nine one never conceived that a relation with you may have any trace of a relation to a mother-substitute (am I (an unborn) not always told by women of *whatever* age, due to my losing things often, etc., "I don't want to be your mother"?!)([*added in 1991*]: You cannot imagine how excessively old I was while writing *(Vampires)*: age-difference is the possible objection to a relation between us: not the fact that you are thirteen years older than me, but that I had/have become infinitely older than you).

The seduction in asking someone to write a dedication on a book he did not write: if it is alright to write on another person's (the writer's) book, then it is alright to try to have a relation with a woman who is already another's lover.

One dedicates the dedication.

Jalal O Toufic

He videotapes the auditions he conducts. This gives him that minimal concentration that the frame of the image is, but what is framed are distracted things, or else it is the camera itself that is distracted and keeps moving. This is what differentiates his use of these distracted images for concentration from the critic's use of existing concentrated images as concentration. He cannot, though, choose certain parts of what was shot on video and show them to his cinematographer, actors and actresses to duplicate them on 16 mm film (certain smiles, gestures occur, like Hiroshima, like Auschwitz, like the Israeli invasion of Lebanon, once). It isn't that he tried to do this and discovered that he or his actors and actresses or his cinematographers can't do it (his acceptance of certain forms of imprecision, those that have to do either with the description of what already exists or with sync, was known to his crew (most actors come to the filming considering it as one thing among many others (If one sometimes seems arrogant it is the arrogance of the one who risks in relation to the one who does not (courage is tied to risk not to danger (when tired (or/that is resting) one is more exposed to danger, but there is no risk). A situation in which one is threatened by even an imminent danger to one's life, but where there is no risk involved, makes it impossible to react with courage, since in such a context courage has been automatically transformed into mere indulgence. There is no way of showing courage at a Syrian military checkpoint in Beirut)) and not that they are distracted people (*tag-team cinematography*. This expression made the part-time cinematography of his non-distracted cinematographers acceptable to him). The distracted person knows that distraction is not one thing among other things). He is a one-take director (the ratio of *Night for Day* is almost 1/1 (one of my favorite thinkers is to speak today (people show up early to be sure they'll get a seat). The crowded noisy auditorium. The empty waiting until the speech begins, like the few feet that are wasted at the beginning and end of the film roll)(one-take shots, and one notices that one did away with the out-takes (a two-minute shot of Eliot writing turned out out-of-focus. It is not discarded, but is cut into shorter segments which are inserted in the credits sequence: alternation between in-focus typeset names and out-of-focus handwritten words) only to get off-takes (the ratio of what he felt/perceived and noted as something he wanted to put in his film to what he put in his film is high (his cinematographer tells him jokingly that he'll end up having a ratio of more than 1))). In *Night for Day* there is the additional ratio of fast-forwarded to normal-motion sections), so that one had to translate, i.e., blow the video images he had chosen, to 16 mm and have them in the film. That is what gives his films their documentary feel despite his refusal to use extras (who play an equivalent role to that of presence (ambient sound) in the case of sound). Reproduction, and with it the chance to alter and perfect what took place, was barred to this person who changed so much, passing through many a bifurcation point.

One must be laconic or (the same thing) extend things for too long. Extended for too long, hence laconic compared to eternity.

Lebanon is so small there are no internal flights between its cities. A country without sky, while the U.S. —

A dancer is a noiseglass (the reddish-orange sunglasses over her blue eyes. The reddish-orange suntan over the rest of her face). S/he absorbs the noise of a too loud music away from anyone looking at him/her.

An extremely attractive woman walks to the dance platform (her walk is a dance in slow motion) and dances badly (he had the same feeling moviegoers must have had in the early thirties on hearing their stars speak for the first time and discovering that they had terrible voices). She is most probably more attractive without make-up.

Her hand, her skin, next to mine, not touching it. I am chapped lip skin that has fallen off, that can longer touch the tender skin.

Laura's party. The phone is ringing. The person nearest to it picks it up, shouts: "Who's Laura?... phone call for you". I am in the room farthest away from where she is sitting. I know that my presence disorients her like the sound of myriad invisible beetles at night. Coming into the room where I was, she must have perceived my presence as the sudden cessation of the beetles' sound: equally annoying and disconcerting.

Her hand the in-focus plane of my hand. [Telephoto lens]

— Your hand the in-focus plane of my hand.
— Which one of my two hands?

My body next to hers, almost touching hers. My body is my frozen body (I can't feel it), her body is my warm body.

Christ: «Let your left hand not know about the good your right hand has done». That is don't applaud (unless you're a Zen master). Or else, applaud (once more to his amazement those fingers fluttering without flying) them not after they finish speaking but while they are speaking. Others learned how to stop applauding by getting drunk (clapping yet the two hands never touching). Omran Omran, due to a car accident, had one hand shorter than the other. One can always listen to the rain.

It's the jump that separates the earth from the earth. The jump is the real mountain. The bird flew (like a zipper that is being unzipped), the far away mountain became a valley. Even the ghosts of the cemeteries have left these small towns for cities.

I hit a small cockroach. Intense feeling at seeing the half-squashed cockroach still advancing very slowly. I hit him again. Speaking about him I would not have said *cockroach* but *like a cockroach*.

Never use regret ("You'll regret not having tried this one day." Don't tell stories, don't indulge in suspense) to convince someone not to judge *a priori*, to try to try things (not to try to try is thriftiness, thriftiness is the real injustice, is cowardice. Sahar: "poverty rather than thriftiness") for this threat of regret is an *a priori a posteriori*. But trying to convince people not to judge *a priori* with "try it, you'll lose nothing" (a curious woman is not seductive) is even worse, since the idea was to lose one's chains-limitations. It is not through curiosity that one tries things and changes (the higher the resistivity at room temperature, the more likely it is a metal (with comparable densities of conduction electrons) will be a superconductor when cooled. *Critical temperature* in the case of the onset of superconductivity signals a phase transition to the absence of resistance. Possibilities as idle curiosity, as easiness, in the normal state; possibilities as real in quantum physics (for instance in quantum interference), which is against curiosity since the latter collapses the Schroedinger wave equation), it is by getting lost.

Laziness should be related to rest and not to how low the energy level is: superconductivity (resistless uninterrupted flow of electrons) is a lower energy level than the normal state.

Nightclub. Asked three women for a dance. Three nos. Now waiting, like a woman, for the idea to come to me.

I saw her on West Fourth street, New York. That's how it all began and that's how it all ended (an expression as laconic as a heart attack).

Cafe. Scattered light on trees' wooden fruits. Strange faces like condoling hands. A smile not answered even by a hindward look. I wonder about silence, whether it is a mute or a deaf person.

The white page originated in trees, in fertile life, only to become the sterile semen of the beach's foam (foam surfing on the waves (the foam's teeth of emptiness)). As soon as one tries to write on it one discovers things had been inscribed on it and then erased, endlessly. Only ink is blank.

An image must remain for much longer than its function requires, or disappear so fast that the *persistence of vision* makes one feel it is the eye itself that subsists for too long.

A blind man has no shadow but his stick has one for it sees.

The first limit to disappear: the borders of the lips.

Her body a part of my body still under the effect of local anaesthesia. I want badly to feel it. Metempsychosis?

A woman dancing alone is the figure of fidelity, the fidelity of the music to her.

The beach, the whole skin turning very gradually intense red and the sun making one see red even with the eyes closed. Should one use sun lotion over the dark inside the closed eyes?

Lying in bed the earth is flat, it is only when one stands that it becomes spherical (Running for a long time very fast then stopping to catch one's breath. How come nobody thought to use this as the proof the earth is round?).

Dilution is not help. Dilution is a weakening that makes one need others' help.

Wenders' *Nick's Movie*. A sad, pessimistic film for a cowardly film. Dying is a foreground whose background has dissolved to become the withdrawnness, detachment, of the foreground itself. Dying is a search, because the body itself is falling into pieces (and not necessarily due to old age or sickness), becoming heavy, of a no-piece or -pieces anymore. It is meaningless to say that since the body is disintegrating into pieces that fall away from one — on one —, one will attain this no piece or pieces merely by waiting. There is an infinity of pieces. Death will always interrupt the futile wait.

To speak here about weakness and consequently about help, or rather to speak about help and consequently about weakness is obscene. Nick: «And I started out as strong as I could and then there was a great relief when I surrendered more and more to you.»

Wenders comes to help. All one can hear in the changing rhythm of one's breathing is from time to time the piercing — for constrained between the "action" and "cut" — sound of Ray: help me, anybody, get rid of Wenders' help. For that's when others need help, and that's when one should help them, when one has a duty to help them: when they are being helped. People need help only when they are being helped, they need this further help precisely and for no other reason than to get rid of the former help.

Gogol burnt the second volume of *Dead Souls*, Joyce threw the manuscript of *The Artist As A Young Man* into the fire, Kafka asked Max Brod to burn everything he wrote after his death. One still has never heard of a filmmaker burning his film: it belongs already to the producer (unless the filmmaker himself/herself financed his/her film) who will never throw it in the fire: too much money is at stake in making a film, so that it becomes almost impossible to put it to the stake. The condition for mixing with dying people is that everything become so mixed up that death may strike us instead of them. The producer of the film is a link with an outside safe world (although the relation with him is not so safe. One has heard of filmmakers committing suicide because of the bad *treatment* they received at the hands of producers). *After all* after the shooting stage, when one may mix with the dying, comes the editing stage. Wenders reedited the version that was edited by his editor and shown at Cannes.

Like Odysseus almost all filmmakers have crews. Odysseus «has found an escape clause in the contract, which enables him to fulfill it while eluding it... he has himself bound. He listens to the song... he cannot pass over to them, for his rowers with wax-stopped ears are deaf not only to the demi-goddesses but to the cries of their commander» (Adorno & Horkheimer). Exactly the same can be said of Wenders and most other filmmakers, except that now the contract itself (with the producer and the crew) is the escape clause. One must leave this «fulfill it while eluding it» behind as part of youth, that period when the creative fulfills his/her destiny while eluding it (exceptions: Rimbaud…). «My ape nature fled out of me, head over heels and away, so that my first teacher was almost himself turned into an ape by it, had soon to give up teaching…» (Kafka). An experiment cannot but begin or end with the undoing of contracts. The film opens with narration by Wenders: «I had been given two weeks off from the pre-production work on my next film», and then later in the film: «the next morning I had to make a phone call to the production office in Los Angeles… They needed me back… for decisions about the budget and script of *Hammet*». Shot of the plane leaving New York; panning shot from the air of Los Angeles; shot of a plane landing back in New York, then Wenders' words: «It was four weeks later when I came back to New York». (Some people missed seeing in the film the actual moment in which Ray died: a pornographic audience that wants to see the soul leave the body, as it, in other films, has to see the semen coming out of the erect penis). Why skip showing in the film his stay in Los Angeles, why skip the interruption that Los Angeles represents, if not because Los Angeles is not really the interruption but *Lightning Over Water* is, and a false interruption, since it lets itself be interrupted by the continuity. The contract, the contracts, subsisted and no experimentation took place.

Ray knows he let Wenders steal from him what he himself did not possess but had the possibility of experimenting, his dying. But really nothing has been stolen except counterfeit dying since one can never steal except the forged. Those ever increasing in number cancer cells (he shaves his bald chin in abhorrence of a posthumous proliferation (hair continues to grow even after the body has become a corpse). If one entered a fully silent anechoic room in 1951, one would have heard two sounds: nerves' operation and blood's circulation. Two sounds heard and one has become their friendship) have already inhabited every place except the grave. The hospital room: the light light outside, the heavy body that is becoming even heavier as it becomes skinnier, as if the bones themselves were eating, feeding on and digesting the flesh.

Ray on camera asks Wenders to cut the shot the latter is directing. Wenders replies that it is he, Nick, that should say "cut". This exchange is repeated three times, then Wenders says "cut" (Safa claps the slate, throws it, walks away, and says "action". Cut to him in continuity walking back and forth. A little later, he says "cut". The shot is cut but edited in continuity with a different shot. He turns toward the camera and says "cut". The shot is cut but edited in continuity with a different shot. He says "cut"…). One watched. It was in another film, Patrick Bokanowski's *L'Ange*, where animation techniques were used, that one screamed *stop* while a man was repeatedly stabbing a puppet dangling from the ceiling (in animation films puppets, clay and other sorts of objects become animated, alive (if not explicitly then potentially). One has to know which medium (film, painting, writing…) and which modality of the medium in question (animation…) one is dealing with before considering one's feeling that a puppet is alive to be the result of vague sentimentality induced by a metaphorical way of thinking). And yet the other spectators in the cinema do not seem to have heard the scream, did not in any way react to it. Was it that one's shout was edited out by one the same way "obscene" words are edited out when they occur during interviews on TV documentary programs? Was this because one somewhat intuited that one must not try to stop the interminable, for that would only replace it with a more infinite interminable: a maid carries a milk-filled pitcher and deposits it on a table (in this animated film one cannot imagine/conceive that there is liquid inside that pitcher. Indeed, when we later see shots of a liquid on the stairs, it has the character of something either melting or having just melted, that is, of something that was *very recently* a solid). We see, over ten times, shots of her bringing the pitcher to the table. She deposits it firmly on the table and it falls and its fall is decomposed Marey-like into almost as many frozen pitchers as there were shots of her carrying the pitcher to the table. The shouted *stop* would have increased the number of frozen frames of the falling pitcher and that in turn would have increased the interminable number of comings and goings of the maid with the pitcher, which in turn would have increased the number of immobilizations… That is most probably why one either did not scream or edited out one's scream.

Her way of exteriorizing her movements as if she has just given herself a manicure and is waiting for it to dry.

He's sitting looking at something. Pov into which he enters, exits, the shot continues for a time, then he enters the frame, leaves it, the shot continues for a little while longer. Next shot: he's sitting in the same place as in the first shot, looking.

They hate words in films. Since words are underexposure, they think they may underexpose the whole film. The temporal precedence of words-in-the-form-of-the-script over the image echoes the fact that the sound recording of a shot begins before the image recording of the same shot (—Sound. —Speed. —Camera). Slug.

Drunk, one feels every stability to be a stroboscopic effect.

In TV programs shot with a film camera the mouth is the TV frame, the shout the film frame; in 16 mm films the mouth is the 16mm frame, the shout the wide-screen frame; in wide-screen films the mouth is the wide-screen frame, the shout the cinemascope frame. Only the distracted (forgetful) can be outside while still inside the film, only he can resist either being thrown out of the film (how can the non-localized be thrown out?), or reduced to decor (extra), or used as insert (temporal decoration) to avoid jump-cuts. The *outside while inside the film* is a jump-cut.

The air's stillness. Then rain, the air dissolving in the water. At last, touched by the air.

It is not by accumulating limitations that one becomes lean. Neither is it through inertia: what I am writing is becoming flat, a flat horizontal line scratching out what I wrote before: An obese emptiness.

"Stop smoking words."

Drunk. Every sound a sound-over.

One may, being in sync with one's time, become a (so-called) revolutionary just because everybody seems to be during a certain period in history. But sometimes everybody has become a revolutionary, everyone is not in sync with his time.

Don't show the person in the film changing from a young man to an old man through the use of make up, but through a degeneration and deformation of the image: it is the image that has to become older.

Innate: It was born with you. The problem is that *you* are not born yet.

Silence, the sounds not just absent but having been sucked out and continuing to be sucked out. This urge I am feeling to be outside.

The crowded small bar, and yesterday the crowded classroom. If only we are/were being filmed or photographed with a wide lens.

The melted voices and sounds in the restaurant waves eroding the words/ phrases one is saying.

Beirut's night, like ink, does not hide things but erases them.

116

Through the moving train's windows he can see the many stopped trains at Howard station: "Always loved the tops of trains, like the backs of whales. A *Moby Dick* Whitman could have written." Father telling his child: "Parallel lines meet at infinity." Shot of two parallel train tracks that converge. The child: "Is this infinity?"

Full Metal Jacket: It is not the perfect sync of the movements of the army units that really scares one, it is the absolute sync in the reactions of the film spectators.

As black as a tear in a blind person's eyes.

Walking always, as if so painted.

She's asked to dance not by you but by the music.

— When should I come back? [said before leaving].
— Now.

Night. Greyhound bus passing by twin Amoco stations one on each side of the road. The reflection of one of them on the window glass opposite one's seat hides from one the mirror image station which one knows is there since one saw the two stations while the bus was heading in their direction. Hiding behind one's twin's image.

That man's gaze stuck to her, circling round her, like a horsefly one sweeps away and that keeps coming back. Fly circling around the light and around me. I drive it away; it comes back. Repeatedly. Then it bit me. This urge to scratch. The hand circling around the place of the bite then scratching it. Repeatedly. This concordance between the behavior of the cause of the bite and its effect on the behavior of the one bitten.

After writing about slug, he looks from the window of the moving train: "Was what passed by while I was writing, a slug (to maintain sync)? Or is it automatically considered an image merely because it is inserted/an insert between two shots of my open eyes (during sleep, the eye sees images only during the REM period. The same during the day, the eye sees only rarely)?" The slug, as long as it is not used to sync, is the secret.

Someone is smoking in front of Safa's face in the subway train. Safa writes: "The hot weather: like someone smoking right into one's eyes and nose."

Inverse metaphor.

He arrives late for the appointment. He asks the receptionist at the gallery whether she saw a beautiful woman with black hair and sync silence.

Only the etc. is really comprehensive. Its talkative silence.

Her hand right next to mine. If I touch it, all of me would slip. Afterwards I felt like a leper surprised he did not slip when he rested on the stone, that the stone did not slip from underneath him (Drunk, but the frozen slippery road is also drunk).

Her knotted laces the only flower I like (not true: I also like and dread the resurrected flower in Cocteau's *The Testament of Orpheus* and Godard's *King Lear*). The blotch of dried blood on her foot one of the most beautiful pimples.

Have not written you one letter yet. Forgive this sudden patience. Why is it I always end up using the brush as a scalpel? Why this fall into things when one is too impatient even to float (Sauna: floating on one's sweat)? Is it that one is still impatient with one's impatience? To become patient with one's impatience.

I am back in New York. Streets that are numbers, numbers that are bank accounts, yet not one river here has a bank, let alone two.

Naked, except for her eyelids. Beirut: lidless eyes waiting for coffin lids.

Everything moving is falling apart because of the stickiness of the ground.

Hail Mary. The poster of the film shows a man's hand close to but never touching a woman's naked belly. In *Hail Mary* the distance between Joseph's hand and Mary's body is the off-body of the body (as the screen has an off-screen); this off-body constitutes a halo, hence an aura: a religious film. It is not by backlighting the actors, making their hair luminous, light spilling from their heads, flaring around them to form a representational halo, that one can combat the anti-aura, hence anti-halo nature of film, that mechanically reproductive art: the aura/halo is itself mechanically reproduced, hence annulled as aura/halo. That is why one feels there is something foreign to cinema about this off-body and not because it is non-visual (It is a long time now since one stopped equating cinema with the visual), but because it evades the anti-aura of cinema. The halo then would crown not the one who performs (or has the potential to perform) a miracle, but is itself, in the mechanically reproductive medium that film is, the miracle. This attempt in *Hail Mary* to create an aura/halo within an art inscribed in mechanical reproduction is performed by a woman, and Godard should have known that Mary was a dancer (it took God himself to undo her self-containment. A woman is dancing; the stupid attempt by men to regain control, to make a breach in her self containment by fucking her, by playing pinball using their dicks for ball (the penis going in and out of the vagina (not a back and forth movement: it ends in the one way movement of ejaculation), like an implanted organ that gets rejected by the host, time and time again), reducing her to the body of the pinball machine. Dance is not erotic. Erotism is the urge to penetrate the impenetrability of the dancer). This off-body (which has nothing to do with any territoriality)(which has nothing to do with the anti-missile heat blankets around tanks, that the Israeli army used during its invasion of Lebanon and that left the Lebanese and Palestinian fighters (Lebanese guerilla fighter aims his RBG missile at an Israeli tank in South Lebanon. Fires. Sees the missile explode on hitting the heat blanket around the tank (territorial machine, condom-using machine)(the only way to interact with a prostitute is to give her a sexual disease (Molly opens the door of the place where she works in *Working Girls*. The phone is ringing. Without changing the rhythm at which she's moving, she turns on one light, then another; rests her bicycle; puts both the tea cup she has in her hand and her notebook on the table; takes off her sweater; gets a CleanX box from the closet. The phone was ringing all along: it rang a total of eleven times (then she answers it). She's like a turned off message machine. It is almost as impossible to have a dialogue with the former as with the latter). Or else as customer having sex with her, simulate, behind the screen of the condom, ejaculation), sees it exploding upon touching an invisible veil (a wall is not a veil (the bat sends a sonic signal which hits against an obstacle and sends an echo. Almost everything is an obstacle-wall to the bat. Would a veil in this case be that which would swallow the signal, a black hole?) A veil hides the absence of a wall). The same with thoughts, as if there existed between one and them an invisible-unthinkable veil (made of heat? The heat released by actions, or worse by reactions?)) no alternative but to fill a car with explosives and dive straight into these tanks (how to dive into solids?) in suicidal attacks to destroy them) is outside of the spectrum of detection of the human senses, hence a way of undoing the all pervasiveness of the look, and hence of maintaining the body intact. Those who dislike Godard may consider this off-body as no more than a reactionary spiritual condom (we're in the Aids era; I see it as a halo and would relate it to anorexia (more predominant among females than among males): at least some of those who even when they are extremely lean continue to try to get even leaner do so because they are aware of this off-body, so that an anorexic's body seen by other people as already excessively thin is all things (body + off-body) considered not so thin after all, in fact it may be precisely what the anorexic conceives it to be, fat. Maybe even some anorexics want to be all off-body (is God an anorexic?)(If it is possible to have a film be all off-screen, then it would be equally possible to become all off-body. The whole five minute film consists of the credits sequence, with, on the sound track, sounds (subway trains, wind, gulls) and voices of many people. Is it possible to have a film be all off-screen?) This off-body is so strange to most Western males and females living in late capitalist societies, since it goes counter to the logic of capitalism of cluttering space with commodities. The constant message to go on a diet (addressed also to the machines, which are turning microscopic) is the acknowledgement that space is being so much cluttered with commodities that humans now have to make space for them at the expense of their own bodies: become leaner. We've been dealing for some time now with a diet raised to the second degree, squared, since diet itself now necessitates the purchase of commodities and hence entails that humans surrender even more space at the expense of their bodies (this does not though create an off-body). If we also take into account that women have for a long time often been treated as commodities, under such conditions a woman has to make space for herself as commodity — by becoming a reflection in a mirror, a shadow, or an image (on film, video, photographs, posters, retinas): a surface.

Yesterday. I slept with my roommate for the first time. The corridor connecting her room to mine feels today as short as a seven-page paper typed on a wordprocessor that has been compressed to the prescribed limit of five pages without the elimination of one word.

Silent as a reflection.

Time tries to make us blank, for every creation is a hurrying of time.

They felt sometimes annoyed with him for what they considered an attempt to impress them with his ideas (then they would say: "You speak in slogans and aphorisms. You don't facilitate discussions." He used to enter into long discussions, only he discovered very early that, unlike him, they did not understand a discussion to be something that went on even in the absence of the other(s). Since he was surrounded by their culture, he was automatically doing this. Not so in their case), when in fact he was getting rid of those ideas of his he considered merely intelligent but without any necessity (— L'au lieu est le lieu de l'expérimentation. — Oui, le nécessaire (what one does outside of any help (I can't help myself)) est le lieu de l'expérimentation), by reducing them to chatter, drowning them into the anonymous noise of simultaneous conversations where it's no longer clear who said what, who heard what, who did not hear what (the advantage of being solitary is that one does not waste too much time with/on people, but the disadvantage is that one is less able to exclude from the book what should not be included in it but merely said/ wasted in a conversation). Had they not forced him to despise them so much, hence precluding his having conversations with them, his book would have been more laconic.

Nomads are drowsier than others: it is as if they are constantly on subway trains (frames of rest and motion are relative). The sound inside the subway that of diving into water. The fade out in a film should have the same harshness-violence as the obliteration of things on diving in water. Will Hindle's *Watersmith*: it is more to the water than to the diver that violence is happening. The swimmer dives; his hand, as he swims, is constantly diving. To travel inside a subway/car/plane is to dive into space.

She's sitting on the seat opposite me on the subway. Her beat up sneaker and just a little higher the miraculous tenderness, smoothness of the skin of her leg. As if each has gone through a different life.

The modulation of the breaths in the harmonica in the blues tune: giving breath to silence.

Waiting in the plane for the take-off. Outside in the dusk the long cue of airplanes taxiing to the runaway like a pod of whales.

Jalal Toufic
1340 West Estes #3N
Chicago, IL 60626
Summer 1988

To Prajna Parasher:
And if most books now begin with quotations (a habit I dislike), then maybe one would be allowed to write a few lines of one's own on someone else's book, that is write a dedication.

Sincerely Yours

Jlal O Toufic
Jalal Toufic

The last page finished, closing the book. It is as if rain has just stopped and one can go outside.

The distracted must resist being hurried ("I am slowly losing myself in these quick endeavors")(«Helium 4 does not exhibit superfluidity under any and all conditions. These properties are lost if the liquid is forced to move too rapidly»). Hurried by being asked to do something when one is still too young, not having had enough age hence time to prepare oneself; and/or by not being granted enough time to prepare the project one is working on; and/or by not having been given enough time to present (*Alien* was presented to studio executives as: *Jaws* on a spaceship) what one has prepared (never summarize, even if you end up having to fast-forward and hence to become unintelligible (— I don't follow you. — But you are my friend not my follower))(thinkers who appear on TV are not allowed enough time to elaborate their answers, so what they say goes without saying. This permits anyone to feel s/he has the right to be on video or TV or film (the interval between the presentation of the work and the response is shrinking and so is the time allotted for the presentation of the response, with the result that the response cannot be fully articulated, hence becomes necessarily a platitude, and thus cannot expose the inanity of what was presented (the more the time accorded one to produce-receive something is decreased the more we will see the time provided for any kind of discussion of it shrink)). Hence the democratization of video (camcorders). The more video cameras and editing become cheaper the more the time given to each to say or write or be listened to on a large distribution program will be summarized); and/or by being asked to work on and/or present one's project while one is resting; and/or in some cases by not being given enough time to undo one's preparation; and/or because the work is hurried since the audience takes only the time the work is being presented to it to deal with it, and afterward stops thinking about it. Orators in oral cultures often repeated to gain time to think what to say next (the superconductive can't do this for all the repetitions (emphasis is a form of repetition) are superimposed. But whatever has been received at the end of the perforation of a wall, even if it is exactly the same as something that happened earlier historically, is simultaneous with the latter). People from oral cultures speak slowly, eloquently, there is an inaudible echo that follows what they say (aura), as if they did not feel they could be interrupted (can people feel the same in the age of TV zapping?) Postponement has nothing to do with gaining time but leads to forgetfulness and off-takes (due to delaying writing in final form the words that have to be said by the actors, which remained in the mode of fragments (those who attended the 1988 film symposium at NYU were used as extras to fill the auditorium. None of the four directors (Scorsese, Penn, Lumet, Kaige) brought any notes with them. All came without a "script", though none of them would have done so if he were going to see a producer); also due to delaying calling the actors and actresses, I had no occasion to film many of the shots I had planned to get (my acting in my film has nothing to do with narcissism (in immunology they speak of the body's tolerance toward itself. The tolerance of my ear to my strange voice on the recorder). I do it because I am available, while others, in large part because of my postponing, are not)). What was given the chance to meet due to postponement (supersaturated solution. Laziness in contrast to postponement has to do with impatience (and then the book is published (do not publish articles, at least not before publishing your first book, i.e., do not vaccinate others against your book) and then the film is projected and then the video is shown. This *then* subsists after the three are available): an inability to let things meet. One has to give things the chance to meet (the wave equation of two particles that once met insures that they remain correlated however far they move away from each other (*Max Tavern*. Drunk: the body has evaded oneself as its center of gravity, and now, so light, is floating some distance away. Though bodiless (often, the removed limb continues to be felt by the one who lost it), one is apprehensive about hitting against it at any moment. Drunk: the two hands no longer twins. Each hand is solitary now, does not know instinctively where the other one is. One feels that people are lip synching and may go out of sync. Friendship: a drunk person's hand laying on his other hand without floating away. Michael (his extremely nervous face, utterly closed, as he stands there directing his film. Then you feel, to your horror, that the face that you thought fully shut is still closing, your momentary interest in it having trapped you within that closing movement that is dragging you now with it) says: "you may think my film is not necessary, but at least it has integrity." "This table has integrity. Look at it through a microscope, it will dissolve into plant cells. With a higher resolution microscope, it will dissolve even further and be filled with gaps. Until we get to the level of the subatomic particles, and there a disintegration of one of these will send flying two or more subatomic particles that will be related however far they get. It is at this level that one can speak of integrity." His funny laugh. Une moustache de sourire))) is dispersed by the wind that postponement is, this either leading to part of the script becoming part of the finished film (off-takes) or else requiring that the film be shot intermittently. The off-takes are beginning to almost completely replace the off-screen. The option of the voice-over which becomes more urgent, more seductive must be resisted in favor of the off-takes (off-takes make it necessary to think in terms of an off-film (not in the sense of context) that the film then has). It is in this sense that the film should have a script (it is a part of the final film).

Hurrying is a form of fast-forwarding (makes one unintelligible in-sync (on time)) or of zapping (in sync)(jealousy will be more and more important in the age of TV zapping). Rather one must hurry time, becoming out-of-sync. Despite zapping I stutter paragraphs (the parentheses within parenthesis within parenthesis are my stuttering) and time (out-of-sync).

If one applies a force on a vortex, the latter, instead of moving faster, expands (distraction) and becomes slower.

It is not by running that one goes outside. Running, one has to sooner or later stop to catch one's breath, this giving the dialectical movement enough time to catch up with one. The dialectical movement is this catching of the breath.

Workers make one wait at least for the minimum division of the their working schedule (an additional *absolute refractory period*). Both workers and jealousy-inducers function in terms of waiting. They don't think of themselves as receivers. They wait (and make people wait for their decision (j'attends toujours, mais pas pour toujours, ta réponse)) until the timing is good (saturated solution)(those who postpone are not able to do that: We arrived five minutes late at this remote cinema. We decided to wait for the next screening. Went to bookstores. Arrived once more five minutes late for the screening). But to decide later is to decide when the situation has altered however imperceptibly and hence the alternatives have changed and hence the decision is about something else. While postponing has to do with choice, which does not presuppose any already existing alternatives between which to choose but is the creation of the alternative or alternatives (all of which it accepts)(in believing that one receives everything one answers the generosity of the world, or rather the generosity of what in the world resists the world). Postponement is always double: one postpones to get a supersaturated solution, but one goes on postponing even after the meeting of the different elements has occurred (his actors and crew contacted the last moment, with the result that some of them were not available for the filming. The script on the day of the shooting is still in the form of fragmented notes). This second postponement is the dispersal of what was given the chance to meet (for X quickly changes from the meeting of two lines to the sign of crossing something out — in this case, the meeting). Meeting may mean never to be introduced (constituting oneself as one's private property is already thriftiness), never giving oneself or the other person the possibility of becoming thrifty.

We can give *only* that which does not belong to us (evidently, we can give what belongs to us), we can give what belongs to us only when we no longer belong to ourselves (evidently, we can give what belongs to us while we still belong to ourselves), we can dedicate only what we have received (at the end of a perforation of a wall). It is out of thriftiness that they want to have a superficial relation: they want to be indebted, they want to be able to count what is given to them, or that the debtor should be able to. They also don't want to be given things that are in them but don't belong to them (Her ever wet tongue. Not that this can't be said of other people, only of her, but that it occurred to me on thinking of/looking at her. What characterizes everybody else is an idiosyncrasy of hers)(that incredible amount of energy contained in the atoms of her body is like those spirits that speak through the mouths of mediums and shamans)(under the platitude they just said you felt the incredible number of operations that went into producing it (release of neurotransmittors, contraction of muscles, circulation of millions of blood cells). This absence of aura between dimensions that creates an aura in us, the receivers, precluding answering the platitude with a platitude). They don't want to be indebted to us for our receiving (at the end of the perforation) what makes us indebted to them.

It is not infidelity but a losing of things.

Not having excellent knowledge of rock & roll, it is by looking at her dancing that I knew that the live music could have been played better, not that she was dancing to the better version.

This sudden feeling of being in an unknown place, of being ignorant, that seizes one like the sudden paralysis, tiredness that takes hold of a bad dancer in the midst of his dance, making him unable to move his body naturally (this instantaneous superfluousness, obesity, of a body all in one block that is not at the end of an articulation (hinge), but around it), what used to take place simultaneously now having to take place sequentially (too slow for music).

Most people, as soon as they meet persons who don't project, want the latter to get to know them as fast as possible ("what is there to tell?", then they speak endlessly, until one is forced to fast-forward). For a person who doesn't project is highly sensitive to the points of bifurcation in his and other people's lives: those points at which alternatives were present, one or many of which could have been taken but weren't if no people who don't project existed, but which could *still* have been taken if one were later to meet a person who doesn't project. People who project rarely make mistakes when forming a judgement-opinion about other people who project; they make flagrant, gross mistakes (always besides the point (of bifurcation), always simplifying (especially when imputing, adding hidden reasons) whenever they formulate an opinion about non-projectors, but since the latter are so rare (many projectors spend a whole lifetime without meeting one, so that on the whole they can congratulate themselves on not having made many mistakes in their life; while people who don't project do make "mistakes" for they sometimes fall in love or have a relation with one of the alternatives that the person who projects didn't take, but that exists by the mere fact that the person who doesn't project exists (the non-projectors are called the projectors par excellence by the projectors)(one is distracted because one is a non-projector and hence is in the presence of not one reality but two or more alternatives that existed and that continue to exist because one discovered them later). Hence people who project feel annoyed in the presence of people who don't project, for the latter's existence makes them feel that choice exists (seeing people undecided between different alternatives is not what will convince one that choice and decision exist)(at first the latter think that choice is a decision in favour of one of the alternatives to the exclusion of the others; later they'll know that choice is the acceptance of the paradoxical existence of all of the alternatives, and if we want to meet people — not so often (for how many are there who don't project?) —, it is because they may discover an alternative, a bifurcation that has been hidden from us all this time (Cindy Sherman's work?) Also because they may induce a bifurcation that begins at the moment one meets them, or later).

I found out she was completely different from what I thought. I learned later that her sister is suicidal, unlike her who is indifferent and cowardly. Had I fallen in love with her sister? Often when one thinks one is attracted to a person, one is attracted to one or more persons s/he knows or knew (or will know?) and that one may oneself never meet: her sister/mother/friend/teacher/enemy.

One projects on a screen. Hence the world is then experienced at a medium distance, not too close (a wall), and not too far.

This sadness that does not go away, that remains at the same place, like an eye that does not fall like a tear.

Drunk, the light's reflections on the wine my teeth. Highway. Storm. Later, listening to music with the car windows shut: music is a form of extremely bad weather to the distances outside.

Her long hair (her beautiful straw hat her short hair. So that she had both hair styles. People who see her for the first time feel they have known her for at least the average time women spend with one hair style).

Caressing her long hair as black as the night darkness in which nothing, no hair can be seen, he said "I'll never touch you" (*Hail Mary*). Hair with two simultaneous hair styles, longer hair and shorter hair (any hair he is touching has been cut virtually). Temporal image.

Stagnant Evanston, where the grass is constantly mown. Thank you Amy for cutting your long hair. Now it is on the floor wild as grass.

Nasih means both 1) obese = 2) someone who advises.

Postponement is not a strategy of optimization, for postponement is a kind of secrecy, hence less people are interested in working with one (exception: those that have faith and trust), for almost all others need a form of proof (never counter/alleviate postponement, for instance with: "one day I'll be..." Away with stories (and suspense). You can say: "one day I wasn't...", since postponement does away with the destiny inscribed in the first period of one's life (*"dark" rearing*)), when detection collapses the wave function. This leads to a further postponement since not working with many people or working with no people at all means one is not hurried by them to finish (the younger one was the easier it was to finish projects).

It is not enough to be at the right place at the right time, one must also have the right speed. One must be careful when dealing with slow people who arrive on time because they started early.

Asked an actress to read the same text at different speeds, but also at different sound levels: reading it very fast she turned sarcastic, reading it slower she sounded pitying-understanding.

The slap a rack-focus.

I need a film or video camera to divest myself of myself, to stay not merely off-screen, but off-myself. I need to stop hearing or to continue hearing the sounds of the passing cars outside. I need to stop seeing or continue seeing this white light. I'll clean my buttocks with blue ink jutting from a bidet. *Backstreet* crowded with people and beer bottles. The drunk's laughter, like the bubbles coming out of the beer. The silent striking of the clock's second hand the bubbles of time. Yet I am not getting drunk, but feeling anesthetized, as if these people, beer bottles, and bubbles of seconds were the particles in a numb foot one is trying to move. Most blanks are repetitions of other blanks, redundancies that have to be crossed out.

To the blind all that is not an edge is an abyss.

His words cold breath that deposits on the image, that hides it.

Divest possibility from curiosity.

Like borders, flags don't move, at most they go out-of-(video)registration. Once a flag moved, in Griffith's *The Lonedale Operator*, except Griffith, not being laconic, missed its movement by not cutting before we see that the woman's waving is not to the train flag swaying in the wind, but to the operator (what was their shaking hands before parting if not a waving? Why then have them wave again? Redundancy).

At present every action he had to perform feels to him like having to look up in the dictionary the meaning(s) of every word he does not understand in a book. Would the remedy for this (did he want a remedy? Only at times of rest) be to begin finding out the other meanings of all the words in the book?

Worker tilling the ground in Evanston. The drop of sweat at the edge of his nose more annoying to me than the sound of drops of water falling intermittently for hours from a bad faucet.

Many people think writers acquire a facility with written language. On the contrary. And the difficulty now extends even to writing a letter to someone to ask permission to film in his cafe (how about creating performances? Would he then be almost unable to speak?) Is writing this gradual reduction of what one feels should be written, of what one feels is necessary? The process is contagious, one ending up saying little, becoming almost mute, walking all the way to the other end of the medium-length table to get the salt instead of merely saying *salt*, one ending up doing away with salt, one ending... (how much does this *etc.* still contain!).

Everything, the sounds, the air, quantum fluctuations, is seeping out of the lecture room. Everything except the students (my still feeling arrogant in relation to them shows my extreme modesty).

He found it funny, strange (redundancy: funny includes strange) that he thought the horizontal majoring of his room (many a book not on bookshelves but standing, not lying, on the floor; envelopes full of quotations stacked neatly on the floor, the two futon mattresses, the TV, the video recorder and the telephone all on the floor, suitcase horizontally on the floor, two posters of paintings on the floor (like carpets)) as Japanese in spirit, until an Arabic friend came to interview him about exile. Only then did he connect this to the Bedouins' horizontal majoring.

Difference between grace and gracefulness (only the one who has lost the gracefulness of the accompaniment has grace). Music occurs as grace only if it is not an accompaniment, let alone a *conductor* of the emotions or the movement. On the beat: the second hand stopping the other hand midway in its movement to slap the body (do we have two hands so that one hand can prevent the other from often slapping the rest of the body?).

Dancing, she becomes her hair that was blowing in the air outside.

After sixteen hours of work, an image doesn't have enough time to be processed by the time the following one is registered: one gets a superimposition of the two images (Bruce Baillie's *Castro Street*) each becoming a filter that beautifies the other. Sometimes the same beautifying superimposition takes place even though one is not tired. Is the world tired?

The sentimental hug of the horizon. The green trees on either side of the highway posters advertising SUMMER. *Race Road* on the way between Kalamazoo and Ann Arbor with speed limit signs of 10 miles/hour, 35 miles/hour, 45 miles/hour. Orange neon lights in the dark, like floating blue veins in freezing hands. The sky vacant except for three birds breathing; the street empty except for a man breathing; in a vacant meditation room, fourteen people learning how to exhale. Walking in the underexposed darkness, seen only by the red light eyes of a cat.

Film teachers tell their students to turn off the sound of films to be able to concentrate on the lighting/composition of the image and on camera movements. One should turn off the sound track of life, so as to see better.

A pseudo-Marxist present at a meeting of Northwestern University leftist students trying to organize a conference said: "We should have groups that present problems, and others that present solutions."

The fingers suddenly beginning to move at the end of long clothes, like worms not wrinkled with any folds (with rare films the cornea's white overflows on the pupil and lids. It's as if the movie theater's lights had been turned on and the film were no longer projected but injected. A new film has been created, a film without any jump-cuts but that is itself a jump-cut with what preceded it and what will follow it)(*palm reader*: misnomer. The palm has no wrinkles whatsoever. These lines are created by the fast-forwarding that goes on until the palm watcher gets to the part he wants to know about. Due to advances in technology one can now fastforward video without any lines jarring the images passing by). The darkness under the tongue oozing out and flooding the eye. All the teeth lost (the mouth no longer guarding the rest of the body from the teeth). The fear they'll jut out in the eye (terrifying eyelashes), the ear, the nose.

Postponement does away with suspense; there is no longer even the suspense of when postponement will end. Those who postpone are against waiting (waiting gives at best a saturated solution). A car came to a standstill at the Stop sign and waited for him to cross the street. He moved toward the car's rear and crossed behind it (this having also to do with the unobtrusiveness of the unborn, their hatred of being forced to have a pseudo-existence by becoming a trace on someone's retina). A large part of the actor's and actress' day during the shooting is passed waiting for the lighting to be ready, the dolly tracks to be laid, for the sound person making sure the microphone does not appear in the shots; how can he be a film director: how can he ask others to wait, or rather (for they usually didn't mind the waiting that much), how can he withstand the waiting of others?

Why is he filming snow on and on when his film is about Jane? Is it because he felt the snow had the whiteness of her tennis shoes? Her even whiter than the snow tennis shoes overexposing his eyes, he preferred to go outside and shoot snow overexposing his film.

Going back to Lebanon after such a long time may mean that all the images one acquired through changing abroad would not be used as images, would not be seen, hence may be used by others on the soundtrack as slug to maintain sync (secret: what is not seen because used on the sound track as slug).

Things have become hard and impenetrable. I feel in their vicinity that I am oozing.

Drunk one must dance so as to, in a sudden gesture, get rid of the body, like a ballet dancer sending the ballerina up in the air. This beer drink passing on my tongue like a tongue. When sounds exist on their own, divested of their sources, we begin to touch things. The distinction private/public is unintelligible to the solitary. Color animated films should have different touches (coups) of colors, to constitute the flesh, otherwise the colors are mere reflections (black and white films screened in bars, over which pass the multicolored stroboscopic lights). I am on vacation only when I have the flu. The detective's room resembles a motel room. The whole finger has the leanness of the part surrounded by the ring. Is the impossible easier than the very difficult?

How can one choose between two alternatives when each contains so much that is aleatory; how can one choose between the unknowns contained in these alternatives?

She's not available, but open, an openness where both of us get lost.

The ear should often get clogged (like a sink), words and sounds flooding out of it.

She's using hand gestures to further explain to me what she's saying. I understand what she's saying; what I don't understand is why she doesn't give me her hands. When I am not touching her lean hand, I feel I am wearing gloves.

Autumn. Leaves crossing the street like school children.

An EL train passes nearby. The knots of the body dissolved. This remote control massage.

Moving her tongue like lipstick over her lip.

Projection is the contagious element in stagnation.

The straight hair of the dancer the only distracted part in her. Strange to see texture in a dance film, for at first dance seems to be the metamorphosis of everything into surfaces (gravity being wrinkles in space-time), the toes of the ballerina becoming, as tip, a surface. The camera in this experimental dance film is itself doing the balancing through high, low, and strange angles, so that the dancer no longer needs to balance himself/herself, becoming the camera's tripod. Her hair lying on the floor without resting.

From the fast moving train, bright house windows pinned to the night like laundry. The hand extending to touch the things in the water never touches them, a so thin layer of fluid on which they are imperceptibly reflected is on it.

My backpack, containing notes assembled over a period of five months, stolen. I feel like a cat whose claws have been extracted, surprised now its teeth don't retract when it is not using them; it finds chewing strange, as if it were doing it with its claws. What use anger (— If I had bought a backpack just because one of my favorite writers carries one, it would be an imitation, but not so much of the writer — he doesn't imitate (against the *tabula rasa*. Rather the derivative: the interval tending towards zero, but never totally reduced to zero (Joseph's hand not touching Mary's body in Godard's *Hail Mary*). Taking things to the n+1 (the opposite of obsession, which is even "the first time", n+1. With it, as with spaceship launches, we have a countdown) 'th degree (acceleration the derivative of speed the derivative of movement). In that sense to be a derivative is not to be an imitator. To be called a derivative of someone is the highest praise, and if we don't sometimes accept to be called a derivative it is out of modesty. Always to inject time. Derive: to divert the path)(imitating Warhol? But he's done even that: he imitated himself so successfully in his last years (one must read and experiment enough while writing one's first book, so as to diminish the danger of one's spending the rest of one's life repeating oneself/it. That's also why first books take such a long time to finish). That's one way of fighting imitators) — as of the ape, for it is the ape that imitates.

— I was joking, you shouldn't get angry.

— Anger as a good antidote to inertia. What you said was a good occasion for me not so much to get angry as to exercise my anger.

— Then you were acting.

— Not if what is not acting is distracted, not looking on as a spectator) now when all it can achieve is permit me to write a line, maybe two, even a paragraph, even a page or two, when I've lost over twenty-five pages?

The meeting line between land and sea is frozen. The horizon, junction between sea and sky, is also frozen (a white line).

The summer timing is upon us. It is as if I suddenly found myself transported to another time zone with one hour difference from Chicago, and sleepy as I am it feels I have now to drive for an hour and a half to my apartment in Rogers Park instead of just walking for seven minutes.

His words like your long hair falling intermittently on your eyes. He kept removing them away from your eyes.

The voices of many old people in this huge restaurant, like school children during break, are the only thing that is young here (I feel I am raising my head from under a sea wave having inadvertently swallowed much water).

A pointillist rather than perspective way of forming a meeting, through simultaneity not chronology. In *Mrs. Dalloway* the strokes of the clock a pivot from someone's interaction with it to another's, a sort of party given by time. The instant is timeless, as the point is dimensionless, hence one is affectless in it; it is the affectless state that is the duration of the timeless instant.

Can one speak about the universe experiencing a certain event at a specific moment when we know [special relativity] that two events that are simultaneous from one frame of reference can be consecutive from another frame of reference, with the order in which they happen in relation to one another depending on the frame of reference from which they are considered? So that though one should not repeat or do anew what someone else did/experienced, it is nonetheless true that from a given frame of reference one can truly say that what has from other frames of reference been already done many times was done for the first time by oneself.

But even in the case where from one frame of reference a certain event has already taken place, we can, still in the same frame of reference, through an altered state tap into the event exactly as it happened the first time.

Postponed having money transferred from Lebanon to my account in Chicago. A friend lends me a thousand dollars. Postponed for another month having money transferred to my account. My friend no longer has any money; neither do I. It will take ten days for the money to get here from Lebanon. Both of us have to borrow money. "I didn't think someone could be so irresponsible." "Don't take interest on the money you lent me."

Poor inducers of jealousy have the same face whether in profile or straight on. Their profile is their non-relation with one, hence one does not feel jealous when they gaze at or speak to someone else. While jealousy-inducers have a different face depending on whether one sees them in profile or straight on, so that they have more than one face, and hence they can be in a relation with you with their profile and simultaneously in a relation with the one they are facing. The cubist faces of jealousy-inducers.

People usually don't like mysterious persons, for there is nothing obscure in the latter, nothing to form the dark backdrop of a mirror.

The truly shy person feels shy even in front of himself/herself in the mirror.

I am sitting in the back seat of the speeding car. Behind, in the visible past, other cars. One of them gains speed, enters the present, then passes into the visible future, then into the off-screen future. Shaved fields. Wind floods car drowning my breath. The clouds visible, odorless smell.

The superimposition of all the silences in the case of the superconductive creates a distortion in the silence: too high of a level if all the silences are superimposed where and when one is; too low of a level if all the silences are superimposed away from where and when one is. The company created by even the solitary superconducting person. To the sound technician he said: "I think you forgot to adjust the silence level." (Manhattan seen at night from Brooklyn Bridge, an endless digital vu meter). The filmmaker ended up having the same spectra as his film stock and lens, his sound recorder and microphone (the nagra's and microphone's spectra are different from that of the human ear. The final sound track in almost all films is not a transcription of what has been received by the sound recorder, but a description: many films have forty eight sound tracks mixed in the final track (he does not hear or see most of what is happening according to others, except sometimes when he's in a superconducting state with its superimposition of light and of sounds (a form of sound mixing). Often in the superconducting state he sees and hears much more than what is heard in normal life). It is his refusal to describe that gives his film a science-fiction feel, since the audience perceives then a world perceived through sense spectra different from those of most humans). Almost all science-fiction films are deficient in that they don't change the senses' spectra. How not to describe (the film does not describe thinking, does not try to recreate how a paragraph is assembled from fragments received at different times, and if it shows someone writing, it shows him writing at the speed at which a lecturer in the Middle Ages would have recited the text to his students-scribes. Not that the film accepts the existence of an already finished text-script), not even in the minimal manner, through metaphors?

Spitting, watching the saliva floating in the rivulet is a gargle. It cleans one's vision so one sees the quiet flow of the water that would otherwise pass unnoticed. *Tropic of Cancer*: «This is not a book... this is a gob of spit in the face of Art». One can go on spitting in the face of Art (whether it is written with A capital a or no), art will still be there behind its vitrines. One must skip art. It is those who don't know how to skip (Henry Miller does) that spit and profusely on their fingers so as not to miss inadvertently any one page of the book given to them as a gift.

— I like *The Subterraneans*. — I thought that, being an aphoristic writer, you...
— The blanks between aphorisms, or, at times, between the phrases of

aphorisms, or, at times, between the words of aphorisms (right handed people's left hand, the hand that does not write while the other is writing, if distracted, corresponds to these blanks), like the aphoristic white patches on this highway we're driving on, allow gaining speed, crossing from lane-paragraph to paragraph-lane and overtaking (a continuous line indicates that one is prohibited from doing that). Both have to do with Kerouac's dashes.

It is a war. There is no time to lose, otherwise timing becomes important; that is that which we were fighting would have won.

The violence of sounds not anchored by their images.

One can respond to generosity only by doing something that is not a reaction, something that comes out of the blue, a surprise (surprise creates the stranger)(generosity presupposes forgetfulness). Generosity is a beginning, it cannot be a response, it cannot be responded to: it is the gratitude of the forgetful. Generosity is always towards strangers, it even makes of people we know strangers, rather than the other way round. It is aristocratic to accept generosity. Only thrifty people take full advantage of a situation (extremists don't). But to the non-thrifty the situation itself may be generous. Neither the generous nor the distracted squeeze a situation; they slap it.

One can't go back to a strong relation since a strong relation changes one.
Can one say to a person one has never met before: "I miss you"? Yet I miss you very much.

The tip of a dancer's feet the insulator separating the two superconducting parts of a Josephson junction.

The projector's sound (like matte box edges appearing in all the wide angle lens shots of a film) beneath the diegetic piano music. It is as if a feverish man were playing the piano.

It does not follow from the fact that one person is following another that the former is the hunter. Often it is the one that is being followed that is the hunter. Trapezist going back and forth in the echoless air (the way her pupils advanced toward you when she spoke, like a trapezist performing his acrobatics with no net beneath him, and you constantly felt that something in her is in danger). His decision to let go of the bar (no safety nets) is simultaneous with the second trapezist's decision to go to meet him. The second trapezist cannot say that the moment of decision for him takes place

135

once the first trapezist has let go of his bar (this applies only in the quantum world (Wheeler's delayed-choice experiment)). And yet she —

So many people in the room (drunk, one's bones and flesh usually so compressed together, now spaced as in a butcher's place) where the film is being shown. She has to move her chair to avoid having her gaze blocked by the heads in front of her, so why is it that being myself a crowd, she does not move away from some of those towards others, but rather moves away from the whole crowd altogether.

Antonioni's *The Passenger* begins in the desert and ends in a "very dusty" place. In the beginning was the wind. A desert wind constantly howling (the other sounds dispersed by the wind's sound), and like a headache preventing one from talking or having a readiness to listen to others. To this place comes a reporter ready to ask very elaborate questions and to listen to equally elaborate answers. The wind, the corresponding silence of the people and the devaluation of time (as if the idea of using every minute was as absurd as being interested in owing stretches of the desert (before the discovery of oil in many a desert site)). In the desert, time is the mirage, and is treated as such.

A conversation takes place at the beginning of the film between Robertson and Locke, "It's us who remain the same. We translate… every experience into the same old codes…" Yes, Mr. Locke, we are to a certain measure creatures of habit. And yet — ();?!:,. Locke then will change his life to prove this cannot be done. How does he go about it? He exchanges his identity with another European! Having the same language! The same culture (he even reads Locke's articles)! Even the same way of living (always traveling)! So that when Locke answers the woman's question about his future occupation: "I think I am going to be a writer in Gibraltar… maybe a novelist in Cairo… a gun runner…" one wonders if he'll continue "… or a reporter in London." The story about the blind man is not gratuitous. The interchange of personalities is caused by a kind of blindness, a blindness stemming from the total indifference of the motel room. Nijinsky instinctively shrank from contact with an inn room, «I wanted to stay; but God told me to leave.» It is to protect the arrival from losing his identity in the anonymous room that he's made to sign his name in the motel register (*Stranger Than Paradise*: They arrive, the three of them, at the motel parking; the two men go inside and register for a two-bed room. As planned she sneaks into the room a little later. But not having signed the register she becomes absent. The two men go on several outings without taking her along). Locke is neither murdered nor commits suicide; he dies like Robertson of a heart attack. Yet Antonioni's film does not deal primarily with blind men. At first Locke prefers men to landscapes, unlike Robertson who prefers the latter (in which men appear) to the former. Later in the film, Locke asks his female companion about the view from the motel room's window: "A little boy and an old woman..." A little later, he repeats the question hearing an answer he accepts, "A man scratching his shoulder, a kid throwing stones, and *dust*." The ability to see the landscape rather than the ability to "see" a person (a blind man can do the latter with his hands) is what differentiates the normal from the blind person. Opposite to Antonioni's stress on landscapes is Bergman's blind person's way of seeing: Liv Ulmann and Erland Josephson stand in front of an off-screen mirror in *Cries and Whispers*. They are illuminated by a table lamp. His words: "Your fine, broad forehead now has four scratches above each eyebrow — no, *you can't see in this light*... And under your eyes the sharp *almost invisible* wrinkles of boredom and impatience."

Beyond blindness, portrayed differently by Bergman and Antonioni, there is a healthy dissolution of the self that stems neither from blindness nor from hypnosis (the overlap of familiar voices is an unknown solitary sound made not of their *mixing* but of their coexistence. Recording each of the voices separately then mixing them gives a sound hypnotized by the silence of the other sounds around each)(when Cindy Sherman standing behind her camera looks through the viewfinder, she sees a view from which she's absent. Then she sets the camera on automatic, goes and positions herself in front of it. Would this explain the use of the rearscreen projection in her work? For her absence from the view she sees through the viewfinder as she sets the scene gets transferred into the use of the rearscreen projection (shot earlier) from which she's absent and with which she does not interact. There is an absence of association on her part with the past that is behind her as her environment, which leads to hysteria (the background can be added later if one uses a blue matte instead of rear projection. Hysteria due to a future trauma). Undiminished-in-freshness events happened to a hysterical world, and it is a hysterical contagion that makes them Cindy Sherman's events (her stills of the fourties, fifties...)).

I saw her in the library. She left. I ran outside. I found her. We're meeting tomorrow. This evening I walked much longer than if I had missed her and searched in despair for her in this foreign city.

Milk under concentric ripples of the nipple.

Empty stalls in vacant public toilet. I feel like a soul that has found a body in which to incarnate. In all the shots in which he appears, he is a reflection in mirrors or water or is fully framed, becoming his own image, something that does not feel pain. The halo around the faces of Christ, Mary, saints: a frame that makes of them a painting or a reflection of themselves. The flight from pain.

The image does not feel pain but one can by looking at the distorted reflection in a drop of water on a table or falling from a faucet see a confirmation of the abstract pain one is feeling.

Not to mistake being slower than oneself for laziness.

In-sync artists who say they don't care whether the audience understands what they are doing or not, being themselves their first audience, are liars (if one is in-sync, one fights against oneself whenever something new is to manifest itself: one is fighting that part of oneself that was the audience and that is slower than what is being received, since what is being received is out-of-sync with itself. Hence one is amazed that one still has to fight against people to let it manifest itself. Why this redundancy even in the case of the introduction of the new?). Only people who are out-of-sync with themselves can really not give a flying fuck about glazed audiences (the spectator thinks that in front of any work of art there are two spectators: the spectator plus the artist-as-spectator-of-his-work. All one can say to the spectator who tries to apply this in the case of an out-of-sync with himself/herself artist is that a dirty person has two shadows: one of his body, another on his body). But if one is not one's first spectator, how can one discriminate (between what is in sync and what is not in sync with itself, between what is simultaneous and what is not)? Spanish poet reading his poem. Not one word understood. One listens to the music of the words. But is his poetry necessary, was it written without his being hurried by himself or others? And if it wasn't, how come I don't hear the all too familiar-annoying sound of the fast-forward, instead of hearing the music of the words?

The prohibition against looking at the camera transgressed by jealous people trying to include you in the scene. What the jealousy-inducing woman does (she includes a third), the jealous person achieves by looking into the camera, including you as the white billiard ball. Sickening atmosphere of the confession. Jealous people are curious people (the vigil over possibilities has nothing to do with curiosity, since an act of curiosity-observation is what collapses the wave equation into one actuality. Quantum physics has been the branch of science that has gone furthest in acknowledging possibilities precisely because it relinquished curiosity: it can say nothing about what goes on between the source and the detection device in a measuring apparatus).

138

Unfortunately, the jealous project that everybody else has curiosity: the jealous person looks at you to see in the expression on your face signs about what is going on *behind his back* (Munch's *Jealousy*)(there are eyeglasses (advertised on cable TV) that permit one to see what is going behind one), but being not the jealous type myself, I look at him (the Kuleshov effect would have been of help to him had I looked with even disinterest and detachment at what was going behind him), never at what is eliciting his curiosity (the awaited expression on my face, and what is going on behind him). Cafe. Sudden loud sound. Everybody looks in the same direction, I look at them rather than at their povs (most often when faced with a bad film, I do not leave the film theater, but spend the rest of the time looking at the spectators looking at the film). Standing on the subway platform at the Fullerton stop one notices that the traffic light of the street perpendicular to the platform and in its direction is facing one instead of the cars. A Parajdanov shot (in Parajdanov's films the main characters often look toward the spectator. This is somewhat counterbalanced by the fact that the animals (*Suram Fortress*) inhabiting the same shot do not look at the main action, are oblivious to it. Were Parajdanov to shoot a film in the streets of a city, real passers-by would not look at the camera, while the actors themselves would continually look at it).

The devil's tuning fork. A misnomer. Jealousy has to do with merely *the devil's advocate's tuning fork*.

Whenever one buys something a coin toss should take place. One pays only if one loses.

The bad critical: a critical that has nothing to do with a phase transition.

Forgetting does not presuppose one has lived what one will forget.

His hug as rigid as the eyeglasses' clasp of the ears. The traces of leaves in the pavements' stones.

Music is sound-over. Music is headphone music even before headphones were invented.

I blew the match, she blew its smoke. This annoying humming (as if one were listening to it with headphones) inside the airplane, like a contagious headache. The eye of the dead holds the camera on it, no reverse shot is possible: the dead's eye is a grave. No description by the modulation of light. Nor by means of acting. To be continued because it was not intended to be begun.

Occidental surprise oriental freshness. Kneeling to pray, making oneself shorter (are old people always kneeling?), as short as a child, and can God not forgive a small child? He's reading poetry; his voice the echo of my silence.

Two professors (a student is not good enough if he remains a student, writes Nietzsche. Nor if he remains (later) a teacher) called my parentheses within parentheses within parenthesis a stream of consciousness (not to use the different fonts and letter sizes of the word processor to hierarchize the parentheses) when in fact they were received at different times and met through postponement: simultaneity.

Rack-focus from image to subtitles to image.

In interviews, one is asked to repeat part of the question so that the answer should look self-sufficient and not like a reaction ("How long have you lived in New York?" The correct answer is not "Three years", but "I lived in New York for three years."). Laconic writers find this excellent, since it eliminates the external context forcing the interviewee to *take irresponsibility* for what he says. We are irresponsible only for what we receive at the end of a perforation of (or, only in some cases, a tunneling through) a wall, otherwise we're responsible not for what we do but for projecting.

Not even: "The question may come before the answer only if the answer will enter in a 'chemical' reaction with it, changing it". Due to his slowness, the disciple will, on hearing the Zen master's answer, find the question he asked stupid, then retrospectively perceive that his stupid question was transformed into something else by the answer (for the master there is no *first* and *then*). A satori will not occur without the disciple's seeing that there was no question in the first place, but only a koan (otherwise the disciple will remain merely a student, someone lagging behind the master, someone who appreciates excellent answers and thinks he asks stupid questions).

People who lose things and events (we lose the world every time we lose something important. If we lose another important thing, we lose the world we've already lost, again. Losing the world twice without having found it in between!), find the editing process strange. It is at the editing stage that one finds (and hence finds out where one is again after not so much having been lost as having lost a world), while before, one received. Receiving has nothing to do with finding. It does not permit one to locate oneself in the world.

Not even to want to be "rich by the *opportunity cost*s he forgoes".

These are traumas of the world, events that have not been inscribed in its consciousness. Each is simultaneous with itself across time and space. One should not associate-react if one is strong enough not to have hysterical amnesia-repression (in which case one turned the event into a narcissistic event), so that the event should remain fresh-simultaneous.

That slowness of the feet, of everything that touches, of everything in touch.

TV programs are ads, not to help sell something but to buy from one one's in-sync time.

"I am flattered." How unflattering is this response. Did Mary answer the annunciation angel: "I am flattered"?

1) hands outstretched up. 2) 1+hand arching back till it touches the ground, then the body kneels forward. 3) 1+2+ left foot moves to the right side of the body, right foot to the left side of the body (as if the feet now part of the brain)... Someone suggested that the dancer's movements followed a progression of contrasting movements. In that case memory was not really needed, for no real variation was taking place. But in a dance that changes in an aleatory way from one move to the other, memory would be needed if each following move has to include the previous ones and then add to them. How to make that invisible movement (memory) part of dance?

Moving fast, but hesitating (ornamentation). Territorial instincts as far as time is concerned (refusal to be hurried). I don't touch people easily (aura: beneath the platitude that was uttered, I feel the millions of microscopic operations that went into producing it); I accept being touched (always forgot my umbrella). Used to sleep with my whole body under the covers, like a vampire. Each leg forming a pyramid so that more air could be present under the covers. Were I then to have been moved and put on a chair my body would have automatically been in a seated position. Yes, it seems I slept seated. Otherwise, being seated (a nomad has to walk (back and forth. Walking back and forth creates a lot of space (how long is the distance between Rogers Park and NU? It depends on how many times one has covered that path)) a long time before he arrives at sitting) is the most unnatural position for me (only dancers (and meditators) can be seated without giving the sensation of stagnation).

She both creates a lot of space (being thin), and uses a lot of space: her ever unlaced shoes. She always walks as if against a light wind (territorial and distant, for one is walking in a different weather even though one is only inches away from her). Like dancers, even when standing still she gives the feeling she is on an escalator, so that one has to constantly move just to remain with her (in her presence one is nervous). Ornamentation of the words with the lips and tongue.

Bill Viola's *Migration*: The sound of a bell or of a hard object hitting against metal has a resonance that does not so much propagate, as *dissolve* the distance between things. It is this resonance of the sound that matches on the level of the sound the dissolve from image to image. Bill Viola has found a ready-made natural dissolve (the shots in the totally white snowy areas in Canada that begin *Chott-al Djera* provide a natural *white balancing*. The desert is a natural special-effects machine (the distortion in colors…) that turns the video image into a mirage). The drops of water falling from the faucet in front of the chair on which Viola is sitting, a strange kind of Sauna. No narcissism in Bill Viola's videos for the camera is there to record all the screens in which we are reflected-distorted-dispersed (Janalle Joseph's dream: one of her teeth is loose. She pushes it with her tongue, but now the second one is loose, and then the third one, until all her teeth are loose, and they all begin to disperse. It is the same with Viola: he is dispersed in all the reflections (at all the levels: whether in a drop of water or in a desert mirage) in which he appears).

The first shot is of snow-covered landscape, totally white. Snow preserves what is underneath it, maybe also because the abstract whiteness of the snow-covered landscapes is a forgetfulness. One then sees a faint blotch that gets clearer until we merely recognize it, rarther than see it, to be a tree. Then there is a zoom-out until the tree is no longer recognized, but remains there as a lag not in the video image but in our minds.

In *Migration* and *Ancient of Days* the dissolve is not used as a way of making a smooth leap in time, but rather as a kind of *petit mal*, so that one or the world disappears for a while and then one or the world is back. Uninterrupted zooms-in/-out are used in conjunction with the dissolves (which do not apply to them but within them), for time has continued meanwhile its linear movement. History is an escalator on which time may be immobile or moving.

The silly expression I kept repeating in my mind "I love this woman". Like the visibility of breath in the cold. And now that I have to phone her, the same way that on hearing one's voice on the recorder it seems foreign, the same with speaking to her, what was going through one's mind seems foreign.

Not the laconism of barbers who cut one's hair too short without stopping speaking (one kept on saying "cut it short", and he kept on cutting one's hair shorter and shorter until one became totally bald and one kept on saying "cut it short". He began cutting the moustache).

She's sitting outdoors at the cafe. I enter and sit indoors, my back to her. Rain as simultaneous condensation of water around particles of dust or other material, and the dispersion characteristic of rainfall. And she moves indoors to the table opposite mine, as if she's just arrived at the cafe (rain become a time machine).

The proper setting: for the first week of my stay here, the town revealed itself a desert in beauty. Then suddenly, you. After leaving the cafe in which I saw you and wandering in the streets, I saw at random good-looking women. Are they really good-looking? If yes, you are attractive, for you attracted them to appear at that time and vicinity, to be your photogenic aura; if not, you are charming, for it is because I was charmed by seeing you that they looked good-looking to me.

His constant looking at me without reason. I feel he's looking at me through the keyhole of a door. Drunk: No frame, hence no focus; no off-screen, everything part of the screen. Weariness is the ultimate mask: a hand taking off the masks one after the other on and on until it became itself a mask, something rigid, no longer feeling-felt, an idiosyncrasy of inertia. The clown's make-up hides his laughter.

To feel how drunk you are, you have to move to shake the world in you so that it melts like ice in the drink.

Six in the morning on July 15, 1988 in Michigan. The major part of the life of some people happens in this 6 A.M. state. Part of what it means to have changed is that most of one's life occurs at a different hour-season-place than that at which it used to occur. One should experience as many of these hours-seasons-places. A lot of persons manage to be in a 6 A.M. Michigan Summer state without ever having lived in Michigan or ever having been awake at 6 A.M. Three people driving in a car in Michigan at 6 A.M., one in a 2 P.M. New York Spring state, one in a 6 A.M. Michigan Summer state and one in a 5 A.M. Michigan Summer state.

An attractive woman is the hysteria of the world: in her presence and *her* absence the world itself has multiple personalities. A *conversion* of the world (as far as lighting, sound levels) takes place to make her look more attractive: her aura. The advent of mechanical reproduction in photography/cinema does not do away with the aura: to be photogenic is to have an aura.

143

The *Orbit Room*: not the light of natural sunrise and sunset decomposing through a prism into different colors, but darkness passing through a prism and decomposing into Warhol's cool colors. The doom of bad dancers has it that most nightclubs now have huge video screens: the extremely rapidly changing shots of politicians giving speeches, women giving birth, people dancing, etc., though not cut to the beat of the music, are far less jarring and contrary to the flow of the music than the bad dancers' movements. Bad dancer sitting in the nightclub listening to music. It is as if he were listening to a phone message. Late.

Every thick color is lipstick.

What we're dealing with in extremely quick cuts in film and video has nothing to do any longer with jump cuts, but with images that are out-of-sync with each other (it is no longer only sound/voice and image that can be out-of-sync with each other).

Only by joining to the sobriety of the writing the awkwardness of the body (or dissolving the body until there's just gradations in the waft of the wind) does one flee control.

Then twittering birds. A hole swallowed by a stone's shadow.

Weariness is a waiting bereft of something to wait for.

As a child, whenever visitors came to his family house, he retired to his room. Hotel rooms remind him of this.

In Daguirre's time it took half an hour to take a photograph: the person being photographed had as it were to become cataleptic for that time; the result, the photograph, was/is a catalepsy of time. *Cliché* means both *photograph* (catalepsy) and *stereotype*. Indeed, in cases where the hand of a hysteric becomes cataleptic/paralyzed, it is the hand as understood-delineated in common language and not in anatomy.

Difference between Rocky's way of being hit continuously in the beginning of the match, and that of La Matta in Scorsese's *Raging Bull*, who intentionally has himself beaten in the beginning (Dostoyevsky feel to it)(for a time it looks as if he has been bribed and the result of the match has been decided beforehand. Humor).

144

Nam Jum Paik's *Buddha Watching TV*'s Buddha should be zapping, with the same image showing on all the channels.

Producers in Lebanon still speak of *target audience* when considering making films about the dividing areas in Beirut that have been emptied of any audience because they were and still are targets (producers are waging war on us and we have to wage war on them). How can they still do that when everybody here is a target: does not the notion of a limited target audience become meaningless? What does *target* mean when we have film images of fighters walking to the edge of walls at the dividing line between East and West Beirut, quickly advancing for a few steps in the open and shooting without having enough time to see (not only civilians, most fighters also die of stray bullets! (only Vito Acconci, who in 1969-70 shot stray photographs (holding his hands above his head and taking a photograph; bringing camera to foot and taking a photograph; taking two photos while falling; while lying in a field, taking five photographs from five different positions of the camera on his body), would have the right to do this). I for one don't criticize the Israeli army for putting veils over the eyes of captured fighters) and then as quickly retreating behind the walls (only the filmmakers shooting these fighters have them as precise targets)?

Shots of destroyed buildings are almost mandatory in any film on Lebanon: the only taxes that have to be paid in this country that has none.

Her ankle bone *Adam's apple*.

A percentage, however small, of the guerilla operations directed against Israel should be directed against the studios that make Arabic and especially Egyptian soap operas. It is not only the ground that gets occupied, but also windows (TVs) and doors (so many military checkpoints on the roads of West Beirut (the only remaining movement is that of dilation caused by the heat). So many speed checkpoints on the roads in the U.S. (15 miles/hour; 35 miles/hour; 45 miles/hour; 65 miles/hour)).

They listened, were convinced. Later they try to reproduce his arguments and the way he said them (the absence of emphasis…) They find what he said absurd. Once truly convinced, one should not try to reproduce (even if one is trying to reproduce what one oneself said but at a higher, stronger, more intense state). One should have faith (until one changes radically again). When tired, faith in oneself-when-non-tired to cross tiredness (the average: what is always missed for it arrives late, because it never postpones).

Elias Canetti: «A nightbook, a "nocturnal," no line of which was written by day. Parallel to it a real daybook, a journal, always written by day. To keep the two apart for a few years, never comparing them, never confusing them./ Their ultimate confrontation.» Written during the day or at night? Is their confrontation to occur at sunset or at sunrise? Or would it occur when both are co-present but separate, each occupying part of the field of vision: daylight sky sprinkled with white clouds over a night landscape in which can be seen a house with lights on and a lit street lamp (Magritte's *L'Empire de Lumières*).

The smaller we make the basic element (1/1000 shutter speed in photography) the larger the portion of secrets. But also the parasitical increases, or the danger of the parasitical.

Last 1. Last 2. Last 3. Last 4. Last 5.

Beyond a certain point, when a book is considered finished is as arbitrary as a word processor instructing one in the midst of a paragraph "this addition will make paragraph too long".

The distracted don't need entertainment except when concentrated. The two meanings of *distraction* exclude each other.

She keeps speaking about love as madness, yet what maddens you is that she reasonably wants to deduce from the fact you've fallen in love with her, her value. Were she in love she wouldn't do this.

During the editing stage, you read your manuscript five times, discarding parts of it. Does this mean they are bad, or does it just mean they are not good enough to be read five times? The former, for necessary writing precludes one from reading it enough times to become familiar with it. Postponement. It is not only we that resist the material, once it has changed us it resists us.

On May 21, 1985, Israel released 1150 Palestinians in exchange for 3 Israeli prisoners caught during the Israeli invasion of Lebanon. Racism. An Arab should not feel happy that so many have been freed in exchange for so few since the casualties ratio would be equally high: for the $\approx$ 655 Israelis killed during the Israeli invasion of Lebanon $\approx$ 17835 Lebanese and Palestinians were killed (*al Nahar*). Were *all* the Lebanese and Palestinian war prisoners freed in exchange for the three Israelis who were *all* the Israeli war prisoners at that time, one would not speak of racism however high the ratio.

The parentheses within parentheses within parenthesis train one to a way of reading that maintains all the aphorism's meanings/tendencies, that makes one know an aphorism is never a phase toward something else, cannot be reduced to the one meaning majored by the progression of the paragraph in which it has been inserted (aphoristic writers never edit in the *assemble mode* only in the *insert mode*).

Artists who think of themselves as creating rather than receiving can slander what they in fact received. One has the duty then, if one is not going to do anew the art-work/event (this second time is neither a parody nor a critique, for it is the previous one of the two presentations of the art-work/event. The former is the parody or the critique of the latter), to describe it as it should have been (description is then legitimate).

He dislikes the easiness of the scream; his only scream is his cough.

"Have you ever played Mastermind?". "No", "No! Oh my God! I'll show you how. It's not hard." A few minutes later. "No way, nobody wins by the second guess." After the game, she and her female friend leaf through a fashion magazine. He writes: "To be told by two women — teaching one how to play Mastermind —, *Close your eyes, don't look!*" He looks at them, then resumes writing: "Never bet against someone playing a game for the first or second time. For at that stage he's so intimidated by the game, so outside it, that it is the game itself that is playing against/with you." She turns towards him and says *shekkit*: his mouth and fingers become numb.

Second floor of the Art Institute of Chicago. Standing in front of the receptionist's pupils I felt I was standing in front of Reinhardt's *Abstract Painting #11* or Stella's *Painting*. Heard some persons speak about the beauty of her eyes, but never saw them amazed in front of them as they are in front of Reinhardt's painting, though her pupils too are of one beach of color (like a wing made of one feather) surrounded by the cornea's museum wall white. "I am shooting a film. Would you act in it?" She says with annoyance, "I am not an actress" (three possibilities: she turns out to be a good actress; she's really a bad actress but gives me things I didn't ask for, mistakes; she's both a bad actress and unable to come up with new mistakes). Now if in the same museum where she works one can see Joseph Beuys' *felt suit*, and read books on Bresson and on neo-realist directors (many of whom used non-actors), one wonders if she is not acting being in this place. Walked to the Beuys *felt suit* and put a *sale* tag on it.

Her way of closing her eyes like a Moslem's kneeling during prayer.

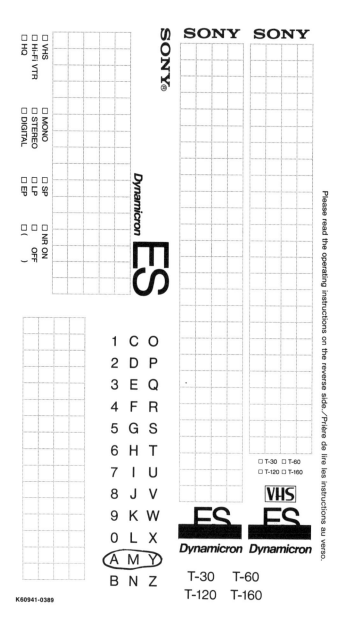

148

How to hug her voice? How to hug what hugs (is it by turning, like a coat or a glove, inside out?)?

The tip of the dancer's feet (and, in the case of Balinese dancers, hands) are fluctuations. To stand like dancers on fluctuations.

a sentence that begins with a small letter, like walking barefoot.

The room, the open window through which breeze passes swaying the curtain. Time, in the static film shot of the room, like gas. Suicide (did I open with the Santur music a window into time/the static film shot? Or did suicide take place?).

She asked me to wait for a month (he would by then have moved to another city, she would not hurt herself because she would not have hurt him. Yet her bringing him into my notice made me despise him (the brutality of his movement, as if he were pushing aside-away from his path his previous positions (the grace of any Marey series); his "I like competition" (three containers needed: one hot, one lukewarm, and one cold. If one puts one's left hand in the hot water and one's right hand in the cold, and holds them there for a minute, then plunges them into the lukewarm water, the water feels cold to the left hand and hot to the right one. Three persons are needed in lukewarm relations, but that only shows that she's lukewarm (diluted hot or cold) herself)(he thinks that since he is her lover and I am attracted to her, he has entered a relationship with me! He thinks that he has entered my off-screen space, and indeed he has, but contempt is a joiner (In Godard's Contempt the jump cuts between medium shots of a continuing action, taken all from the same angle, are part of a sort of joiner): A halo is created by the fact the same thing has two off-screens, one provided by another photograph, the other a homogeneous extension of the first photograph, but hidden beneath the other photographs)); this is of no importance to him, and thus to her. She, so quick to feel guilt, will feel no guilt whatsoever over my contempt for him. That shows with whom I am dealing.
He says he thinks everybody is wicked. He is lying, for otherwise he would not include strangers (people about whom one cannot project) in his diagnosis: solitude would become too great (coming out of the cinema, I tell John we should finish editing Ashoura. "Is it so people may see it? There were only six people in the cinema today." It dawns on me that fourteen people saw the film during its two-day screening in Chicago, while fifty persons saw each student's final project in the film class at Northwestern University. Gallery Emit, which just opened, is interested in selling films to private patrons, the

same way paintings are sold. I would sell a film if no other has been sold before. Only one film, for though selling a film might provide more viewers for it in Chicago (people look at my actors and at the camera during the filming, but none come to look at the finished film), considering that Bresson's *L'Argent*, which was shown at Facets and which may not be shown again in Chicago for a few years, was seen by only five people on the first day of screening and by four (three of whom were the same as on the first day) the following day and that the buyer may have a large family, many friends and relatives. But to have one's film shown in cinemas is to feel that a stranger also may be seeing it.

Maxwell's wave equation for light has two solutions: the *retarded solution* and the *advanced solution*. Retarded light waves travel forward in time, advanced waves travel backward in time. In conventional radiation theory, an atom can emit a wave of light even if the latter does not get absorbed in the future, but in the Wheeler-Feynman *absorber theory of radiation*, in order for light to be emitted, a half-sized retarded wave must travel from the atom to the future absorber and a half-sized advanced wave must travel from the absorber back to the atom (this back-and-forth movement). If there are no absorbers in a particular region, light will not shine in that direction.

Every time one creates something, one knows there is a stranger somewhere who has received it. Many a time one stopped writing or perforating a wall for no reason, and went out with boring people who have money and time to spend, and felt wretched. Possibly because there was no stranger to receive the new we might have created if s/he existed. An ethical imperative: to be available so that what has the possibility of being created can be forwarded to us rather than *blocked* (there may be only a tendency to exist for the stranger (one who aborts a tendency to exist [I am not writing about fertilized eggs and fetuses] is mean; one who tempts it to actualize is cruel, for life is strange, solitary, and maybe endless))(being blocked is different from facing a wall, since the latter is part of the process of creation)). The one who despises most people (I shot the whole film without actors or non-actors. The camera pans from a table to another one in an empty cafe: "he walked nonchalantly [hence lagging behind the pan that began with him leaving his table] to my table and..." Can one speak in this case of a voice-over? When I am quoting something to them I feel I am paraphrasing. They intentionally make one angry, hence hurried enough to say "I despise most people" instead of writing it, for when one says it, unlike when one writes it, they are still part of it) cannot despise strangers, for they are the last possibility he has of not despising. The two extremes of solitude: that experienced during a bad LSD trip when a zoom-out of the world occurs and humans become devoid-of-life extras (not that their life and energy was sucked out of them to infuse the remote world with its newly acquired intense colors. One is certain they were always devoid of life) in which one has to project/inject life; and that of no longer believing in the existence of strangers (strangers are the world's generosity). One should avoid reaching this state: when one not only no longer meets/sees strangers as one walks in a not so crowded subway train or street, or sits in not so crowded cafes, but has lost them in general, one has to invent/create them (to succeed in creating a stranger, in giving the world a stranger, is to know that what one achieved was possible only because another stranger was there already, that the world had already given one, unbeknownst to one, a stranger. This simultaneity of generosity)(strangers, those who are changing, entering in a relation with the unknown, who can no longer be known even in the form of Feynman's *sum over histories* or the probabilities of a quantum wave function, becoming an unknown for the duration of the change, are elitists toward what can be compared)). My response is: we'll have to wait an additional twenty-eight days (we are not in early January), changing the previous month of waiting into postponement (I am against waiting (exception: man running down the street up the stairs to the train platform at Southport station. No train there or in the distance. Did he want to extend the time of waiting for the train?) and making others wait). Postponement must be accepted: that I should write or say or do something that she can appreciate, if at all, only much later is totally acceptable to me (don't tell me that I can postpone because I have money (only in-sync *time is money*), and that you can't, because you don't have money and hence don't have time, for you forget that I am suicidal and hence that it is as difficult for me to postpone, if not more, as it is for you). What remains uncertain is whether when she understands what I said or did she would still accept postponing, so that the simultaneous that was separated by a time lacking any sense of timing, a time that always arrives too late or too early, or suddenly on time (too early or too late on time), can still meet. One should not maintain oneself in a particular state (an exception, where the maintenance of the state has nothing to do with fidelity, is superconductivity), for instance remaining with the same person (fidelity), but maintain a state beyond itself (the camera should be turned on just before the transition from being awake to sleeping, or from not eating to eating, so that the continuous filming would induce a continuous fasting (no cutting from non-eating to eating) or non-sleep (no cutting from non-sleep to sleeping). Viola's *Reasons for Knocking at an Empty House* against Warhol's *Sleep*)(Seen in a documentary on cable TV: a certain kind of sea water animal swallows a very small fish, which maintains itself in it, just irritating it; meanwhile the animal itself is swallowed whole by a bigger fish. It moves wildly in the body of the bigger fish to force it to eject it. Indeed the bigger fish ends up ejecting the animal which in turn ejects the smaller fish (the instant diet when this happens). The same logic is at work in my writing almost whenever two or more parentheses are side by side in a larger parenthesis (in a few cases these parentheses within parenthesis may be a sign of hyperwriting. A warning to laconic writers: the hyperactivity of anorexics can become their form of bulimia: one study on forty-four female anorexia nervosa patients found hyperactivity associated with greater weight gain[4]. One must guard against both rest (the obesity of time) and hyperactivity). Something undead (Jonah in the belly of the whale) about that. No decomposition of either the vampire inside the earth or the parenthesis inside the parenthesis). I am so sad I keep ending up in front of the waves' back-and-forth on the beach (this artificial respiration (shots of the masts being filled with air in *Potemkin*: an attempt to fill the image with air)). My friend forgot where he parked his car; I reminded him where it is (me who almost always forgets where he parked his car)! Is it that sadness is the *station* of memory, the state that does not want to forget itself? Maintaining a state beyond itself always has to do with/permits/demands forgetfulness, is what one fights/short-circuits projection with. To maintain a state beyond its phase transition threshold has nothing to do with fidelity and hence nothing to do with inertia. One should maintain the other person's inaccessibility present (while s/he himself/herself may be diluting his/her solitude (workers are experts in this)), by not trying to absent oneself from his absence through TV, films or friends (it is not by adding one more habit (that of being with the person, getting used to him/her) that one has a strong relation with the person, it is by killing (at least temporarily) the other habits (not even to urinate or drink). Being unobtrusive also means not making others get used to one (he said "I like competition", while making her used to him (habit, the leveler)!)("It never occurs to Safa to say hello when he enters [Julia Lesage prefaced a film by Godard, the director who used so much the jump cut, the no-preface between two shots!] or bye when he leaves." Safa's politeness showed itself in his speeding up when the yellow light began blinking (so that the car behind would have time to cross while the yellow light was still flashing), instead of driving at normal speed, as most drivers do when having enough time themselves to pass the light just before it turns red).

Every intense relation paralyzes one, devastates one (he was drowning in something that did not touch him, submerged him without touching him), yet as one ponders what is going on, whether there is a relation at all, one finds nothing, the non-existence of what paralyzes one (only in the absence of habit

---

[4]S.C.Goldberg, K.A.Halmi, R.Casper, E.D.Eckert, and J.M.Davis, "Pretreatment predictors of weight change in anorexia nervosa," in *Anorexia Nervosa*, ed. R.A.Vigersky (New York: Raven Press, 1977), p.35.

is this non-existence not veiled)(this void is not freedom. The received, though experienced as the necessary, is the only time one feels freedom is possible, for these instances of something received are the only new), and one knows then that what has total possession of one cannot exist except if one has *also* created/invented it. This knowledge allows one to turn in spite of one's paralysis (not fidelity but paralysis), which, rather than being itself the wall, makes one unable to receive (even a wall). This turning creates the wall that has to be perforated so that something can be received. It is at the level of the anti-dilution that the exercise of will should take place so that the other and the affects that the other has created in us is/are not diluted (she said: "give me time." She's making me wait. Not to dilute the other person is to draw an equivalency between him/her and time (a sure sign that that person will change us, for it is time (not to dilute time with itself, with repetition), undiluted time, that changes us)(how often is the ability to make a decision or to be insensitive to something the result, rather than of a power that confronts that thing, of the dilution of the latter (by mixing him/her with more time, TV, friends, films. I did this at least once: according to her we'll meet on Sunday. Saturday. What to do but drive for four hours to Detroit and then drive back to Chicago, reducing time (as workers do in another way) to a metrical distance one can gradually diminish (75 miles/hour) but cannot jump over, divesting the other person from an equivalency with time))). The two kinds of will are in inverse proportion, the more one exercises one's will not to get distracted from the other (one must also not become distracted from the other by the other), the less one has will in relation to deciding concerning the relation with the other person. This imposition of waiting on me, this training in impatience, goes together with making me hurry in my writing. A youth having a relation with an older writer has failed if s/he made the latter become quicker in his/her writing, made him/her postpone less, gave him/her the ability to finish things (as a youth one could so easily finish projects. The time required to make them was of the same shortness as one's age then)(*Khallas* means both finished and saved. Not to have this condescending attitude towards others (saving them) and towards oneself (saving oneself)). Long ago one still generalized, thought that there is something of an ideal progression (reincarnation is the most rational version of that), and the thought would occur to one of an impersonal revenge (it is absurd to take revenge on someone changing (the pain of metamorphosis cannot be interpreted as revenge), since, being forgetfulness, change is the goes without saying forgiveness by the other person): the other person's retrospective regret at having missed an opportunity. But most people don't reach certain states nor certain thoughts: these don't pre-exist, they have to be created; these don't pre-exist even after having been created by someone, for they are not a necessary step on the path of everybody. Either the other consents to enter with one into a relation whereby both are changed, or else s/he does not change, and hence has no way of regretting not having changed (hence the absence of revenge-in-the-form-of-the-other's-reg-ret)), for how would s/he know what s/he missed (unless s/he projects, hence has an abstract regret, a regret that does not change, a static regret: squared non-change) since this something missed was to be constructed through the relation, and did not pre-exist it?

Though I am a distracted person, don't think of becoming a distraction to me. One interrupts oneself so much (laconism) and is interrupted by the ideas that never come on time, one certainly does not need those who understand interruption as mixing/dilution to do that for one. I accept being interrupted by others, not diluted with them (only the interrupted can really interrupt).

If she thinks of using me to make the one she lives with jealous, that would be a case of manipulation, but so would be aiming at and using a minimal part of a person with there being no risk of change (as long as there is that risk, one will in no way think one is being misused/abused if only a minimal part of one is being interacted with). If she at times feels guilt (guilt is indulgence, except when it is a reminder to help the recently undead) over doing the former (jealousy-inducing), she should equally feel it over the latter (misusing). For a while I thought that he had only to let her speak to me, for him to win her back, for I would scare her. Wrong; there is no risk for her since she can always shield herself behind ignorance or low interpretations. Cowardice is not resistance! It is unfortunate that she is not resisting me: one of the most effective means those who trust their experience too much, who learn instantly from their mistakes, have to shield themselves against intensity and the power of things is to try things as soon as possible. The resistant postpones till s/he can be sensitive to the thing's unexpectedness and intensity. Resistance demands generosity. Generosity is also in believing in the existence of what one cannot receive because of the limitation of the spectrum of detection of humans and machines. Faith (whether in the sense of believing in the existence of what one cannot receive — except through faith: either in the sense that it is faith which allows us to receive it, or in the sense that one has to have faith that one received it; or in the sense of undergoing, not thanatosis (are estivation and hibernation forms of thanatosis, the predator being in this case the too dry or too cold weather?), but a real dying before dying where suppression continues until the filtering device is reached and suppressed (the flood), one and/or the others in one experiencing what previously was either filtered out because outside of the spectrum of detection, or rejected whether through repression because recognized or due to the dominance of focal attention: one needs faith to hold on to what one wanted to receive, to the desire to receive it and to oneself to receive it. Sooner or later in one's changes the former kind of faith makes it necessary to have another sort of faith, a faith in the world and time, for both seem little by little (suddenly in a bad LSD trip) to withdraw from us. I can ask her to have (the former kind of) faith in me, for I am not asking her something I am not being forced to undergo myself, (the latter kind of) faith (having to have faith in her, she being part of the world) in the same absence of context) is not projection. One fights projection (not to project even where one knows there is nothing: Fluctuations (uncertainty principle). Nonetheless was the ad I put in the film department at Northwestern University for a cinematographer and an editor a rhetorical one? Is both this and the previous question rhetorical questions?) also with faith.

She seldom reads books (She gave me a book, insisted that I read it and that we go to a lecture its author was giving the following week in Chicago. At the end of the conference, I asked him for an autograph on the one fragment of good writing (I never cut a book into quotations while waiting for the occupied barber) I salvaged from his book). Still she should be more at home in the library than I, not because she works there, but because most books are cowardly, full of petty interpretations.

The letter won't begin with *to Natasha (alone)* for that could be a dedication. It cannot be addressed to one who gossips (she called me at night and asked me what we spoke about, for she saw him stop me in the library and demand that we talk (at several points he said blablabla in the midst of his superfluous talking. This etc. in the superfluous. This etc. in the etc.!)). I'll write it in Arabic. Why not give her the excuse of gossiping — another person has to translate the letter for her — since anyway she will show the letter or speak about it to someone, instead of being angry with her for doing it?

If you are afraid of a particular experience, don't speak to others until you become like the cat your brother threw on you from the top of a tree, all her claws out in an attempt to grab into anything — frightening the person you're trying to speak to; only then if one can still utter something (when one is terrified not only the scream, even silence fears to come out), one has the right-duty to tell others about one's fear. Then the mere fact that they are still there to listen and have not fled is already help/example.

The age of those who don't change is unimportant (Quartier Latin: it is as if the street numbers of the restaurants were designated by the prices of the plat du jour: 32, 34, 39…), except that at a certain stage in old age, the body itself begins to undergo a drastic metamorphosis (the destiny of senility of the old, if not of their mental powers then of the rest of their bodies that lose all control, bark like a dog, howl like a wolf…), imposing change on the person. That she is only twenty-one means nothing provided she accepts changes.

Nonetheless, young people think that many of the experiences they are making an older person go through are his/her first encounter with them, when in fact s/he has repeatedly gone through them. One may still go through them (we tend to repeat things *ad nauseam*, waking up everyday, turning on the water, washing one's face, stepping in the bathtub, turning on the hot water, putting shampoo on one's head (the fade out of the etc.)), but one's writing which has become supersaturated with the subject (one has written on this already through several experiences) will resist this. Writing dissolves the will of the writer, but it has a will of its own. Hence it is dangerous for a writer to be prevented for a period from being a writer, for instance being forced by circumstances to be a teacher or a student, or because of a repetition a la Fitzgerald, for being himself without will, he is then devoid as well of his writing's will (a will that undoes any will-testament). If that period is prolonged, he will no longer be a writer but merely a teacher or a student, slowly developing back his own will, so that there will be no danger, the danger of the lack of a will, but equally there will be no longer any risk.

Her saliva in my mouth. Restaurant; I park, then drive again, hungry, without eating. Her saliva must remain in my mouth. How long will the fasting last (is one more attractive because more people are attracted to one? Is that why she wants me to be attracted to her, so that her lover...? Are we going to have *l'addition*, even though I am fasting?)? Not only fasting, but also not swallowing one's saliva, as if one had a sore throat. I move my skin over her skin, she stops me with her hand; the skin of her fingers (all my skin's layers want to be touched, the surface tanned and falling off instantly so the deeper skin layers can also be touched). Her tan. Is it to signify to me that I am not touching her but only the layer of dead skin slipping off her body? Not true, for the smoothness, tenderness of her tanned skin has the untimeliness of what has not seen the world, never been touched by it, of skin that has just emerged to the light, to the touch, to the light touch. I look at her tanned skin falling off to the air, never to the ground. Her dry lips on which her ever wet tongue passes like a zero viscosity superfluid, leaving them dry. One wants to wet them with one's saliva.

A relation changes, changing one. Even if in the end one or both persons are the same as before the relation began, this recurrence undoes the repetition of security and absence of change (only what does not change (the *control sample*) has control. Sobriety has nothing to do with control). One cannot "use people as pretexts to write," but can at times use them as catalysts. An enzyme has not changed if we look abstractly at the quantities of it on both sides of the chemical equation, but has changed during the reaction (most aristocrats are catalysts, they change during a relation, but are the same at its end as at its beginning (we have to *become* (*befit*) even what we are. The most beautiful complement: *becoming becomes you*)). I liked her at the beginning of the relationship, and I know that the relationship will change her, but she may be changed into the same person she was before the relation began. Is this what one calls destiny, to be changed into what one is by passing through all the risk that change entails (standing in the presence of the child one was, oneself (letting loose to float on the water another sort of boat, saliva. Hole in the left shoe force-feeding small stones scratching an unfelt itching in the feet) the only one among the grown-ups present he cannot establish any relation with), which differentiates this from the usual repetition which is a matter of absence of risk? To say: "even if the relation does not change her, it will change me, making her look changed to me" is false, for to change is both to forget how the other was (though change is the memory of forgetfulness) and to become the measure (it is not the one who is not changing that is the measure) of whether a change occurred or not in the other (and hence of whether the other will be missed), hence able to differentiate between the two repetitions: in the bad repetition where she did not change, my having changed and she remained the same, will mean that I'll miss her, whereas in the second case where she has changed into the way she was, both, she and I, have changed, and hence I don't miss her.

I cannot sleep when I am next to her. Is it that sleep contains NREM periods, where no images, affects pass through one (different from the paralysis in her absence (and in her presence when she is not diluting herself, which she often does), but also from the anaesthesia (this utter intensity that rises in me as her lips come closer to my skin, the skin becoming all of a sudden anesthetized. Yet her kisses are still felt: is this anaesthesia conjoined to a posthypnotic suggestion?)), and how can I be next to her and be without affects and images, without commotion?

Her way of closing — like an umbrella — when you touch her, so that the world (she also being part of the world) opens.

The way she closed her fingers on a secret, the fist not closing completely because of the long fingernails. Vampire ('s teeth).

She will remember me (this having to do with projection, which is the opposite of the maintenance of a state beyond itself (beyond the point where even inertia stops), for in the latter case the state comes to one in the past, rather than come to us in the present as in projection). But I can/will not remember her, for this separation is death, the death of her to me, the death of me to myself (the exile of the survivor)(the Aharonov-Bohm effect applies only with strangers or those who knew how to remain strangers with us)(we may have after all more lives than cats do, we who have no memories, who have no ghosts, who have no photographs or rather who enter telepathically with the deformations to the photographs created by the refractory periods).

How to be close and open? Must one be broken? Her her her her her (dragonfly way of seeing her (*I love you* repeated for a reason)(her "OK? OK?", as if to cover the two meanings (knowing I am interested in phenomena near zero Kelvin)))(**er** as in sadd**er**) hair not in braids (like her ever undone laces (like the blue veins conspicuous under her skin in the region of the neck and the forehead)). Hugs, the body's braids. Detached strands of her long blond hair on my sweater and/or jacket and/or shirt and/or socks trousers. Are all clothes of all colors made of this one color-material that I both can and cannot remove as if my jacket had become a photocopy of my jacket (hair on the photocopy machine's glass)? A strand of her hair in my mouth, like the string of cello between the teeth of the improvised music performer (Tom Cora at *Woodland Pattern Bookstore*).

[He] criticized her for going out with foreigners. How to, if one is not rich enough, travel, except also by meeting foreigners in one's country (this travel in place)? Except that with the increasing homogenization of the world most foreigners are already adapted to the U.S. by the time they leave their country (the only remaining shock is that of the disruption in the body rhythms due to the time difference between the different geographical regions. The body fully recovers in a matter of days). A foreigner passport wise; this he thought a blessing, for it meant that the other foreignness, that of being a writer, can hide behind the former foreignness, since people who have already gone out with foreigners think that they can easily handle the tinge of excitement that the geographically foreign can elicit. Then maybe gradually one can disclose art to her. But what if art is the sudden? Nonetheless one gradually moves toward the sudden.

Those who are too much in contact with the bottom, who are quicksand, need the cold surface of snow. She rested her head on my shoulder! Me who always considered myself to be quicksand.

The palm lines of the forgetful, of the one who, rather than growing old, passed through the many generations of a photocopy degeneration (the different shed skins of Brundle in *The Fly* are the consecutive (film/video) generations of his skin. The repetition of the same words on and on during Sufi *sama'* is a photocopy degeneration to achieve *fana'*), change (washing away the map from my palm). Palm readers who profess to be able to read the palm of such persons are liars, for the degeneration of a given image results each time in a different abstract result, different palm lines. I like the two greens (the photocopy machine's green light passing over the plant leaves at *Kinko's*), maybe even the three... — What's the color of your eyes? — Blue. — Though in color on the monitor next to me videotaping you, the image is black and white in the viewfinder (looking at your eyes, it is as if I am the viewfinder of a video camera).

There is something nostalgic about beauty, which has to be dissolved, while one must not write *therefore* at the end of aphorisms (the sly know that one cannot write *therefore* at the beginning of an aphorism, so they dangle it at the end, like a bait, so that when another aphorism is laid next to the previous one *therefore* links them). Walking back-and-forth while the photocopy machine's light moves back-and-forth over the pages being photocopied. This back-and-forth movement of the photocopy degeneration is the movement by which one achieves the derivative (the new has nothing to do with beginning or beginner), by which one moves towards the limit, and the difference moves toward zero. Anorexics read standing (Virginia) and authors I like write standing (Woolf) and I do photocopy degeneration standing.

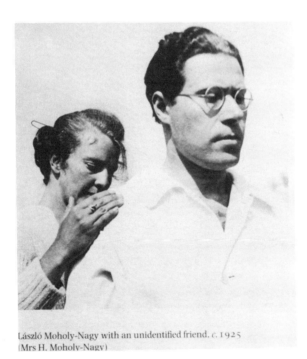

László Moholy-Nagy with an unidentified friend, c. 1925
[Mrs H. Moholy-Nagy]

159

Natalia Goncharova (*seated, left*) with the composers Léonide
Massine and Igor Stravinsky and the stage-designer Leon Bakst at
Lausanne, 1915
(Visual Arts Library)

"I want you to take photocopies of a page from my manuscript on which
I will place one then another photograph of yourself." The first photograph
covers a quarter of the page. She photocopies it. I add the second photograph
to the photocopy. She continues photocopying. She ads a photograph to the
fifteenth generation photocopy. I write *nostalgia* on the newly added
photograph in the photocopy that comes out, and ask her to continue
photocopying. She says, "why aren't we using one of the photographs in
which both of us appear?" "My writing, next to the photographs, is going
through the same process of degeneration". I don't need to go through a
photocopy degeneration, for I have somewhat already disappeared:
unobtrusive, not even an unknown (an *x*) or an unidentifiable person (it is
strange to have disappeared when one is still simultaneously a trouble-maker
(this back and forth that mixes the elements. But not always; at times looking
at the clouds of milk, as strange as boiling hats (*speedy ennuie* in Chicago has
the best milk clouds in the coffee, that is why I recommend it to friends),
without stirring the coffee)), like the two other objects next to the pear in

Nicholas de Stael's *Poire jaune* (in the painting *Bouteille, poire et cruche*, all the objects shown are listed in the title). The generosity of many a famous writer, painter or film maker shows itself also in their making it easier for us to be unobtrusive (in one photograph the painter Mary de la Villet is blocked by another person, yet the caption reads *Mary de la Villet*). On page 112 of Edward Lucie-Smith's *Lives of the Great Twentieth Century Artists* (New York: Rizzoli, 1986), five people appear in a photograph whose caption mentions four. This omission is not due to the fifth person being an unidentified person, since we find on page 190 a photograph of two persons with the caption: «Laszlo Moholy-Nagy with an unidentified friend». In Agnes Angliviel de La Beaumelle's *Yves Tanguy: Retrospective, 1925-1955* (Paris: Le Musée, 1982), three persons appear in a photograph on page 229 whose caption mentions only two. Here too the omission is not due to the third person being an unknown, for on page 196 there is a photograph where three persons are shown and whose caption reads: «Y.T. en compagnie de Jeannette et de X».

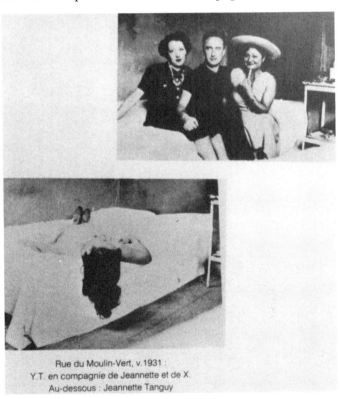

Rue du Moulin-Vert, v.1931 :
Y.T. en compagnie de Jeannette et de X.
Au-dessous : Jeannette Tanguy.

Devant la grille
de la rue du Château en 1925
Jacques Prévert, Y.T. et Florent Fels

Jehan Mayoux et Y.T., Paris 1953

Like vampires, these persons do not appear in mirrors and photographs. This is not the same as layering, where one has disappeared from one place but is in another place and/or time, be it non-localizable. By means of matting and overlaying one can seem to be at a certain place (a university classroom) while in a different place and/or time (those who are adapted (to the two or more places in which they either are or appear), who, as in digital layering, don't change because of generation loss (the danger of hysteria), are the easiest persons to fool by layering). Layering allows us to show those who otherwise would not believe us that we were elsewhere than where they saw us. Up till recently layering was still done in an analog way, which meant that it did not really work since there was a generation lag between the first image and the n+1 image. The equivalent to digital layering has always existed, is not a postmodern device: the double in sorcery: Castaneda's Don Juan in two places at the same time through *dreaming*.

Rather than Hitchcock's fleeting appearance in all his films, Fritz Lang's hand (in close-ups) as extra in some of his films; or even better, Bresson's disappearance as extra as he stands in place of the off-screen character in shots where someone on camera is speaking to someone off-screen.

She says while photocopying: "the page is becoming desertified". I part my hair at the sides: "See, I am slowly becoming bald." She continues photocopying. She stops photocopying: "I would have thought one would do this at the end rather than at the beginning of a relation, to forget. I don't understand why you're asking me to do this. I told you it wouldn't work between us, we're very different."

The conversation between them filmed with the camera pointing at her. "With you, I experience how a film actor feels during the first phase of the shooting of a conversation that is to be edited in a shot-reverse shot manner, having to say his lines for the entire conversation with the camera on the other person. Except in our case the camera is not then aimed in my direction with the conversation repeated".

His back and forth movement windshield wipers that made him again able to see the world (so why is it sometimes he still banged himself against the wall either interrupting or at the end of his back and forth movement?).

Nothing, inability to think, to feel, nothing but the screech of the spoon used by my roommate scraping the almost empty bowl for the remaining soup.

The self-reflexivity in Bill Viola's *I Do Not Know What It Is I Am Like* resides both in the shots in which he is taking notes while looking at his footage on a monitor or those in which we can see his reflection in birds' pupils as he stands behind a video camera resting on a tripod; and in the close-ups of birds' and fishes' faces and of a bull's eye: *bull's eye*: a simple lens with a large numerical aperture; *fisheye lens* (a 180⁰ field of view wide-angle lens, giving prominence to central objects (*bull's eye*: the target's center), hence distorting the image); *bullseye* (an Australian food fish (*Priancanthus macracanthus*)) relates *bull* to fish; *bird's-eye view* (a far away overhead shot, as from a helicopter); *bull-eye* («an eye (as of a pigeon) having both iris and pupil dark in color») relates *bull* to a bird. The shot of the fish attached to the side of a helicopter was videotaped with a very wide angle lens, giving one a bird's eye view with a fisheye lens. Since the fish is part of the bird's eye view, one is not surprised that in the final shots birds eat the fish.

A fish is eaten. This strange diet at the end of which its face does not become uglier than it used to be (as happens in most extreme diets). All that remains of it is the head (the head contains the brain whose cells, unlike those of the other parts of the body, are not continually replaced by new ones). All that remains of it is a close-up. When I see close-ups even of human beings, I sometimes have the feeling the rest of their body is being eaten, or has already been eaten, unbeknownst to me or to them. Viola is eating the fish placed on the plate. Fisheye lens reflection of his face in the plate. For one eats also part of oneself (saliva, enzymes, acids that decompose the food) while eating other things. After one has eaten all of the fish except the head, one sees oneself in the fish's eye.

Can an anesthetized corpse give other than a totally bland taste (and if it does, would that not show that some component of the anesthetized still feels)? Is a minimal amount of feeling requisite for there to be a taste to what came from a living organism? That is, do corpses, since they still taste when eaten, feel pain (and/or other sensations) when decomposed by other animals? Terrible tooth ache. Is this the pain animals felt as they were shredded by the teeth?

One tries to evade pain by moving from the body to its reflection, and if this reflection itself still feels pain, however paradoxical this may seem, then one has to revert to reflections of reflections of reflections by sandwiching oneself between two mirrors.

Faith is needed in the ceremony in the Mahadevi temple in Fiji, not so as to evade pain (God protected Husayn and his followers (massacred in Karbala) from pain (in a sort of divine hypnotic analgesia). He did this also in the case of the martyrs of Badr), but to evade the danger to the lives of the participants (no blood spilling from their bodies perforated by needles), so as to divest pain from danger, preventing danger from masking pain (many wounded soldiers and warriors felt no pain until the extreme situations during which their lives were in danger subsided).

So many needles stuck into the body of the participants in the ceremony.

The pain is so extreme that their bodies become one ear to receive the cry, yet there is no longer a mouth to utter it (needles, like earrings, making lips an ear, hence no longer a part of the mouth).

An egg cracks open. The absolute solitude of that chick laying on its back (the dead fish was eaten-decomposed by birds and flies; the chick is attacked by sensations). The strange absence of names in this shot (hormones-secretions can be names (female bats recognize their infants among millions staked in caves). But here there is no chicken, and *we* cannot call the chick). Lost. In the absence of the chicken, there is still one thing that knows him (the same thing that is already in part destroying him): time.

Bull eating in prairie. The camera pans with him when he moves. A fitting pan, for suddenly as the camera stops when he stops on reaching another bull, who is grazing, one has the sensation that the camera is one more member of the herd.

Nam Jum Paik says video is not I see but I fly. Shots of extremely white birds flying in black background. Closer shots of extremely white birds flying in black background. The shots get increasingly close until all there remains is a black and white screen alternating at the rhythm of wings flapping. A meeting of Paik and Viola.

Yes, **CIA Off-Campus**. But also **Teachers** (One can try to ignore their pettiness but how to ignore that they want to steal one's time. The latter ignoring is IGNORANCE. Waging *class struggle* in classrooms) **& Students** (extras) **Off-Campus**.

The price of one of Christo's wrapped objects at Gallery Zabriski is $330,000. One can subvert this price by putting something worth more than $330,000 in the wrap, or by giving the latter as a gift to someone and looking at him/her unwrap it to see his/her present.

"I've seen it all", a lassitude like a massage by time, or as if time were a massage that made us always relaxed. Then one sees a performance (Kylian's *Les Noces*, a Pina Bausch piece), and the world is again expanding (like space-time).

Kylian's *Les Noces*. A man's raised arm is held by another man; both men take a step forward and another man advances and holds the first man's arm which twists 360°, then the three take a step forward and another man advances and holds the first man's arm which twists another 360°, then the four men take a step forward and another man advances and holds the first man's arm which twists an additional 360°, then the five men take a step forward and another man advances and holds the first man's arm which twists another 360° (to go on enumerating things one by one until the one before the last, only then putting the *etc*.). His hand laundry being dried of blood.

The somnambulism of a dancer walking backward (also the somnambulism of a dancer still continuing his/her dance after the music has stopped) without bumping against anything, not even himself/herself (the temporal bumping against oneself that hesitation is). Nomads move back-and-forth, dancers move forth and back. Both back movements have nothing to do with memory.

Dancers standing hands up. The hands slowly fall one by one like autumn leaves. Kylian should have collaborated with Moses Pendleton: as a member of Pilobolus, Moses performed dances (*Shizen*...) where two or more dancers form one body that dances alone or with another body formed of two or more dancers. Pendleton had a skiing accident and felt an urge to get rid of the leg that was hurt. In a piece he performed while a member of Momix, he stands on one foot while trying to get rid of the other (having formed one body with one or more dancers and at the end of a given interval of time separated from him/them, and having carried another body on one's two feet (hence two bodies on two feet) it is natural that one would feel both that one needs only one leg to carry one body (Laconic: the heron rests on one leg) and that the body can rather easily split into its constitutive parts). Had Joke Zijtstra then, instead of standing still, moved slowly in divergent directions, her dress twisting-flowing (one felt the wind), the fallen arms-leaves would have been swept away from the other dancers' bodies.

It is not only by the hand that one dancer makes another dancer turn, but also by the long hair.

The tallness of the dancer means that his/her head cannot rest on the ground: the *ground level* (as used in chemistry and physics in relation to energy levels) of the head is not the floor but the palm, and the ground level of the palm is the thigh (this slapping of the thigh). The long feet of Joke as if the bones were wearing a too large flesh (while the feet themselves are wearing the right size shoes).

Her head is leaning on the palm of her hand and we are standing motionless on the tightrope of her neck's tense veins. The head parts with the hand on its own rather than being pushed by it. Why? So that the hand would be able to follow it, which it does, rather than be forced, if it had pushed it, to go in the opposite direction in compliance with the law of conservation of momentum. Or else the two movements have to happen simultaneously so that a push is only that in appearance, in fact it is an accompaniment, like hands that do not close in a hug, but remain barely touching parallel to each other, and we know that the hug will happen at infinity.

The art of getting to a derivative of the jump, to a jump of the jump (like driving over a road's Adam's apple). The male dancers jump, but within that first jump they do another jump, extend the first, and fall smoothly on the floor in one jump and harshly on the jump in the second jump.

Ancient Egyptian posture of the palms. The moment is eternal, hence eternity should end in one moment. The logic of pain. It is projection that makes the moment not eternal, that makes it drag.

These open palms like Edvard Munch faces looking at you.

These hands that jump on the thighs they slap.

An Autumn-Winter feel to Joke Zijtstra's tallness, as if a tree had lost all its horizontal leaves.

Gravity is but the shortest path between two points in the space-time continuum curved by matter-energy. So that to take the longest path (the hand almost touching the ear on the other side of the head, instead of almost touching the one on its side) is to be oneself and one's movements, less heavy. The angularity — which shortens — of movements taking the longest path.

She's in pain, her body contorted; behind her are female dancers on their tips moving back-and-forth as if her fever. While dancing with them she suddenly drops like the shout of pain from someone sick who was speaking with us normally until then.

Males dancing, and in the background a female dancer moving backwards like a curtain closing.

She sees something. In terror it is not her hair that stands on end: being a dancer, it is her feet that stand immobile on their tips.

This *ney* sound, as if the breath of the person playing it was being sucked out of him by it.

She goes down slowly and reaches ground and one feels she has to go even lower, and indeed the male dancer stands on the tips of his feet, raising the surface with him.

In front of many a photograph or video/film shot, the question poses itself: what is the temperature in the part of the diegetic world shown in the shot? The black between shots in Vito Acconci's video *Red Tapes* ends up controlling so much the impression one has of the subsequent images that they seem to be after-images not of things and landscapes but of aleatory events in the brain and the camera. Not only is the world absent, but even the noise is taken at one remove so that what we perceive is not the noise but the after-noise of noise, the lag of the noise on the receptor, the noise of noise. The asceticism of many of those who pursue the derivative. But irrespective of whether the latter are ascetic or not, only by getting to the derivative can one become original.

But is the noise of noise, is this semblance of repetition when we deal with the derivative (acceleration is measured in centimeters *per second per second*) a narcissism? Derivatives are the furthest from narcissism, the closest to reflexivity.

The exclusion of all sounds except the voice is not narcisstic since the voice becomes a stranger to itself through the whispering, the loud shouts, the neutral description. Narcissism would rather reside in the temptation the spectator may have, especially in the section in *Red Tapes* 3 where the black screen continues without interruption for more than twenty minutes, of treating the video with black screen as a radio, his/her eyes wandering then in his/her room.

In one shot, Acconci describes some photographs in color terms: "farm: green", "pasture: green". Since this is a black and white video, the photographs may in reality be themselves black and white. Painting with words.

The tree outside the window. For a while today there was no boundary between us and I knew that the shit *in* me is manure for it.

The applause of many. I need an umbrella for my ears.

To have taken LSD and seen the world so distant, so withheld, to have seen how far objects can withdraw. Three weeks later in a cafe: to see the coffee cup so near! This happiness at feeling one is going on a date with a cup of coffee. For one knows now that objects can be absolutely far, or on the contrary go on dates with us, accompany us.

Things are reflections (in a lake) in Tarkovsky's world, one cannot move without destroying them.

A minority is always of less than one. A minority is formed of myriads: 1,345,783/3,345,967.

We project because the other did not change.

At last the train in which I am sitting moved. This feeling of melting.

You're the nearest to me or rather the distance separating us is so near to me.

Only schizophrenics have the right to use voice-over since they suffer from it.

At best you can, not so much dance with the dancer (no mixing of music with men/women, not even as ice in the drink), as dance to her/him.

Our being lost is one way two immobile things can vary the distance between them.

The way you cut the film determines the kind of space-time not only in the film but of the spectator and the movie theater in which s/he is. The spectator watching many a Chantal Akerman film is in long shots that continue for long times... (identification with the character is quite secondary in importance).

Haven't slept since yesterday. Looking at the papers in front of me on the table, I have the clear sensation that they belong to a film pov, that is, if there were another person who hasn't slept since yesterday looking at the same papers, there would be an ambiguity as to whose pov that was: for the duration of the look we may both have the exact same vision or one of us may go blind or undergo a lapse.

   Drunk, one apprehends the gesturing with the static parts of the body: this long nose is not a static thing but a continuous gesture. So many of people's expressions are not caught by others; they are destined to you, the drunk. We perceive, unless drunk, only the poses other men and women reveal to us (even the secrets we discover are poses). Voices like flies. Will she be memory in this forgetfulness (will jealousy be her way of making me "sober", of detaching the person she is speaking with from this mixing of voices-persons, the re-establishing of sync?)? This liquid quality of the voices that spill behind one as one leaves the hall. As soon as one rests one's head against a wall, trying to get away from it is like trying to disengage from a hug. We project almost all the time (projection does not work by extending as by first short-circuiting, then extending in a homogeneous way what it cut short), rectify. Once one stops/neutralizes projecting, whether by getting drunk or otherwise (these themselves though often have attendant delusions/hallucinations), one sees that non-matching gazes don't exist only in amateurish or in experimental films and videos, but also in reality itself and all the time. One then knows how false all acting is (exception: Dreyer's last films). Over her fingers my fingers become a tongue. The way one walks when drunk, as if accompanying oneself. His loud laugh like an umbrella over our talk.
   The beer foam in the just filled glass from which I am drinking. The foam vanishing little by little. And little by little the voices of the persons becoming foam.
   Space like glass: the closer the people come toward one (they don't have to come very close), the more their faces distort, the same way faces do when

pushed against the glass of a door or a window (opening the train window, my face no longer against the glass but against the wind, it is now my affects that have become distorted).

Laurie Macklin is against explaining (explanation is a form of incarnation). She incarnates music! This incarnation can only take the body of the composer: he walks on the stage playing his wind instrument. By doing that Macklin localizes the music: the composer playing the wind instrument on the stage moves away; she follows him, though the sound of the music did not move away. The problem is that when the musician stops playing his instrument for a while, there is no incarnation of silence. The incarnation of music in a person makes jealousy possible again (disembodied music saved the dancer from ever being part of jealousy).

That other puppet, the tightrope walker.

An aphoristic problem: how to, without introducing the parasitical, give a temporality to what comes in flashes, without that temporality being merely due to the persistence of vision, to refractory periods?

Houses with unfilled walls where knocking on the wall produces a hollow sound. Dancers that go to the ground (the crest covering the still burning center of Earth is very thin) and listen after merely walking (that other kind of knocking).

It is not enough to be without clothes, all the body's parts must be light enough so as not to drown in the music and be hidden, but to float on it. Only dancers are truly nude. That's the innocence of dance: nothing is hidden; an innocence that never verges on the obscene because of dance's seduction: everything that is not part of dance's and music's meeting is excluded (the dancer's way of exposing herself/himself to your gaze defiantly (the defiance of what excludes exchange: one can watch a dancer, one cannot have an exchange of gazes with him/her, an exchange is not fast enough for the music) as if standing head on in the blowing wind, or as if turned back and forth by the waves that have become vultures circling then plunging on him/her). Dancers are ignorant of jealousy.

A culture of jealousy hence of competition, of competition hence of jealousy. He tells her «look in my eyes, *don't blink*»: like uttering a word in one breath for as long as possible. And then the only way to evade the obstinate other is to dilate the pupil to let him/her better see his/her reflection there and be lured by that third from one («Be more feminine, caress him, and caress yourself». This makes for narcissism, and for the jealousy one feels in the presence of the narcissist, in whose presence the number of persons is at least three. In a one-man dance called *Farucca*, the gestures and moves have a great strength but also a slowness, the latter insuring that they have enough time to go back on themselves, almost cancelling themselves as far as the other person is concerned. Male narcissism, unlike female narcissism, does not invite its disruption, since one would then be putting oneself between the force and its return on itself). Since the eye doesn't blink, the blinking gets transferred to the feet (this stamping has nothing to do with the one in aboriginal Australian dancing where the simultaneity of the consecutive stampings generates so much momentum in the opposite direction (to float as an immaterial spirit, one's body must have been buried in the earth) that the aboriginal dancer leaps in place without pushing hard against the earth.

Standing behind her, he tells her «embrace me just as if I were in front of you.» Behind her, so that even when she turns back to look at another man, he would be there.

Twyla Tharp's *The Catherine Wheel*. Frozen image, covering one third of the frame, of four dancers; at the other side of the frame Sarah enters and looks. The image of the four dancers moves slowly to the ground (Tharp should have shown Sarah dancing on the superimposed-on-the-floor image of the four other dancers still dancing), and the computer-generated dancer appears. The electronic dancer: the modern puppet (Saint Catherine wanted to be a puppet of God), a puppet not only moved by but also formed of hypnotized lines lying on emptiness (the electronic dancer a sculpture not in space but in emptiness). Rather than the other members of the family, it is Sarah, who is learning from the electronic puppet how to dance ideally, who is accompanied by a chorus of dancers. For the law of the digital is reproduction.

Shot of the house becoming a moebus strip. Does gravity apply to a moebus strip?

The curtain inhabited by shadows has different laws, is a different world than the stage on which the dancers are moving: the lights are placed at different distances from the curtain so that the dancer, moving between them and the curtain while trying to get hold of a pineapple which keeps going up and down, seems of different heights. The use of the curtain replaces the factor of weight (the shadow on the curtain has no weight), by the factor of size and height. A dance of dilation and contraction. So that the dancer has to work on his distance from both curtain and light as s/he had to work before on the distance of each of his limbs to the center of gravity of his body. This doing away with the importance of gravity at the level of the dancer's body('s reflection) signals though the majoring of gravity outside his/her body: a myriad of pieces of garbage fall on the members of the family (poltergeist effect, quite natural since we're dealing with a saint); garbage, assembled in a net in the air, may fall on Sarah; metal wheels with spikes almost crush Sarah lying on the ground. It is no longer the body that falls (the family members often *mime* falling (the mimed pushing and shoving in the comic sections (Tharp seems here to be following the suggestion of words: *light* means entertaining, frivolous, not heavy, and «to fall unexpectedly») major that other figure of gravity, inertial effects))(for a dancer to try to perform a jump and not to get at the right elevation is to have fallen) but objects that fall on the body.

Much of the information processed by the brain does not enter consciousness. In a one-person dance for two dancers, one dancer becomes the preconscious information of another dancer: she lets go, falls, only to be steadied by him just before hitting the ground; the same phenomenon as when someone reading while walking suddenly stops and looks up seeing that he would have bumped into something had he walked one more step.

Both dancers are lying on the ground. He moves upward in a peristaltic manner. Attracted by his upward extension, she (her nervous tiny gestures, her trembling) moves up like shreds of paper attracted by the static electricity created by the peristaltic movement. Then he pushes her, and since the law of conservation of momentum must apply, it is not him that moves/is moved in the opposite direction to her movement, but his shadow that lengthens enough to counter not only the momentum of her move in the opposite direction, but also that of his move in the same direction she's moving in.

The dancer playing the maid emits at times what sounds like fast-forwarded speech. So that two sound tracks are present: the music in normal speed, and the talk in fast-forward. This discrepancy between the two speeds of the sound track should have been reflected in the dance in that section.

Three moments in Lynn Blom's dance piece: A young dancer playing the role of an old man enters stage and walks in front of a curtain (behind the curtain is as it were his past, of which we can see nothing, only hear about it from him), speaking about feats he could accomplish as a youth: jumping a given height and length... Then, stretching (getting back the body size he had as a youth), he jumps the same length and height. One feels that, as if by telepathy, one has suddenly seen something that happened behind the curtain.

An old man supporting a ladder gestures, with his cane, to a young man to walk up its steps. The young man first refuses, then goes up the ladder, the old man lets go of it, the young man falls. The young man goes up the ladder alone and tilts it from one side to another thus walking with it a few steps. Man evolved from walking on four limbs to walking on two. That change is evoked in Lynn Bloom's piece by having a person who already walks on two walk with a ladder: from two limbs touching the ground to none.

A man throws in the air three scarfs one after the other, watches each fall and as it gets level with his eyes uses his breath rather than his hand to prevent it from falling to the ground and to send it back in the air. Who would have thought about using instead of three balls (as is in the circus) three scarfs, except a dancer?

If one is a laconic aphoristic writer, i.e., going through an anorexia at the level of writing, will one's writing have the non metaphorical equivalent of (some of) the unusual perceptions, affects and other symptoms (no menstrual blood, hypothermia, hyperactivity, sleeplessness) that are part of anorexia? Then one may want to include a section on laconic writers in any book on anorexia.

Her hair seen from the back an Arnulf Rainer Overpainting. Like afterimages in the just closed eye where blotches of space appear.

Overpaint the Overpainting.

The scratches on the Rainer photographs like the hair on the palm of the vampire.

I am a few feet away from her sitting with both feet resting on a chair. I have a fever localized not where I am but at the place where she is. This telepathy that one may experience in very intense moments is conjoined to a separation from *most people*. They are *a priori* against us. Strangers are with us, even when they do nothing but exist, that is be available.

Waiting for the bus on Wisconsin Avenue and 5th street. This very strong impression I have that the passers by are extras. Seven joggers running together, some of them speaking while running, three of them without shirts and sweating profusely, give me back the feeling the people I am seeing are not extras. Five minutes later another group of runners pass by. They are extras. Everybody is an extra again. Until a man walks by holding a cup of coffee in one hand and a cup of soup in the other. Reality again (and not because a man holding two cups instead of one looks more realistic (the Ketchup bottle on the TV in the last scene of *Paris, Texas* is an extra, turns the shot into a matte shot)).

I take the bus and stay on it the whole day and the part of the night during which it operates (the transformation of Milwaukee into Venice). The same scenes of Milwaukee appear on and on (as if I were a film editor in front of the flatbed). It is no longer the driver that sees me come on the bus then leave, but me who sees the bus drivers replacing each other. At one of the stops, a man got in, walked through the totally empty bus, and sat right next to me (people in Milwaukee often do this whether in cinemas, busses, or when sitting at the counter in cafes). I felt the bus is being videotaped with a telephoto lens. These deformed, retarded, slow, worn down people filling the bus, stop after or before stop, the bus a trash truck circling round and round in the city, and me writing, and feeling that what I am writing will be grabbed by a homeless person, sniffed at, studied, reversed upside down, then returned to the fat garbage can from which he took it.

The title of an Arnulf Rainer Overpainting is what creates the secret. A secret is the telepathy between nothing and something.

She attempted suicide (rather than her boyfriend's blackmail phrase: "I can't live without you", "You can't die without me.") Something utterly strange in the suddenness with which stable people, people who thought they would have children, attempt suicide. There is no necessary link between suicide and the suicidal. A person may attempt as many suicides as s/he chooses, without that necessarily implying that s/he is a suicidal person. Nonetheless at times attempting suicide turns one into a suicidal person, which may mean that one may no longer attempt suicide.

Northbrook Hospital. 10:40 p.m. She is accompanied by a woman who did not leave us alone. What I encountered in the Middle East only through films (in *Yol* a woman is accompanied by two relatives on her outing with her fiancee), I met in the U.S. tonight.

With suicidal persons, it is their normal state that is suicidal. They may commit suicide when they feel that they have been forced to no longer live as suicidal persons. With the others, suicide is a murder: a state arises, takes possession of them, and kills them (three multiple personalities or three states, all played by Maya Deren, play cards in *Meshes of the Afternoon*. Is it to see which one of them will commit the suicide? Or is it to see which one will murder all the other personalities or states, one or more of which may be a suicidal one? One criterion that may help one answer this question is that with the suicidal there is no trace of surprise while s/he falls mortally wounded after shooting himself/herself; but in the case of the one who kills himself there is, however minimal, a surprise of the same sort one witnesses in films and books on doubles, when one suddenly realizes that while/by killing the other (state) one has killed oneself). The suicidal *live* as suicidal

174

people (can they die as suicidal persons? The church stipulated that those who committed suicide did not disintegrate in the grave but became vampires, the undead. I repeat: can they *die* as suicidal persons? Or will they, after an encounter with the double, dying before dying, opt for trying to transcend the cycle of redeath-rebirth?)

Did it really happen or did I imagine/hallucinate/confabulate that it happened? This question is also asked whenever something has also to be created.

The way they walked, slowly, as if accompanying a space that shifted faintly, that slid, so that at times they would stop, look back, as if they had preceded it and now had to wait for it to catch up with them; at other times, they would suddenly walk faster as if to catch up with it.

One is cornered between the impossibility of stopping thinking (one knows, having undergone a bad LSD trip, that this is not always in the form of the generosity of the world (the unfolding of an event on its own is a form of the generosity of the world in the case of the samurai's sword fighting by itself or the Zen archer's arrow hitting the target by itself)) and
— a thanatosis of thinking (through suppression (as in *binocular rivalry*)) that makes thinking closer to primary processes (focal attention is, to a large extent, inhibited, this leading to proliferation of the associates activated by any stimulus…), minimizing to a large extent repression. Thanatosis of thinking can be also a mode of the utmost thinking, while the impossibility of stopping thought during a bad LSD trip can be an absence of thought.
— a blockage of thinking due to the absence of strangers (different from the blocking of thought in fear).
— the refractory period. The absence of strangers, hence the blockage of thought, is radically different from the refractory period, hence the stolen time, one's becoming a hostage. The latter, which is thought's rest, can and should be fought by telepathy and postponement (Arnulf Rainer deforms/ metamorphoses the photographs produced by the presence of refractory periods)(preventing thought from resting even during the refractory period), the former cannot be fought, except, maybe, by going through a dissociation a la Alan Gray in Dreyer's *Vampyr* (but then there is the danger of one of the dissociated entities turning against the other (the most widespread form of the double: the malignant)). The latter is a non-thought that has been imposed on us by those who perceive us and by our own bodies, and has to be cancelled, the former is a non-thought that is a necessary part of thought, of that which has to do with the new, hence with strangers, hence with the

unexpected, since one does not know when one will meet a stranger. One has to change into a stranger as a condition to be changed into a stranger by the meeting with the stranger: from stranger through unpreparation (this unpreparation is not at the beginning. One has to prepare the unpreparation), to stranger through postponement, the two linked by telepathy; telepathy is their simultaneity. One can no longer rest from thought through non-thought also because non-thought is no longer also the state of someone distracting himself away from thought, but the state where one has only two sensations-thoughts: how totally devoid of thought or sensation one is; that one's body is, for that interval, being decomposed by everything that continued to move in it (the body is not eaten by worms that infiltrate it from the outside. The body is degenerated-decomposed by the parasitical inside it). This body-as-corpse is the worm eating-decomposing the corpse of (a hibernating) time. Hence the necessity of disappearance: the white letters on black background in *Night For Day* show the time that elapsed for others (*Two days eleven minutes thirty seven seconds (later? Earlier?)*). These intertitles have nothing to do with shortening a scene's real time through editing nor with averting jump cuts: the actor cut his hair yesterday though we are scheduled the coming week to film additional shots that are to be intercut with those filmed three days ago. The jump cuts could be averted by inserting the temporal intertitle between the two shots in the same scene, in the first of which his hair is long, in the second of which his hair is short; rather the written intertitle that states the time that has elapsed occurs between two shots that are continuous. The vampire, vomited at night by an anorexic earth, does not *under*go the decomposition-dissolution that would permit him or the constituent elements of his body to become part of grass, ashes, snow, clouds, bums in the cold. What permits the vampire to avert this total separation from the others, human and inhuman, is his ability to become all these things through metamorphosis, thus extending his spectra beyond their merely human range. Whenever spectra are radically extended (for instance by dying before dying), one should, as in suppression, be two (and this not so as to have competition (the stupid term *binocular rivalry*): there is no rivalry between master and disciple): the two eyes (one conscious, one suppressed (in binocular rivalry)); the two ears (in dichoptic listening); the two states of the vampire: living and dead (Eastern European vampires have «two hearts, or two souls... one heart, or one soul, never dies»).

In Marcel Duchamp's *Etant Donnés* the nude has to be constructed (Duchamp leaves specific instructions on how *Etant Donnés* should be assembled). Nudity is arrived at by an addition of pieces rather than by a subtraction of veils.

Judaism and Islam not only prohibit representation (When one reads one

176

does not get images but "in the image of", and were one to be asked to formulate what images were going through one's mind during reading, the images one gives will be "in the image of" something that has no image, as man is "in the image of" God in Judaism and Islam), but also don't have the institution of confession, hence are less prone to pornography.

Appearance has been so much disregarded in the rare porno films I've seen, that acting itself is discounted: there is no pretence of acting in the midst of all these scenes that are supposed to be instantiations of the imaginary. Because of the absence of seduction in these films, the persons, who cannot seduce each other due to the facility/fastness with which sex between them begins, sometimes look awkwardly, with boredom, at the camera, and it is in this look that an infinitesimal unintentional direct seduction between the person in the film and the spectator watching it resides.

Close-ups permit a miniaturization of the dimension used to measure space, but also a miniaturization of the dimension used to measure time, hence the orgasm in porno films stretches for an extremely long time. The price is repetition (fractal self-similarity).

What is obscene about pornographic films is, in large part, that they put an artificial stop to the denudation and penetration (while its extension into infinity means that the measuring device is getting smaller and smaller and the observer is getting closer and closer and hence the privilege of vision (which presupposes perspective, be it nothing but the internal perspective of the eye, with the messages moving from the rods and cones toward the blind spot of the eye (its vanishing point)) is vanishing). Cronenberg understood that the body's surface-membrane is a false limit that has to be penetrated, that has been penetrated by science. While in his earlier films — and in parts of *The Fly* (the continuous peeling off of Brundle's membranes, until he has none) — Cronenberg reached only the inside of the body (the inside of the body can be merely another way of veiling the surface of the body), in *The Fly* teleportation is the dissolution of what is to be teleported into its constitutive basic elements in one pod and their reintegration in another pod to reconstitute the person or animal or thing. For the time interval, however infinitesimal, between his/her/its disappearance from the first pod (a device that can serve, better than cryopreservation, for indefinite preservation) and his/her/its appearance in the second pod, that person or thing cannot be seen, has been withdrawn from the realm of the pornographic (Brundle's "catch me if you can" does not apply to speed as much as to non-locality, when he's nowhere between the two pods. A new off-screen space).

One fights pornography either by continuing the process of penetration-denudation until one gets to the nonvisual (elementary processes cannot be seen (the six dimensional wave equation of two interacting elementary particles cannot be visualized), only the traces that they leave when measured) or one respects the aura, the latter alternative being extremely difficult since the aura has been dissolved by mechanical and digital reproduction (exception(?): Godard's *Hail Mary*). *Hail Mary* has nothing to do with pornography; but in the interview Godard gave about it in *Art Press*, he said that had he had enough time he would have literally shown Mary having a child while still a virgin. To show as proof is pornographic. Nowhere is the obscenity of the look and proof (gotten through measurement) more obvious than in quantum physics where a given elementary particle has no definite qualities until one makes a measurement. It is only when a measurement is made (that is, only when traces are detected and amplified (close ups)) that the wave equation collapses and the particle is found in only one place. Obscenity: the cutting down of dimensions (the wave function for the interaction of fifty particles exists in one hundred and fifty dimensions (three for each particle)). The obscene presupposition of the classical paradigm: measurement results manifest dispositions inherent in the real world whether measurements take place or not. So that with that model the look is always there even when it is absent, to make sure that the thing has an inherent value that the measurement will merely declare.

Laura Mulvey posits an antagonism in cinema between the narrative function and the erotic/spectacle function, the latter linked with the female (both Nietzsche's distance which makes woman distant from herself, and Hegel-Freud-Doane's lack of distance which posits her in absolute proximity to herself (the fear she might implode) turn woman into spectacle, the former through the idealizing effect of distance, the latter through narcissism). Sexual liberation can be part of capitalism's imperative of fluidity and exchange, but this function it can have is in conflict with another model/ means of implementing this fluidity, that of narrative action (in pornographic films there is a stagnation if not a total disappearance of narrative progression). Conflict between these two ways (both have a progression towards a climax (the multiplicity of objects, colors, persons is not needed because it will not be perceived as long as there is an action-potential as erection (in the pornographic film) or as duel (in the narrative film) and hence no need for background and extras. This poverty-homogeneity is necessarily linked to capital's extraction of a currency from all the objects so that the multiplicity of objects is always reduced to that of their homogeneous abstract equivalent, money) and then a release of the tension) of actualizing capitalism's demand for circulation. These two means clash together only so that no monopoly by any one element as the sole manifestation of capitalism should occur. This clash does not further any revolutionary change. The reconciliatory dialectical movement between the two can only be interrupted by the obscene, by that which transgresses its own finality; but then this obscenity that permitted us to get rid of dialectics can only be fought with what? The inertia of obscenity and the obscenity of inertia, by what can they be fought except by the suicidal, by that which disappeared before reaching its own finality.

Ads are tests of whether we have the information that will permit us to decipher them. The ads sections that are part of TV shows like *Jeopardy* are transparent, don't need any deciphering, since the show has been about proving that the winner knows the reference system.

In Hitchcock's *North By Northwest* the main character who works in advertisement gets mistaken not for another real person but for a non-existent person who was invented by the police as a decoy to fool spies. «We construct a self from the data given (the paper, the cards, the ticket, the hat, the location), the correlatives for a particular character... These "clues" signify a person — but he is absent; and so are we. In this shared absence we can easily merge: we can become the absent traveller» (Judith Williamson, *Decoding Advertisements*). We can identify with the absent person of the ad only because we will then become absent ourselves. That's what takes place in the case of Thornhill. He puts on dark glasses, changes his name (not to Kaplan), acts as if he were a porter in a train station, so as not to be identified by the police, who are now on his tracks for a murder he did not commit. Whereas he was mistakenly taken by the spies to be Kaplan, he is now though identified by the police as Thornhill still mistakenly taken by them to be a murderer. On both sides he is mistaken as/for another person. By taking the place of Kaplan, an absent non-existent person, he has himself now to become absent so as not to be killed by the spies or imprisoned by the police. We do not take the place of the absent person, only his absence. Otherwise the differences (Kaplan's trousers don't fit on Thornhill, the former has dandruff, Thornhill doesn't...) between the two persons between whom the substitution is to take place wouldn't be irrelevant.

Many people do not want to undergo the process of producing the different skin that the lotion is to give them (massaging one's face with the lotion three times a day. Washing one's hands. Putting the towel back where it was), they just want to be mistaken as having it, they want to have it at the level of the consumption of themselves by others. Change demands much energy/commitment. Hitchcock asks his actors to act minimally and be neutral, which means not having to portray/embody/produce a different personality, that of the character; rather they will become the character through Hitchcock's direction of the camera movements and the editing, that is, they are to be mistaken by the audience for the duration of the film as being the characters portrayed by its plot and as having the emotions the story calls for. It is thus also that they can as the film characters be so easily mistaken in the diegesis of the films for the *the wrong man* or woman.

Nam Jum Paik has a strong relation with found footage. Hence he can't use found machines (and circuitry). While mainstream media use found machines, machines that are never tinkered with, and hence can't use found images. In *Good Morning, MR. Orwell* (1984), interactivity has been, unfortunately, extended so much as to become an interactivity of the artist with the material: *live mix* (Paik is not a Zen electronic painter). In this he is extending the demise of the aura. The live program was shown simultaneously in New York, Paris and South Korea. This additional step in the demise of the aura was resisted by planet Earth: though the video signal travels at the speed of light, a distance/detachment is still maintained between these different places due to the different time zones (12 a.m. in New York corresponds to 6 p.m. in Paris and to 2 a.m. in South Korea). If, as Althusser wrote, ideology constitutes us as subjects then Paik's dissolution of the image of the dancer in *Global Grove* into so many distorted images that more or less resemble it, can be a way to fight interpellation: we move from the clearest image — the one which would have readily answered the "Hey, you there!" Althusser speaks about as constitutive of ideology — to the least recognizable image — the one which will not recognize itself and hence would not answer the interpellation (the technology exists, in the case of many media, for having a two-way communication so that the receiver can become sender then receiver then sender (Enzensberger's interactivity). But the actualization of this presupposes that the reproduction of the means of production be possible even though in that case an enormous amount of the population's energy and time would be spent in "communication". In the absence of a radical change in the infrastructure, the sender would not have the requisite time or energy for creating anything original, and then we would have fallen into the worst form of ideology: the exchange between the constantly changing poles of sender and receiver would be reduced to a continual interpellation, an endless closed circuit "Hey, you there.")

Nam Jum Paik, by his use of found footage, is a documentary video maker (other documentary video makers use found cultures, found situations, found mannerisms), who then manipulates the latter visually. Bill Viola's *Chott el Djerid* is a documentary on the desert that makes the subject it is portraying do the *special effects* (mirages...).

[written by Zaid Omran and Jalal Toufic] Without the plastic wrap around the book being removed, time had already used this in-part calender — Gerhard Richter's *A Calender for 1990* — which Jalal bought on 4/15/90. Once

1991 begins, should the book have a tag on it that says *used*, and hence should it be sold for less? Can one title it: *Doubly Used*, by time and Jalal Toufic? Although we see Jalal at the start of a film adding, on the calender pages, the following items,
"Daily Northwestern (reward for anyone who finds or returns my stolen backpack)
Satich (keys lost)
return videos
Buy hamburger for Michael (see the bone at the upper edge of the cheek moving while he eats)" to a list of other already scribbled reminders of things he has to do the next day or so, almost none of them are done by the end of the film. Was the calender used by Jalal Toufic?

What is a face? In SITE's Peeling (Richmond, Virginia, 1972) the facade peels, a section of the wall detaching in a curve from the cement underneath it, which becomes exposed (or should we rather say *overexposed* since the peeling wall does not leave any traces on the cement behind it?). There is a huge difference between this peeling wall and the walls photographed by Deidi von Schaewen on which we see the traces of the wall of the adjoining building that was demolished or crumbled on its own. When the face of the building detaches, one would expect to see with horror a Rilkean absence of the face[5]. Instead all one witnesses is a clean painted cement. And there is a reason for this: the outermost layer of the facade is treated as a mere wrapping detachable from the building (become one more of the consumer objects it contains, a ready-made (the basic building prototype of BEST is unchanged in the different SITE projects for the department store)) in the most easy and ephemeral way. But this absence of the absence of the face behind what has peeled can lead us to postulate that that may be because in SITE's vision behind the face there is always another face, be that face a mask. And indeed looking at some of their other projects one finds many corroborations of this hypothesis: in one of the proposals for the Molino Stucky (Venice, Italy, 1975), the facade of the building is seen as progressively drowning: to achieve this effect they had to have nine facades each representing one progressive stage of the drowning. And in the other proposal for Molino Stucky though the facade has been laid bare, what is behind it has once more been occulted, this time by what can best divert the attention of the onlooker, reflections. Hence

---

[5]Rainer Maria Rilke, *The Notebooks of Malte Laurids Brigge*, trans. Stephen Mitchell (New York: Vintage Books, 1985), p.7: «She had completely fallen into herself, forward into her hands... she pulled out of herself, too quickly, too violently, so that her face was left in her hands... I shuddered to see a face from the inside, but I was much more afraid of that bare flayed head waiting there, faceless.»

the wall of water that is to fall from the facade. The original facade that has fallen made a somersault on its way down and landed face up so that it faces the pedestrians rather than giving them its bareness.

The peeling of the wall is interesting for two more reasons: — It represents a schizophrenic moment: a poster or skin is a surface, but so is a wall. Since they have a similar predicate, they are/become identical. — Since in many a project by SITE (the acronym, with its capital letters, is already a poster, a sign board on the page) the facade functions as a poster (hence the flatness of the part extended beyond the roofline of Indeterminate Facade), we can see how one can, consciously or not, associate the facade-as-poster to a peeling (these facades-as-posters are each more a sort of prosthesis than an organic part of the building). What is somewhat missing here is the kind of poster/billboard art of the sixties, with the posters on street walls, some torn, some superimposed on others, forming a spontaneous collage.

These facades that function as images do so not only in the manner of billboards and posters, but also as film frames: the multiple sinking facades in one of the models of *Molino Stucky* are like the consecutive frames of a film shot; in Cutler Ridge (Florida, 1979) the facade is fragmented into four layers, the third of which is extracted from the second and includes the three main doorways, while the fourth layer, which is made up of the frames of the doorways, looks like three blown-up film frames[6]. Indeed this cinematic mode permeates many of SITE's projects (SITE is not only the homonym of sight but is already a sort of time-lapsed word), hence for instance the false objects as on a film set in Laurie Mallet House (New York, 1985). Broadcasting of images is replacing transportation, therefore the majoring of the images in SITE's work produces as a symptom this freezing or burial of modes of transportation: scattered on Highway '86 Processional World Exposition (Vancouver, Canada, 1986), in what looks like a remake in a Vertov key of the bridge scene in Eisenstein's *October*, are cars, boats, motorcycles, space capsules, airplanes, rockets; in SITE's Ghost Parking Lot (Hamden, Connecticut, 1978) twenty automobiles are buried under the paving surface.

In many of Gehry's houses the original house having become unusable for its user, other buildings are added to it. It is these protuberances that stop the sudden obesity of a house become a ruin [an obesity that can suddenly change into an excessive thinness, unobtrusiveness, one's own, as one disappears in the presence of an absolute ruin], that is, become a protuberance on nothing, a prosthesis of nothing. We do not feel this obesity in many of SITE's projects

---

[6]It is as if one is witnessing here something similar to the process by which a Cantor set is produced. Hence one is not surprised when one encounters self-similarity in Door Within a Door Within a Door Within a Door Within a Door.

of ruins: we are dealing not so much with ruins as either with a mummification of ruins, hence the pyramidal shape of the stack of bricks in Indeterminate Facade, the burial of the cars in Ghost Parking Lot, the tiles of Frozen Archeology arrested in their fall, wrapped by eternity; or with buildings camouflaging (see SITE's forest project) as ruins. Camouflaging from whom? Not from humans, since, as we have seen, they function as posters/billboards in relation to people. From time, from what ruins. But, it seems, one can only camouflage from time to time. Hence in some of SITE's projects the aforementioned obesity undergoes displacement, appearing in the form of reproduction: in Best inside/Outside Building (Milwaukee, Wisconsin, 1984), the mummified false merchandise items in monochrome gray displayed outside the recessed glass wall reflect the merchandise items inside the building; the waste bricks cascading in the BEST Indeterminate Facade Showroom (Houston, Texas, 1975), but arrested in their fall as in a photograph, are as it were an Arman piece.

It is almost as strange to see someone walking in a ruin as to see a person walking underwater without any supply of air. Hence a project such as Swatch Retail Store (Nantucket, Massachusetts) — an architectural equivalent to Leonardo Cremonini's painting *Les loisirs de l'eau* (1973), which is rendered from the perspective of someone underwater (only the part of the swimmers immersed in water is visible): only the lower parts of the mannequins' bodies is visible — would have been perfect for rendering the sensation one should have had on seeing customers walking in a project such as BEST Indeterminate Facade Showroom, except SITE did not manage to create ruins.

There are three degrees of *fana'* according to Junayd: The first one is that of the obliteration of the individual's attributes and characteristics. Thus, the elitism one associates with Sufism counteracts itself. If *fana'* is the dissolution of the form of the subject, how can one explain the major role of the covenant in Junayd's Sufism, and hence of memory (itself a trace, hence a form)? How can one still speak of *fana'* as the *return* to the state «in which one was before one was» (the state in which one answered the *alastu* (Quran, Sura 7:171: «When thy Lord had brought forth their descendants from the loins of the Sons of Adam… "Am I not (*alastu*)," said He, "your Lord?" They said: "Yes! we do testify."»)), when return and memory is a trace/form? How can a trace (in this case the memory of the covenant) motivate the pursuing of *fana'* (the obliteration of all traces and forms)? Can a trace be suicidal?

This attachment to something that was in the "past" (the stage where one was before one was) and that has to be remembered, clashes with what many sufis saw as one of the definitions of *faqr* (poverty): not to let another *moment* enter one's awareness while in a different *moment*.

The covenant shows that the primary speech act is not the *be* (*kun*) of God, but the creation of the position of addressee in the question, hence in a phrase that automatically presupposes that the addressee of the first phrase will become the addressor of the second phrase (the covenant, this movement of the individual from the position of *you* to the position of *I* or *we*, facilitated by the fact that God asks a question, so that even silence would have been a *batin* answer, cuts down the transcendence of God but maintains the separation of God and the sufi: by having a state in which the sufi was before he was, Junayd insures that *fana'* would be a going back to that being before one was, rather than to God). And it is this position of addressee (and the presupposition, expectation, of its transference to the position of addressor in the response phrase) that is this being before one is.

Heard so many people speak about doing away with movements and schools, with all the *isms*, but to do that these people have to lose their names (the Arabic for *name* is *ism*).

«There are four kinds of thoughts: from God, from an angel, from self, and from the Devil»[7]. But once one ('s body) dies, the self *has been* expelled, becoming as external to one as the other three sources. Then thoughts originating in the devil are no longer seductions that one can resist falling for, but are imposed (hence the injunction of the prophet, «die before you die»). Perhaps if the *murid* is, as he should be, as passive in the hands of the master as a corpse in the hands of an undertaker, the sheikh may be able to help him (telepathically) on the journey of union with God, even after the disciple has become a corpse, but if so what makes the sheikh not a veil between the dead disciple and God (to be as unobtrusive as a vampire in a mirror)?

For Muhasibi the heart contains a part he calls *sirr*, which may be translated as secret or mystery. It is at the heart of this Sufi's theories on psychology, this Sufi whose name meant self-examination, that we find this *sirr*, this dimensionless-timeless meeting point-*moment* between the divine and the human, unknown to the person who is experiencing it. What remains of the person in his union with God is this *sirr*, a *sirr* to the person who went through it, because of «the obliteration of the consciousness of having attained the vision of God» (Junayd) in the third stage of *fana'*. One has to do an analysis to differentiate the eternal from the temporal before one enters in *fana'* but also an analysis by/in the *sirr* (for one has lost one's attributes) in the ecstatic experience to differentiate the eternal from the eternal, for God Himself may manifest his *makr* (on the mount the devil proffers three temptations, one to the Son, one to the Holy Ghost, and one to the Father): Bayezid: «He said,

---

[7]Kalabadhi, *The Doctrine of the Sufis*, trans. A.J.Arberry (Cambridge: University of Cambridge Press, 1935), p.80.

"What are you, if not the Truth? You speak by the Truth." So I said, "No! You are the Truth..." Then I said, "I am through You." He said, "If you exist through Me, then I am you and you are I." Then I said, "Don't beguile me by yourself from yourself. Yes! You are You, there is no god but You."»)

Biography deals with the name and the temporal and hence does not deal with *fana'* (the dissolution of the name and human individual attributes), *fana'* being a form of *tauhid*, «the separation of the eternal from that which has been originated in time by the covenant.» So it was all too natural that revisionism should happen in Sufism largely at the hands of the biographers (how to include the Sufi in a chronological order from which he has been withheld during *tauhid*?).

The covenant plays the role of the constitution of ideology (Althusser writes that ideology interpellates individuals as subjects) in an Islamic context. In a way *fana'* is an attempt to regain the position of the subject of enunciation through the *He* (Bayezid: «My "I am" is not "I am," because I am He»), for it is a *He* that can say *I*. The Sufi loses the power to say *I* so that God would say *I* and hence so that the Sufi through *fana'* can say *I* («and when I love him, I am the hearing whereby he heareth and the sight whereby he seeth...» (hadith qudsi)). *Dhikr* is hence the interpellation of God, and as Althusser wrote, it is through interpellation that the subject, the one who can say *I*, the subject of enunciation, can be created. Hence the great importance of *dhikr* in Sufism, for at the same pace that the Sufi individual as subject is dissolving (to someone who came looking for him, Bayezid replied: «I myself am in search of Bayezid»), God as subject must be constituted, the progression in the difficulty of saying *I* by the individual Sufi subject taking place at the same pace as the progression in the ease with which God says *I*. It is intriguing that Junayd would view *fana'* as a way to reach the state in which a person «was before he was», the state in which one was interpellated by the *alastu*, that is constituted as subject, for the name and form are dissolved at the third degree of *fana'*.

For many of the early Sufi ascetics, asceticism came to have value in itself: since *fana'* is part of *tauhid*, to almost totally extinguish one's body is to have arrived at an earthly *sort of fana'*. It is no longer the world that hides God from the ascetic, but earthly *fana'* (the states that the early ascetics were experiencing are earthly states, are part of the world)(asceticism does not divest one from the body: spectra are not undone, only extended (telepathy, being in several places at the same time...)) that hides from him the *fana'* in God. Going on a fast, as the Sufi ascetics did for such long continuous periods, is a way of being self-sufficient, the body digesting itself, feeding off itself. Is one's own body *halal*? This self-sufficiency is somewhat against the *faqr* sufis advocated.

To accuse Hallaj of speaking in public of things that should not be mentioned except to the Sufi elect and only in *isharats* (esoteric allusions) is to forget that Hallaj had to deal with a *batin* more *batin* than the distinction between *batin* and *zahir* («No one can claim God in any way except by faith, for in reality, there is no claim [to having attained God]»)(esoterism applies not only in relation to others but also in relation to oneself (the obliteration of the perception of the vision in the third stage of *fana'*)(one penetrates mystery only by becoming oneself a mystery)), the latter distinction still allowing the person to choose whether or not to reveal what he knows to others or just indicate it by *isharats*. One who has to often deal with a *batin* of *batin*, will, on the occasions when a choice between *zahir* and *batin* is possible, turn — almost as a compensation — to *zahir*.

Many Sufis played *the devil's advocate* (Hallaj considered Satan and Muhammad the only true monotheists, and Ahmad Ghazzali viewed anybody who did not learn *tauhid* from Satan as an infidel)(Satan a precursor of the *malama* people); became, at time, the Devil (the three other kinds of thoughts, «from God, from an angel, from self,» having totally vanished), had then to try to regain the devil's advocate's playfulness, only then really becoming the devil, for the devil is just the devil's advocate, playful.

May 1989. LSD for the first time: Three of my friends are speaking while sitting next to me. Sudden (with the suddenness with which a film (most film departments have bad projectors) vanishes into a burning circle that divides into black perforations that then take the form of lava (suddenly these become a sensation in one's mouth). The lights are turned on, the damaged section bypassed, and the film continued. That's how sudden, after taking LSD and waiting for something drastic to happen for forty-five minutes (nothing changed except the brightness of colors), reality itself burns. The lights turned on, and to one's surprise everybody is still looking at the screen as if nothing has happened, and if one were to speak to any person, he would react as if one were interrupting his viewing. It is as if now everybody, except oneself, were wearing headphones, and all heard the same thing. And now a dog is startled not when one hears a loud sound but when all these people with headphones give the indication they hear one) utter fear: everything has receded in the distance (a zoom-out has taken place (in this state a dolly movement would be artificial and the zoom-out the natural movement), distance itself has receded, everything has become frozen except space which is slightly waving like a flag or a leaf of grass. I call to them. The three turn, look at me without recognizing me, totally annoyed that I have disturbed them. I walk away on the sand; my feet begin to become, up to the ankle, sand feet. I pass two policemen; the sounds of the passing people change in loudness, totally cease at times; people walk in slow motion. I walk farther. Again this detached/

withheld/distant distance as I see four persons standing a hundred feet away. No sound between us (as if space itself wanted to utter a sound but couldn't (as one can't when one is terrified)). The four persons are so far away one can send or receive from them letters. The vanishing point is between us (if I can still see them it is that I am looking at an X-ray equivalent that cuts through the horizon), infinity is between us. To walk towards them may bring me closer to them, but just as probably, away from them, depending on whether they belong within the same frame or not, for space is now an endless joiner (Robert Frank's *Another World — Nova Scotia — Canada)*. If they are not within the same frame in the joiner, the off-screen of the frame in which the persons one is heading toward are located would be hidden beneath the frame in which one is. One is lost since one has no way of knowing whether they belong to the same frame, and if not, what the concealed off-screen hides from one. It may be also that it is because of that that one does not commit suicide, for one *may* be buried in the covered off-screen. This underneath is the real between. The joiner as overphotography (as in Rainer's overpainting). Persons are so distant that one's seeing them twice seems unnatural: encountering more than once a person separated from one by infinity! A sign of conspiracy? Only in the case of plants can one cross them again and again without feeling a weird sense of repetition. For one's mind to take control (it takes control not only over the world, but also over one, who is part of the world), the world has to withdraw (if during the LSD trip all one is seeing are hallucinations, what happens if the mind stops, what remains, since the world has been so distant that it no longer exists?), and this one feels physically (one's ears largely clogged so that they wouldn't be able to hear reality).

We are not forgotten, not because we are remembered (If one stresses the origin and memory, one will end up being the origin of many things and will be remembered much. There is almost no Sufi pedigree that is not traced to Junayd: he is near the beginning of the *silsila*s of almost all *tariqa*s: *Abhariyya, Suhrawardiyya, kubrawiyya, Nuriyya, Rukniyya, Hamadaniyya, Ightishashiyya, Dhahabiyya, Nurbakhshiyya, Lahjaniyya, Jibawiyya-sa'diyya, Ni'matallahiyya, Mawlawiyya*...)(memory is what forgets the past. An event in the past need not send its ghost to us in the present, as in voluntary memory, but can come (to us? To us as writers) in the past, that is not in the form of memory. The relation with the past has nothing to do with memory and everything to do with telepathy. It is in similar ways that one (as a writer/film maker) can enter a relation with an event from the past that comes to one in another region of the past and that the work of Arnulf Rainer (*Kreuzigung*...) creates a connection between the person and the deformations that will happen to the photographs taken of him (whether these be traditional photographs or those created by refractory periods). These immobilizations-images stolen from one must live/be lived rather than merely be resurrected (life regained *posterior* to the resurrection); one has to enter a connection with them, not through image magic, but through deformation or other means of telepathy. That connection means that the person through the affects his image is undergoing through the deformations has an after-life/survives (provided either that the future deformation was already being felt when the image was taken (the «What is this music?» in Godard's *Sauve Qui Peut la Vie*)(there is an advanced signal (as in *advanced wave*) from the future deformation to the person), or that the person be someone who postpones, and hence that in his case what is simultaneous is separated by a late time. Otherwise we are merely dealing with a desecration of the corpse (even if that takes the form of performing a beauty operation on it (Fine Young Cannibals' *Don't Look Back*)), or with magic (the desecration of the living)).

If memory is already a forgetting, then one must forget memory. Forgetting the forgetting that memory is. Those who change (change is the memory of oblivion (not only in the sense that what changed one has become part of one for ever (except in the case of amnesic time), but also in that change is one's way to remember that one forgets all the time)), do this automatically. Those who change have no experience, for experience deals not with the event but with its memory. If I am not interested in having relationships with older women, it is that they constantly speak about their experience ("Haven't you learned from experience yet?" "And why wouldn't life, sometimes, learn from us; why is it we should always be the ones who have to adapt to life?" That was merely a reaction, for neither we nor life must adapt. One must even resist letting reality adapt to one). Change cannot be divided into more basic elements, though like the back-and-forth movement, it is a complex basic phenomenon, while in adaptation there is one element, or if more, these occur consecutively, in which case there is no need for postponement but for waiting. We can write about the memory of a thing, hence about repetition, but once we do away with memory, there comes the biggest danger, that of the repetition of the event itself, not its memory, by writing (only when what is going on cannot become part of experience, has one, through writing, to describe it), even in the sense/case where the event blocks the writing (F.S.Fitzgerald)(that minimal turning away, that minimal difference that has to be maintained for the limit for a derivative), by making it superfluous because redundant. Writing (or painting or film) is absolutely needed since it is only writing (or painting or film) that can give us a way not so much to react to the past that comes back to us in the past (one cannot react to it, to what does not act), but of entering a relation with it (otherwise one may undergo a hysterical absence of degeneration (the danger of the digital) or a traumatic neurosis)), but because we are derivatives, have arrived at the derivative of forgetting: people (including ourselves) and time *forget to forget* us. Ashoura is a training to reach the derivative of forgetting, for only then will Husayn be not forgotten but also not remembered (to which answers both writing and the past coming to us in the past). Neither an attempt not to forget, nor a way of remembering, but an apprenticeship in forgetting to forget, hence an apprenticeship in how to become a derivative, the difference tending towards zero, never becoming zero (that difference is not the chronological one between the time at which Karbala occurred and the time of the present Ashoura ritual, but that minimal difference between one's voice as one hears it while speaking, and one's voice as one hears it back on the recorder (strange and somewhat repulsive. One has two eyes, two ears, two hands... (what if the three points already include *and two voices*?) and two voices), this minimal difference that insures that repetition would not become bad repetition a la Fitzgerald: in *The Crack-Up*, he writes that he had developed a sad attitude toward sadness, a tragic attitude toward tragedy... (like a spectator, he is identifying — with himself. The opposite of that: Safa is sitting inside the abstract small room. He feels there is a camera outside the room filming him. This probably saved him from being swallowed by the room). Zen is to eat when eating (nobody is eating nothing), drink when drinking (nobody is drinking nothing). This is a squaring of zero, a raising to the power of two of zero, whereas the other way out is to get to the derivative (postponement and distraction to undo repetition). The danger is to always try to apply and verify one's writing in experience (is there a sort of *"binocular" rivalry* between experience and writing/film making?), since this often results in the bad repetition that Fitzgerald wrote about. Writing does not need the test of the real (writing is close to the relation with the past in the past, this relation that cannot be actualized, so that one cannot try to verify it by comparing it to a reality taken as the control sample)(except if test is understood in the sense of temptation) to become sober)). On that condition is the derivative arrived at, and the new occurs, time is really injected (otherwise one feels claustrophobic)(there are other ways of becoming a derivative, other ways of injecting time). A repetition is always forgotten, for there is no time to forget to forget it (that's why one needs postponement: postponement gives the additional time that the forgetting of forgetting (which is not a forgetting of a forgetting that happens earlier, not a doubled forgetting, but one complex forgetting that cannot be divided into more basic elements) needs in order to occur), in the absence of this additional time, it is no longer time that gets injected but the thing/phenomenon itself. It is not a matter of forgetting the event (but of forgetting the memory of the event), but of placing forgetting between us and the event (not waiting but postponement).

To go outside the conspiracy that was trying to make one think in terms of

189

conspiracies.

The library's resting area: three couples, each at a table, and two men (one of them reading a book on pharmacology) sitting each by himself. Feeling that each of the couples and each one of the two men is sitting on a different porch, far away from the others, as in a film where the multiple screen joins people from different places-times.

The first index (after the heightening in the colors' brightness) is presence (aura) hence distance (aura: what sends messengers in-its-place/before-it-arrives-itself; it is the messenger that falls like lightning. What leaves behind a trail (subjects had to continue bowing until the king and his shadow not only had disappeared from sight, but were space-like separated from them. (In Dan Reeves' *Sabda* there is a rack-focus from grass leaves in the foreground to a man working out-of-focus in the background. Simultaneous with the rack-focus a series of dissolves of the farmer cutting the crop, occur. Seeing this juxtaposition of the rack-focus and the dissolves one feels the dissolve is a temporal rack-focus so that the thing that one dissolved from is still there but invisible (unfelt, unexperienced) because too close temporally (as very close to the camera fence bars would be invisible if one focused on the distant background). To be having this thought-feeling while watching a video on Buddhism and Maya, hence on the illusionary existence of things!)).

My fingers are sticky, latch on to things and to themselves (memory).

I have seen him many times before at the film equipment check-out office. I see him in the library, walk to him, ask him what he's doing; he says he's writing a paper on Jehovah; I see the Bible. Why do I have to hear about his religious interest for the first time only now?

I would imagine that were a beautiful person to take LSD and feel paranoid he would be in a very tricky situation, for people look at him/her all the time even during normal times, a fact about which he would be oblivious then.

He said: "Just remember it is all in the mind, and you'll be safe." But what would have to do the remembering is the altered mind itself, is itself in the changed mind. Once the disjunction (between two parts of the brain?) implicit in "Just remember it is all in the mind" is felt, it becomes difficult to disentangle a suicide from a murder, and all the reservations one may have against the latter one feels now against the former. This may explain in part the non-excessive number of suicides of schizophrenics.

Sounds are excessively loud, and their detachedness makes them even louder, for the other sounds can't cushion them, mix with them to dilute them. Other people can gauge the difference in level between the sounds you're hearing and those they are hearing by the difference between the level at which they are speaking and the very low level at which you are speaking (it is you, rather than those conspiring against you, who speak in whispers (sound levels are now the differentiating mark between reality and hallucination, the difference between hearing sounds under water and above water. In Islam the devil whispers to you, on drugs it is reality that whispers to you)). The whispering used by Acconci in *The Red Tapes* reduces the possibility of the birth of an echo, hence is anti-narcissistic at the level of the voice, which is not striving to contemplate itself. But the use of whispering almost does away with the ability of the hearer to stop listening to it since it is not what is heard but what is overheard.

Using shorter and shorter time intervals (in photography...), the pose of the person can be undone, the variations inside it but foreign to it discovered. Getting to even more elementary intervals the movement's own pose can be undone (beyond surprising the person, it is a matter of surprising the movement, for the latter poses for the photographer as a particular kind of movement), one discovering within it so many other movements: in a smooth walk (somewhere in this whiteness a leaf, no, a color. In snowy Winter, leaves of forgotten trees; in Summer, leaves of grass. Always in contact with the surface. This demands all the ecstatic sobriety, the balance, not of a dancer or tightrope walker but of a saunterer), the sudden stops, accelerations, running, flying, swimming. In *Untitled*, Winograd changes the kind of movement, from somersault to walking, before/in the act of immobilizing it. Going to even more elementary intervals one gets to expressions to preconscious processing of subliminal stimuli (expressions on the level of the larger time intervals and to supraliminal stimuli have their constituent elements which are different from the expressions to preconscious processing of subliminal stimuli. Hockney's joiners remain at the level of the former). These fraction of a second appearences-expressions which usually cancel each other at the level of large time intervals, are seen in an LSD trip. How many of these (1/1000 of a second or less shutter speed) in one hour? To think of the amount of energy needed for all these extremely expressive gestures of the face (one must be dealing with something between molar energy and the mc^2. Additional weariness, once one becomes conscious of their existence)(at last a reason to respect people again). Of four photographs taken at an instant photography coin machine, one showed Michael in a very expressive strange appearance, from which a personality totally different from the one(s) one connects with him, can be projected. Asked my actor to take seven sets of four instant photographs. Not one photograph is expressive. Today I heard Michael saying the photographs he took were posed.

I can see her walking in the library, like an object falling in water. Time has stopped, the somnambulism of that walk, me fixed to the chair since time stopped, me sucked beneath a temporal event horizon, she outside of it. The sounds heard by me now are not those of people and things moving and making noise (in the absence of time there is no succession, hence no cause-effect), but are similar to the sounds one hears at night and that seem to be occurring for no reason (sounds of the tiptoe of time). And if indeed time has stopped, it is her movement (giving the illusion time is still passing) that is saving me from becoming blind.

Hesitation becomes part of bad repetition. A circular path. I am midway and moving from left to right to a specific destination. I stop and consider moving in the other direction. To continue at present in the first direction is to enter bad repetition, to feel one is repeating the walk.

One begins turning one's face toward a person before he begins a certain movement or gesture, catching him just as he initiates it. It is this telepathic ability making one feel always at the source of the other's incipient movement, making one turn or look only at the loci where things are on the point of beginning, that causes one to feel whenever, on looking somewhere or at someone, one sees no movement beginning, either that the person is frozen or that s/he is part of a conspiracy, someone/something following one for his/her/its action will happen after one looked at him/her/it.

Since in paranoia all the energy of association is invested now in linking people, words and events in a big conspiracy, no more energy is left for the associations that in everyday life make things seem normal (or strange in a traditional way (since it is a deviation *from tradition*)). So that one cannot project-associate things/events/people to similar things in the past, to memories, and/or to expectations. Is the car coming in one's direction with its harsh sound going to crush one? Every thing is unique, no generalizations are possible, no projections. No, though it may seem that LSD makes everything strange, one no longer able to project on how it might behave, that experience is full of projection (fear quicker than the telepathic?), since it extends fear everywhere and fear is the projection, so that one has to project to counteract, in however minimal a degree, this all encompassing fear. The lack of association institutes the reign of repetition, for it is much more probable that the sound of a bird should recur than the set of: sound of bird plus the specific images that were seen while the sound was heard plus the other sounds that were heard in conjunction with it plus what one was doing then. Repetition everywhere.

Silence should be included in any discussion of schizophrenic overinclusion. Minor ambient silences also.

You decide to phone friends to take your mind away from paranoia for at least a few minutes, before they begin not so much to sense that you're saying strange things, as to feel strange, and little by little the conversation has turned to strange subjects; but you can always end the phone conversation and call another friend. Speaking at a public phone, looking through one's phone book to decide who to call next, one sees people slowly gathering around where one is standing (the faces on the street as ugly, as present, as close, as strange, as those seen on subway trains), looking intermittently at one. One is not reasoning very well, i.e., it does not at all occur to one that they are doing so because they "need" to phone. This mind playing tricks on one brought one unbeknownst to one, but not to it, to the place where the real world and its functioning would major one's sense that one is hallucinating.

Flashback two weeks later: I have the clear scary sensation everybody in the ugly restaurant is a devoid-of-life extra (thanatosis. I can see time playing with them like a predator playing with a prey simulating death). I have to project life into them. But has one the right to project?

Real temptation is not of this world, it has (like a psychedelic) always already introduced one for however minimal a time into another world, shown one that the world one lives in is only one among so many.

The world has been so distant from one that now that one can again touch things, to touch them even without moving the hand is a caress.

It happened so many times before, maybe because one was getting very tired, that the lamplight would suddenly become less bright. One felt no alarm. Now, after having once taken LSD, when the lamplight becomes less bright, one has the apprehension that this is the sign that the sudden receding of the world is on the point of happening again. Fear. Also fertile colors of the wet land scare one, for that intensity of color can be the first stage in a continuous strengthening of colors that announces a psychotic experience.

Night. I am hearing voices speaking from the adjoining apartment. Since I noticed them, they have gotten a little louder. The fear they would continue getting louder indefinitely.

I have to digest the words before saying them, redirect them in their physical shape (if the word was facing in the wrong direction when uttered, the meaning would come wrong, or else it would be gibberish). A mouthful of words.

An event that happened a long time ago may happen again but how would I know in which of the two occurrences I am, especially since due to the withdrawal of the world, no *period* indices exist any longer?

He had read the book four years ago and had largely forgotten it. He began reading it again at night. Fell asleep by the time he reached page 34. Recalling the next morning that he had stopped a little farther than page 30, he opened the book on page 32 and began reading. He read a page and a half, remembering the paragraphs he was reading. Suddenly the horror (which includes in itself a suddenness (that may be sudden or gradual)) that on reading each paragraph for the rest of the book, he will remember it (a day after having taken the drug and after its chemical effect has been digested by the body, one is still extremely sensitive to repetition, and hence astounded at its excessive recurrence in the world).

Knowing the page (having marked it) at which one arrived before one interrupted one's reading, one turns back to the book, starts to read, discovers one had already read the first two paragraphs. Time also sometimes (during some drug trips…) interrupts its progression and then resumes it (the interruption often, but not always, coincides with/translates as a lapse undergone by the person), but it may resume on the same history page (a page that may be much longer than the life of the individual), but on a previous paragraph (possibility of incarnation), so that events that were supposed to have occurred some time ago, happen again now. An overlap that is a temporal lapsus, but that does not destroy chronology. The shallowest way to undo the *once and for all*: by the n+1 or the forever. But the temporal lapsus may take one back to a bifurcation point giving one the possibility to take a path other than the one one took the "previous time", in fact, the other time (this other sort of incarnation. One has many secrets though one is the opposite of a secretive person)(instead of one, many chronologies). The individual may *choose* the same path from the event in the past. This latter recurrence undoes both the *once and for all* and the repetition of the *forever*. One must be careful and know that the temporal lapsus and the bifurcating time are not the only eventualities of experimenting with time: there is the risk, for oneself and probably for time, of the amnesia of time, of time getting lost; for then one can no longer depend on the forever of what has been accomplished. Yonder one thought, "I have written 150 pages, have several unfinished videos, a partially edited feature film. Now I'll go through an experience that will most probably change me *from now on* (on such a trip one may be taken hostage by time or madness (an incentive to finish the projects one is doing before one undertakes such radical experiments))." But one knows now, having taken LSD, that the last refuge from change, namely that not one's memory but time's is there, can no longer be counted on (some people may be smug enough to try to undo the delirium and amnesia of time with their memory! They will fail): in this case one's change includes time's change, and hence by changing oneself one is maybe changing time (the highest risk), so one ends up with an amnesic time that may totally deprive us objectively and not merely subjectively (the risk/danger to others) of all one has done prior to the altered state (the book one is writing, the film or video tape one is editing, may in horror of its own possible disappearance due to one's experiments with time try to drive us to suicide (postponement is not also a defence against that)). This may indicate that the almost irremediable separation from the world (experienced during a bad acid trip), can be canceled, not by one's amnesia, but by time's (Grace? Ivan asks his brother in

Dostoyevsky's *The Brothers Karamazov*, «Are you fond of children, Alyosha?», and then tells of the massacres of children by the Turks and Circassians, and of the general who, because a serf boy hurt the paw of his favorite hound, send his hundreds of hounds after the child, who was shreaded by them into pieces. «Is there in the whole world a being who would have the right to forgive and could forgive?» It is not Christ (the one who shed his blood for others so they may be forgiven) that can forgive what happened; only an amnesic time can forgive by taking away from an event its having happened).

We can be the time machine for events in history to travel, we can become, by fasting, taking psychedelics, going mad... the time machine for what was imprisoned within chronology. Will altered states be repressed more and more when scientific and technological research into time travel becomes so advanced as to make time travel a real possibility? Most humans but also many events have ghosts. We are not dealing with ghosts (the recurrence of a past event that remains in its chronological locus) in this case but with a time section that can travel, take a *trip* so that an event that occurred in the past can now occur again, but by being withdrawn from the past (an editing of time. Is there in its place at least a slug to maintain "sync", and would that be space on the time heads?): in its place in the past there is an amnesia, becoming a temporal black hole (with no wormholes constituted) if a "critical section of time" (as in *critical mass*) has been transferred (hence the apprehension of the one who experiences not the recurrence of an event, but its transference (no déjà vu)). What would happen then? Warning to those who want or are thinking of creating a time machine from those (much more radical) who for a time became the time machine for time: be careful lest your machine take you to a time section that traveled already elsewhere, a section devoid of time, an amnesic section: a section where one would be forgotten by time, and to be forgotten by time is not only to no longer exist, but to never have existed.

The paranoid, the schizophrenic, the person undergoing a bad psychedelic trip have experienced the labyrinthine quality of time and have felt absolute terror, disorientation. The reason not all of them commit suicide, or that it takes many of them a long time to do so is that the reason to commit suicide — the labyrinthine quality of time — is itself what prohibits the belief in a death that would happen at a specific time, ending everything. Nothing can assure that person that he did not already commit suicide an endless number of times and is back where he was prior to the suicide, or that the suicide has not already been committed many times and each time forgotten (a forgetfulness between one and the event); or, a more scary hypothesis, that he can never commit suicide because the suicide he thinks he committed is always either a hallucination or a hallucinated memory (while bifurcation is a way through which a possibility left behind in the past can be actualized, we are dealing here with a figure of time that on the contrary potentializes/ virtualises what one wanted so intensely to render actual, what one could otherwise easily render actual)(a stolen suicide): in one case, one decides to commit suicide, then one hallucinates committing suicide, then one asks oneself why is it one is still alive after having committed suicide, no longer sure whether one is in the same world or in after-life; in the other case, before one commits suicide and at the point of committing it, one undergoes a lapse, one's mind has switched off, then one is back with the memory of a suicide already committed (you phone, ask one of your friends to pick you up at a certain time. He's ten minutes late. Already you are no longer sure whether you really called him, or whether the conversation either was a hallucination or is a hallucinated memory you are having now. Like those distracted persons who walk whole blocks then remember that they parked their car next to the place they walked out of, except that now these persons are no longer sure they had a car).

One suffers in a bad LSD trip the separation that Christianity and Islam portray as the state of all at the Last Judgement (when everyone is absolutely on his/her own), a separation infinitely more intense than being pushed from one room into another, during the Israeli invasion of Lebanon, by the pressure coming from the bomb dropped, by a warplane, which demolished the building next door killing seventy persons (in the U.S.A, vertical parking places; in Lebanon, vertical dwarf cemeteries) forgetting for that interval about everybody else's safety (in my mother's case, it was a lapsus in her priorities, for were she to have been asked just after that "If either you or your son had to die, who would you chose to die?", she would have answered "Why, me" (the *why* in her answer indicating that their question was none as far as she was concerned. In Bergman's *Persona* the shout Elizabeth utters, in reaction to Alma's gesture of throwing the hot liquid at her, is a lapsus of silence, since Alma totally disregards it and later asks Elizabeth to speak to her just once, even if in the form of reading from a book (a little later, coming out of the house, Elizabeth crosses, without injuring herself, the sandy space in front of the door where Alma hid a broken piece of glass and in front of which she sits. Elizabeth then goes back-and-forth like a pendulum around the *strange attractor* that Alma has become (a movement conversation in which Alma is the silent one since she is immobile). Beyond this incident Alma no longer entreats Elizabeth to speak to her)). One feels so intensely the urge to hug the receding world, the whole world, to stop it from withdrawing further.

Time also has to adapt to history/chronology, but it sometimes mutates, and sometimes that mutation may lead to its disappearance.

Raoul Ruiz's *Les Trois Couronnes du Matelot* shown in Chicago on 6/30/89 and 7/1/89. Saw the two screenings. The film should have been shown only once or else the second screening should have shown a different version of the film with certain scenes totally cut out and others altered, so that the person who saw the two screenings would have been perplexed and scared by their non-matching (a non-matching reproducing the incompossibility between the events in the film).

Thoreau writes that half the walk is retracing our steps: wrong if the walk is a back-and-forth movement, for the back-and-forth movement is a basic unit and hence should not be viewed as made up of two movements; right during a bad LSD trip, when, for the first time, the back and forth movement plays a trick on one, becoming part of repetition: one has the sensation one has covered a lot of space — when in fact one was moving in-place over a small stretch of space — and hence finds it uncanny to see the same persons passing one.

The same person seen again and again. The clear sensation it is not really the same person, but a clone that has only the life/consciousness of the undifferentiated cell from which he was derived.

I walk to the public phones. The three are occupied. I wait... I wait... I wait... Are the persons speaking on the phones prolonging their talk intentionally? Do they all know I took a psychedelic? She ends her conversation, begins dialing another number, then begins speaking. People are walking in slow motion. I can't stand there to see the three of them with my own eyes, or with my own hallucinations, go on speaking for ever. I leave to maintain the thought that they will continue speaking forever a mere hypothesis. Horror that this state I am in will never end, that my friends' talk about the drug experience ending once the drug has been digested by the body at the end of a few hours, was part of a conspiracy to make me take LSD, and now that I have taken it, I am stuck here. Twenty-seven years of my life passed before I took LSD, yet now all these years are sucked in the present drug state in the sense that I remember now any past event either as part of a conspiracy to make me take the drug, or else as a hallucination that I had after taking the drug; but did I really take the drug? Is it rather that I have always been like this, and the events I remember as happening before taking the drug and the event of taking the drug that is still very clear in my mind and that I remember as having taken place at 2:30 that afternoon, around three and a half hours ago, could very possibly themselves be hallucinations. I walk to the phones again. One of them is free (to, at last, speak on the phone with reality. I call Mick. No answer. Janalle. No answer. I call Mark. Mark's voice. "Can you meet me?" "Yes, but I'm going to see David Lynch's *The Grandmother* at 7." I feel uneasy: why did he mention a strange director, and a strange film? "Can you be here in 15 minutes?" 5 minutes later, I begin to feel extremely uneasy.

What if he does not show up? Would this mean that the conversation itself was a hallucination? Later I ask a woman about the time. "6:30." 15 minutes have passed then. I can no longer wait in the same place, for if he doesn't show up in a few minutes, this may confirm that the conversation was a hallucination, so I begin to move. I see him coming. I tell him I took LSD. "Be nice to me. For a few minutes I thought I will always be mad." I suggest we go to Mick and Katherine's apartment and then from there to a restaurant to eat. In the car I ask him not to stare at me. I ask him what time it is. He says 6:30. "Where is your clock?" he points to the dash board, I look, it is 6:33. For a moment, the fear time had stopped, that no time had passed between asking the woman what time it is ("6:30"; it probably was 6:28) and asking Mark. He buzzes on Mick's door, nobody answers. He looks around, says: "strange, their car is here." Why did he say that? did he really say that? He suggests we go to his place to have something to eat. I don't want to be alone with any one person, "No, we should go to a diner." On the point of entering the diner I feel a strong aversion to the closed place. Mark gets angry, "I want to eat here." We find a table. I hesitate to sit, I want to go outside; he insists that I sit. We order. "Don't be tense, talk to me." He says Nancy Griffith is coming to town; he says she's a singer. I feel more relaxed and ask him how old she is; he says around thirty. An interval of silence follows what he said. I feel that he's becoming tense again so I talk. I begin telling him about the trip I took with two friends to Milwaukee. "John wanted to go there because he found out there is an LP by Beuys & Paik that sells in Germany for $1500, and that a record store in Milwaukee has two copies of it, each for $20. When we got there, John didn't buy it. We went to a restaurant. They had an inscription on the glass window that said THINK." I am beginning to feel very strange. Does he think I am delirious? For why would a record sell in Germany for $1500 and for only $20 in Milwaukee? Why would John drive there to buy it and then not do that? Why is THINK written on the glass window? And then how come the young waiter said, when Michael ordered an apple pie: "It is kin'a old, would you like me to freshen it with ice cream?"?

I thought I had hallucinated what Mark did. Three days after the trip, I discovered, having asked him to relate to me what happened, that he did in fact act that way. To have taken LSD and thought one was hallucinating because one could not believe that a normal person could behave in such a totally irresponsible manner. Who is the one hallucinating?

Those who postpone often order their experiences and thoughts *to go*. This is not possible during an LSD trip. If at all, it is LSD that orders us *to go* (flashbacks).

Clouds drifting slowly like anchors!

Is the delirium of time, the travel of time itself, now the only way that life and reason may be regained? A *flashback* of the state before LSD was taken.

That phrase, "Sunday, March 2, 1986. I touched a branch", may somehow save me from the delirium of time.

The secret does not belong to the terms between which the encounter happened (did it happen?), but to the encounter. That the encounter should remain secret because one of the terms wants it so, shows a very shallow grasp of the secretive nature of the encounter itself.

How to know whether one is changing or not when the measure of change, time, is itself changing-mutating?

Years ago he had written: "My distraction doesn't let itself be distracted by any kind of concentration".

A book of aphorisms? To be more precise, an aphoristic book of aphorisms. A book that admits no prefaces; that does not vaccinate against itself, since none of the material in it had already been published (in articles, etc.). But a book that annunciates itself, since a finished part of it, *(Vampires),* hence something simultaneous with it, will be published later; i.e. *Distracted* is published too early, a too early that cannot be circumvented since the telepathic — *(Vampires)* — affects from a distance in time and space. As can be seen (and prior to that, sensed — always the too early), a book *about time.*

It is not clear to me whether the period I am going through at present, a period of editing, is a weakening, or whether it is the lull before a new beginning. A similar state occurred between *Distracted* and *(Vampires).* It is also because *Distracted* continued for a while after the beginning of *(Vampires),* i.e. after the *blue hour* **separating** the two books, that the two coexist.

Jalal Toufic was in Lebanon for seventeen years; father, Iraqi; mother of Palestinian origin. «How does it feel» — does it still feel? — to be related to three countries (one of them in exile) that have become synonyms for devastation? Was *Distracted* simultaneously what resulted from, what was salvaged from and what resisted this devastation (yes, it still feels)? Will it itself manage to withstand the devastation of *(Vampires),* a work that resulted from, was salvaged from and resisted another devastation, dying before dying?